THE TIE~~S~~
US AS...

ANITA BUNKLEY

The trendy soul food restaurant Micere
and her girlfriends started is Houston's
hottest spot, but can it survive her
ex-husband's anger when he
discovers she has a new love?

EVE RUTLAND

How can Becky stand by Millie, the
girlfriend who's been with her since the
projects, when Millie seems determined
to sacrifice everything for money?

SANDRA KITT

Years before, Danika let Katherine down.
Now, she's in trouble, and Katherine is
determined to help her long-lost
girlfriend, even if it threatens
her blossoming romance.

GIRLFRIENDS

Girlfriends

ANITA BUNKLEY

SANDRA KITT

EVA RUTLAND

HarperPaperbacks
A Division of HarperCollins*Publishers*

HarperPaperbacks
A Division of HarperCollinsPublishers
10 East 53rd Street, New York, NY 10022-5299

This is a work of fiction. The characters, incidents, and
dialogues are products of the authors' imagination and are not to
be construed as real. Any resemblance to actual events or
persons, living or dead, is entirely coincidental.

Anita Bunkley, author of *At the End of the Day*:
To Gloria, my very first girlfriend.

Sandra Kitt, author of *The Heart of the Matter*:
*To all my girlfriends, past, present, and future, who
lent me their ears, offered shoulders to cry on, and
gave me a scolding with kindness, and love with
respect. You've all been an important part of my life.*

Eva Rutland, author of *Choices*:
*To Kevin Svilich, with thanks, and Muriel James,
teacher extraordinaire.*

Girlfriends

◆

AT THE END
OF THE DAY

◆

ANITA BUNKLEY

CHAPTER 1

Micere Sendaba closed her bedroom door and started down the hallway, stopping in front of an oval, silver-framed mirror to check her hair and makeup once more before descending the winding staircase. Her dark, glossy hair was swept back into an elegant French braid with feathery tendrils curled softly around her cinnamon-colored cheeks. She scrutinized the cluster of brilliant rubies at her ears, then looked down at the matching birthstone ring on her left hand—the one that replaced the wedding band she had removed three years ago.

Stepping back, Micere turned slowly, pleased by the way her loosely constructed black silk pantsuit made her appear even slimmer than she was. The outfit was casual yet elegant, perfect for the evening that she, Jewell, and Yvonne had carefully orchestrated. Micere hoped their guest of honor would be impressed.

Sliding her hand along the smooth mahogany handrail, Micere took quick steps down the carpeted stairs that spilled directly into a spacious foyer where people were milling around. She glanced at the tall case clock near the entry and saw that it was only five-thirty. The Friday night crowd was beginning to build earlier and earlier each week. An encouraging sign, she noted, pausing to absorb the familiar sounds of conversation, laughter, piano music, and the clank of silverware against china that filled the lower floor of her home-turned-restaurant six nights a week.

Customers waiting for tables sat on overstuffed ottomans strategically grouped for conversation. A collection of nostalgic kitchenware decorated the walls of the wide reception hall where Micere's grandmother's old iron skillets and corn bread molds were displayed alongside antique china platters, pink Depression glass plates, and hand-painted chocolate pots that Micere had found in secondhand shops and yard sales around Houston.

Lifting a hand, Micere caught the attention of Precious, the weekend hostess at Food for the Soul. Precious jotted down the name of a young couple on the waiting list, then adjusted the African print scarf draped around her neck before hurrying over to see what Micere wanted.

"Are the extra waiters here?" Micere asked, admiring the heavy golden loops twisted into Precious's ears. Her exotic appearance and friendly personality definitely livened things up at the hostess station.

"Yes, ma'am," Precious replied. "I schooled

them on the layout, the specials, the menu changes. They're gonna work their butts off tonight. The wait is already forty-five minutes."

"Well, keep a close eye on the tables and try to keep things moving," Micere said, silently offering up a prayer of thanks that the house was packed that night.

"Okay," Precious said, "but it's gonna be tough. You know, once Bertha, Joan, Essie, and their crowd sit down, there's no getting them up until they're good and ready."

Micere laughed, glancing at the round table in the center of the room where eight or ten of her diehard regulars set up court every Friday evening. Bertha and her troupe had adopted a proprietary attitude about the center-stage location that provided the best view of everyone who came and went during the evening. Food for the Soul had become *the* place to hang out for these girlfriends, and Micere tolerated their tendency to wear out their welcome. As for their unsolicited advice on love, romance, and relationships with men—well, these topics were of more interest to Micere than ever before.

Her thoughts shifted to Conrad Winters, the man who had entered her life six months ago. The attractive, mature restaurateur, who owned a cafe in Dallas, had introduced himself to Micere in the hospitality suite of the Restaurant 2000 Trade Show in New Orleans last January. She'd immediately felt a comfortable attraction to him, and they had chatted nonstop while strolling from one exhibit to another, sampling everything from coffee to quiche.

After returning to Houston, Conrad had begun calling, usually late at night, after both of them had closed down their eateries. She loved their marathon telephone conversations, and despite the 250 miles that separated them, they saw each other as often as possible, flying between Houston and Dallas every chance they got, often for no more than whirlwind one-day visits. Their reunions were becoming more passionate, their separations much more painful, and the time apart increasingly more difficult to bear.

"Is everything set?" Micere asked, forcing her mind back to the moment.

"Well, I *thought* everything was arranged," Precious began, "but Ms. Tulane's assistant called two minutes ago from her car phone and—"

"Please," Micere said sharply, lifting her hand, palm toward Precious. "Don't even tell me that woman canceled again." She sounded more annoyed than disappointed.

"Canceled? Oh, no, she's coming. Probably in the parking lot right now. Her assistant said Ms. Tulane is bringing her entire production staff." Precious raised her small shoulders, puzzled. "That makes a party of twelve! Gonna have to rearrange some tables."

"No problem," Micere said, relieved that the popular television hostess, producer, and local food columnist was honoring her commitment to visit Food for the Soul after canceling twice.

Micere scanned the rapidly filling interior of her small but well-appointed restaurant. "Put Ms. Tulane's group along the west wall, and don't seat anyone on the patio," she decided. It was mid-May, and warm enough to seat customers outside, but Micere wanted the main dining room full.

"You got it," Precious replied, heading across the room toward two busboys who were busy clearing tables.

"And tell Ramon to drop that funky rap routine," Micere called after her hostess. The soft jazz she'd heard earlier had evolved into a bantering hip-hop monologue that was making her jittery. "That boy's working my last nerve with all that carryin' on. I want some class tonight. *Class*."

"I heard that," Precious mumbled under her breath, lifting a multibraceleted arm.

Micere sighed, then turned and headed through the double swinging doors beneath the spiral staircase, inhaling the smell of freshly baked corn pudding. She lifted her chin, allowing the familiar scent of the hearty, crust-covered casserole to soothe her.

So Trudy Tulane is really coming, Micere thought, hoping the menu that she and her partner, Yvonne, had created for the television producer would do the trick. *Everything's got to be perfect*, she reminded herself, moving out of the way of a waitress who was shouldering a heavy tray of food. Tonight, each dish that came out of the kitchen had to work overtime creating its magical effect.

Micere moved briskly among the gleaming stain-

7

less steel countertops and white ceramic work areas. She paused briefly to watch Lottie, the main cook, garnish a large platter of Creole chicken with sprigs of parsley and bright lemon slices.

"Looks great, Lottie." Micere picked up a spoon to taste the spicy drippings left in the saucepan. "Great. Just the right touch of cayenne. We want Trudy Tulane to leave our restaurant believing she has just eaten the best soul food in the city. "

"I'm sure we can do that," Lottie replied, heaving the platter onto the serving table before turning her attention to a bowl of yams waiting to be whipped.

"Listen up!" Micere said, raising her voice to get the attention of everyone in the kitchen. "Trudy Tulane *is* coming in tonight, but there's been a change."

"What kind of change?" asked Yvonne, who entered the conversation from the back of the kitchen, where she was icing a three-tier carrot cake.

"Good news, actually. Ms. Tulane is bringing her entire production staff," Micere answered. "We'll be serving a party of twelve."

"Twelve?" Lottie crossed her arms on her flat chest and stared first at Micere, then at Yvonne, frowning with displeasure.

"That's right," Micere said firmly. Lottie had appeared at Micere's front door ten days after Food for the Soul opened, convincing Micere and Yvonne that they needed her help. Desperate for a cook who could modernize the traditional recipes they planned to feature, Lottie's culinary prowess was put to the test with Micere's grandmother's recipe for red beans and rice. It was a success, and Lottie's cooking kept the customers coming back, so Micere put up with her sassy attitude.

"Twelve, huh?" Yvonne repeated, shaking her head, swinging her mass of locked twists away from her neck. "Well, we'll just add a few racks of ribs to that platter of chicken and throw some more shrimp in the jambalaya." She made eye contact with Micere, cautioning her not to risk upsetting the head cook that night.

"Okay. If that's what you want," Lottie sighed, leaving the mixer whirring in the yams to pull a bag of shelled jumbo shrimp from the freezer.

Yvonne shrugged and returned to her three-layer carrot cake. When a buzzer went off, she hurried to the wall oven and yanked open the door.

"Where's Chloe?" Micere asked, taking stock of the scant kitchen crew. Besides Lottie and Yvonne, only Martha, the part-time cook, and the wait crew were there. "Wasn't Chloe supposed to be here by four?" Micere grabbed a potholder to help Yvonne remove a large pan of biscuits from the oven.

"Didn't show," Yvonne said.

"Damn. I'm through with her," Micere vowed, sliding the glistening brown bread onto a cooling rack before covering it with a red and white towel. "I tried."

"Yes, you did," Yvonne agreed, returning to her cake. "But I could have told you that girl wasn't going to make it. Whenever that crazy boyfriend calls, Chloe jumps. She told me last night he got a gig over in Beaumont, so she's probably over there right now."

Micere bit her lip in frustration as she pulled a chef's apron over her head and rolled up the sleeves of her black silk shirt, ready to chop onions, saute bell peppers, or fry crab cakes—anything to get this meal out of the kitchen on time. She was so tired of dealing with staff problems. Was it the nature of cooks and wait people to move around a lot? Or was Lottie scaring them off? Micere sneaked a peek at her disgruntled cook.

"Please don't look so worried," Yvonne said. "Girl, we can handle this. It has taken six months to get Trudy Tulane in here, and now she's finally going to come check us out." Yvonne stepped back to admire her cake. "I do believe that sweet potato pie and that basket of chocolate-walnut brownies that I sent via messenger to her studio last week did the trick. We'll be cooking on television this time next month. Watch. It's gonna be fun."

Micere said nothing as she took cubed butter from the refrigerator and began dividing it among three small bowls. Yes, she, Yvonne, and Jewell, the financial expert in the venture, had worked hard creating the kind of restaurant that deserved a syndicated spot on the extremely popular *Cooking Live* series for PBS. Such exposure could bring national recognition, increased business, and relief from the mounting debts that they faced.

CHAPTER 2

With a flutter of bright red fingernails, Trudy Tulane lifted her blond bangs from her forehead, then signaled for her assistant to refill her wineglass.

"Sooo good," Trudy said, blotting her scarlet-hued lips on a pale peach napkin. "This is the best corn casserole I've ever eaten. Better than the Harbor Inn in Boston or the Shipyard in Baltimore." She sat forward and made a flurry of notes on the pad at her elbow.

"Our most popular appetizer," Micere said, eyeing the wide leather belt cinched around Trudy's tiny waist. She could not weigh more than a hundred pounds, Micere calculated, wondering how the popular television personality managed to stay so slim when it was well known that she ate and drank her way across Houston, doing research for her shows. Micere doubted the woman had ever paid for a meal in her adult life.

When Trudy drained her wineglass in one gulp, Yvonne glanced discreetly at Micere, who lifted a brow in agreement, then relaxed. So far the dinner had gone

CHAPTER 3

The plane touched down at Dallas Love Field at exactly nine-thirty on Saturday morning. After renting a car and checking her map, Micere headed to the Fairmont Hotel. The Texas Restaurant Association meeting, held at the Lakeview Hyatt that year, had kicked off on Friday evening, but Micere hadn't been able to get away until this morning. Since the Hyatt was full, she'd reserved a room at the spillover hotel, the Fairmont, which suited her just fine.

Thank God for Jewell, she thought, turning off Highway 35 and heading toward town. If Jewell hadn't been able to watch Trina, Micere would have had to cancel the trip, since Roger had unexpectedly been summoned to Los Angeles on business and Yvonne had her hands full minding the restaurant.

The past week had been an extremely busy one. They'd hosted two private parties and catered a luncheon for the senior citizens at the YWCA. Throughout it all, she'd been unable to think of anything but this weekend—her opportunity to finally spend more than a single day with Conrad.

They'd talked on the phone every night this week, and he'd even called her Thursday morning at five o'clock, simply to hear her voice. The long-distance relationship, which had been steadily moving forward for the past six months, was now progressing at a dizzying pace. Following Bertha's suggestion, Micere had splurged on a beige lace nightgown at Victoria's Secret, tucking it into her overnight bag—just in case.

It was difficult to trust again, after the disappointment of her marriage to Roger, but Micere felt this new relationship would last. Something about Conrad made her feel secure, as if she was on solid ground this time. His attentive manner and openness about his feelings delighted Micere. He was eager to express what was on his mind and listened to her with great attention, valuing her opinions, respecting her advice—attitudes that were foreign to Roger.

Conrad understands me, she thought. *I don't have to explain the balancing act that running the restaurant and raising my daughter requires. Though he may not have children or an ex-spouse complicating his life, he intuitively knows how to lift my spirits at the end of the day.*

Micere's feelings for Conrad were exhilarating. The memory of his kisses ignited a fire in her that burned low and steady all week long, carrying her from moment to moment, day to day, until she could see him again. This evening, she hoped, would be a turning point in the relationship, taking them to new heights of mutual desire, where it would be impossible to turn back.

After checking into the hotel and entering her room, Micere grabbed the phone, sat on the edge of the bed, and called Conrad's Cafe.

"Conrad Winters, please," she said breathlessly, glancing at herself in the hotel mirror, wondering if she looked as foolish as she felt. At thirty-seven, she felt as she had when she was seventeen and defied her parents to sneak out of the house to meet Bobby Wilson behind the leafy hedges at the alleyway. Shaking her head in amusement, she caught her breath when Conrad came on the line.

"Yes, I'm in Dallas," she confirmed, trying not to sound overanxious.

"Great! I can't believe we're going to have two whole days together. I've missed you so much. I've been planning this weekend in my head for days," he said, pausing to let his message sink in. "What's your schedule like this morning?"

Micere sat very still, loving the way his voice swept through her and awakened feelings she had turned off long ago. "I'm going over to the Hyatt for the Southwest Cook-off, then I want to track down Trudy Tulane at the NuWay Cookware booth. They are considering sponsoring the cooking show."

"Right. Sounds good," Conrad said. Then in a husky whisper he added, "How could anyone turn down such a beautiful, talented entrepreneur like you? You deserve to be showcased on TV, you know?"

Slowly inhaling, Micere closed her eyes and leaned

back against the headboard of the hotel bed, letting his words wrap around her heart. "Well . . . thanks for the vote of confidence," she murmured, imagining Conrad's full lips nuzzling the side of her face, remembering how they tasted on hers. Swallowing hard to clear her throat and her mind, she told him, "Trudy Tulane has verbally agreed to film the pilot at the restaurant. Once we get a sponsor, we'll be able to move forward."

"It's going to be fabulous, believe me," he said. The phone line clicked. "Hold on for a minute, okay?" he asked.

The line went quiet, and Micere took the opportunity to slip off her black-and-white spectator pumps and tuck her feet under her legs, calculating what she would wear when they went out later that evening. She'd packed two different outfits—a rather dressy pantsuit and a casual western ensemble, along with the lacy nightgown that she'd bought at the last minute. She was definitely prepared for whatever the evening might bring.

"That was Jay, my brother," Conrad said, coming back on the line. "He's going to hold down the fort at the cafe tonight. Saturday is open-mike night for poets, and we usually have a big crowd."

"Doesn't he have a restaurant, too?" Micere asked.

"Yes, but it's a downtown lunchtime deli that's open only during the week, so he helps me out here on weekends. What time will you be finished? When can I see you?" He ran his questions together, creating a sense of urgency. "I've missed you so much, Micere."

Then he laughed. "Did I already tell you that?"

"Yes," Micere said, "but it's okay to tell me again, because I can't wait to see you, too. I'll be back here by six. What are we doing? Going out or having dinner here?"

"Don't worry about a thing. I'll be at your hotel around seven. And wear something . . ." His voice trailed off, as if he was unsure of how to say what was on his mind.

"Nice?" Micere prompted.

"Well, yes. But I'm sure anything you'd wear would be nice. We're going someplace very special."

"Stop teasing. Give me a hint."

"Don't ask. I said it's a surprise."

"All right, all right. I'll be ready. See you later, then." Micere hung up the phone and pushed her feet back into her shoes, grabbed her garment bag, and hurried to unzip it. She took out the blue pantsuit with sequined collar and cuffs, gave it a good shake, and hung it on the back of the bathroom door so that the wrinkles could fall away. Then she carefully unfolded the beige lace nightgown and laid it on the bed. Running her hands over the soft fabric, she tried to imagine what it would be like to stand before Conrad wearing nothing but this silky little number, letting him trail his hands over her shoulders, her back, her hips . . . the most intimate parts of her body. It had been a long time since she'd felt a man's touch, and the thought of engaging in a sensual journey with Conrad nearly brought tears to her eyes. Standing back, she nodded, admiring the alluring slip of a

31

gown that she'd bought especially for him, hoping his expectations for the evening were even higher than hers.

"Someplace special, huh?" she murmured, warmed by her own fantasy. Maybe the special place would wind up being her room at the Fairmont Hotel. Opening her conference packet, she took out her name badge, pinned it on her chest, then hurried out the door.

Jewell rolled out the last batch of cookie dough and handed Trina a cookie cutter shaped like a duck.

"I want the rabbit this time," Trina protested, extending a small hand covered with flour and sugar.

"Okay, one rabbit coming up," Jewell replied, reaching into the bowl that held an assortment of cookie cutters, spoons, and crumpled paper towels. After handing the rabbit to Trina, Jewell picked up a damp cloth and wiped remnants of cookie dough from the little girl's plump cheeks. "If you don't stop eating the dough, we won't be able to make any more cookies. You want to make enough to save some for your mom, don't you?" she chided in a lighthearted manner.

Trina looked at Jewell and nodded, her long braids swinging back and forth. "And Daddy, too," she chirped, smashing the rabbit into the soft dough. "He likes stars. Can we make some stars for him?"

"Of course," Jewell replied, struck by Trina's innocent devotion to her father.

Jewell had always thought Roger and Micere

were mismatched, and their eventual divorce had proven her right. Jewell knew Roger very well—had known him for eighteen years. When they were in high school he'd dominated conversations, taken charge of arranging most of the parties for their crowd, and directed people with a self-appointed authority that earned him an odd mix of respect and deference. He was always determined to control most situations, and she had seen him pout, curse, intimidate, and even threaten those who tried to prevent him from having his way. He had a dark side that he camouflaged very well when the situation required, but Jewell perceived it and had warned Micere not to marry him. *But girlfriend didn't listen,* Jewell thought. Micere had been charmed by Roger's good looks, ambitious plans, and the seductively aggressive way he pursued her until she agreed to marry him.

Jewell hated Roger for hurting Micere so deeply, but when he walked out on her, Jewell never said *I told you so.* Neither had she ever given Trina reason to suspect how little respect she had for Roger.

As Trina pressed into the dough with her cutter, Jewell placed the cookies, one by one, onto the baking sheet, ready for the oven. When they had finished the last batch, Jewell sent Trina to the bathroom to wash her hands and was about to load the dishwasher when the telephone rang. It was Roger, demanding to know where Micere was staying in Dallas.

"The restaurant association meeting is at the

Hyatt," Jewell told Roger, wondering how Micere could stand her ex-husband's constant presence in her life, especially in light of the way he had treated her. After all, Jewell thought, he had been the one to trash the marriage, walking out to shack up with that girl. Now he was unhappy and irritated by everyone and everything. It wasn't Micere's fault that his second marriage was already history. He should have known better than to think that a twenty-year-old model was going to put up with his pompous, crazy ass, even though his bank account could have kept her in designer clothes and diamonds for the rest of her life.

"I called the Hyatt. She's not registered there. Where *is* she?" Roger demanded, sounding angry enough to burst through the phone and grab Jewell by the neck.

"She called me as soon as she got there, so I know she arrived okay," was all Jewell was willing to volunteer. Both she and Yvonne knew how to be vaguely truthful with Roger. Of course, Jewell knew exactly where Micere was, and also knew that she was not only attending the conference but planning to spend some quality time with Conrad—exactly what girlfriend deserved—and needed to jump-start the romance in her rapidly evolving relationship.

"Called from where?" Roger pressed.

Jewell bristled, not about to suffer through a third degree from him. "Don't worry, Roger. If you need to get a message to Micere, I can find her. No problem. Anyway, what's going on? Are you still in LA?"

"Just got back," he said. "I'm in the car now,

leaving the airport. Thought I'd drop by and take Trina out to eat. Maybe Pizza Palace. She loves that place."

The thought of having Roger interrupt the quiet evening she had planned for herself and Trina made Jewell angry. She had no children of her own, and at thirty-nine had been told by her doctor that she and her husband would most likely never experience parenthood. With her husband away so often, she enjoyed the lifestyle they had created and loved looking after Trina whenever she could.

She and Trina had a routine they always followed. Trina would choose the type of cookies they would bake, and afterward they'd watch *Toy Story* on video— Trina knew every line of dialogue by heart. Then they'd have hot chocolate and eat their cookies, consuming as many as they wanted. Then Jewell would let Trina curl up in Micere's satin-covered king-size bed while she read to her from Trina's favorite storybooks.

Taking care of Trina and joining her husband, Tom, on exotic trips were the things that provided a nice change in routine for Jewell. Most of the time she was busy doing the books, keeping financial records, and paying the bills for Food for the Soul as well as several other small businesses in the area.

Wishing Roger were in a more amiable mood, Jewell told him, "Well, we're just fine over here. We're in the middle of baking cookies right now, Roger. I don't think Trina wants to get dressed and go out to eat."

"She can bake cookies anytime," he shot back.

35

And she can see you anytime, Jewell thought, gritting her teeth.

"Well, I'm on my way, so get her dressed. That little blue and white sailor dress I bought her in San Francisco would be nice."

"Fine," Jewell managed, silently counting to ten as she tried to get her temper under control. "She'll be ready."

"Good. I've got another call to make," he said brusquely. "We'll talk about Micere when I get there."

"Sure," Jewell said, slowly shaking her head. Roger clicked off, leaving her staring in disgust at the dead phone in her hand.

The convention floor was so crowded that Micere had trouble finding Trudy Tulane right away. She threaded her way across the convention hall, through narrow aisles filled with booths where cooks offered samples of exotic concoctions, restaurant supply representatives extolled the features of their wares, and a variety of people connected to the restaurant industry, from security to interior design, talked excitedly about their work.

At one booth a popular Chinese chef, whom she recognized from his show on the Food Channel Network, was demonstrating a new type of stainless steel wok. Micere moved toward the front of the crowd, intrigued by the pungent smell of chicken and snow peas he vigorously stir-fried with a pair of chopsticks. The chef finished the dish with a splash of soy sauce, then cheerfully offered samples to the crowd. Micere eagerly accepted, realizing she'd not eaten since the night before.

Looking around as she tasted the Asian delicacy, Micere scanned the busy hall until she spotted the familiar green and red symbol of NuWay Cookware. And there was Trudy Tulane, animated and smiling, standing inside the booth chatting with fans and signing autographs. Micere finished her chicken, tossed the paper plate and plastic fork into a trash bin, then elbowed her way through the crush of conventioneers, trying to catch Trudy's attention.

"Hello!" Trudy waved at Micere. "You found us!"

"Yes." Micere breathed a sigh of relief. "This is a madhouse."

"But it's wonderful," Trudy replied, handing an autographed cookbook to a fan. "Come on in. Meet Ruben." Stepping behind a curtained gate, Micere squeezed into the tiny booth, where a cheerful-looking red-haired man wearing a NuWay apron was holding a gleaming double boiler with both hands, explaining its features to an interested crowd.

"Hello," the man said to Micere, breaking off his demonstration. When he set down the pot to extend his right hand, his energetic assistant took up the sales pitch and continued the demonstration.

"Ruben Wolff," he said, concentrating on Micere. "You must be Micere Sendaba." When he grinned, his bushy red mustache tilted to one side.

"Yes," Micere replied, taking his large hand in a firm shake.

"Good. Glad you made it. Trudy's got me all pumped up about your place. Food for the Soul, right?"

"That's it," Micere said. "We'd love to have you visit."

"He will. Very soon," Trudy interrupted. "I told him all about my fabulous experience there last Friday." She turned to Ruben and smiled, then playfully tapped his protruding stomach in an intimate way that surprised Micere. "It's the best soul food you'll ever eat," she promised. "You gotta get behind this one, Ruben. It's gonna be a winner."

Micere's eyes widened when the vice president of NuWay's large hand shot out and landed on her shoulder. He let it linger there, in a much too casual manner, until Micere gently stepped back, making his hand fall away. She wondered if she looked as shocked as she felt.

"A winner, huh?" Ruben replied, winking at Micere. He chuckled, then sidled closer to put a beefy arm across her shoulder, anchoring his hand on the wall behind her.

Realizing he was much too close, Micere felt trapped, as if he was testing her comfort level with him. With a twist, she smoothly maneuvered herself out of the awkward situation, puzzled and amazed at the man's nerve.

"Well, darlin'," he said in his thick Texas drawl, apparently not at all offended that Micere pulled away, "if Trudy Tulane says it's a winner, who am I to argue? Sounds good to me. NuWay's always interested in backing a winner, so we'll get those cameras rolling as soon as possible." When his assistant interrupted to ask him a pricing question, Ruben told Micere, "You hang around until I finish here so we can hammer out all the details."

Realizing he'd just committed to being her sponsor, a surge of relief swept through Micere, though it was mixed with irritation. If Ruben Wolff expected anything other than a strictly professional relationship from her in return for his support, he was in for a big surprise. She glanced hard at Trudy, who simply lifted her shoulders in a shrug of resignation, giving Micere one of those I-understand-where-you're-coming-from looks. She was obviously not surprised by Ruben's behavior.

This is just great, Micere thought in dismay, moving toward the front of the booth as Ruben turned his attention back to the crush of people clamoring over his newest cookware. *This is all I need right now. A horny white man who wants to play touchy-feely and chase me around my kitchen is not exactly the kind of sponsor I had in mind.*

CHAPTER 4

At six-forty-five Micere entered her hotel room. She and Trudy had sat in the bar at the Hyatt with Ruben Wolff for three hours, discussing the pilot. The planning session had taken much longer than Micere had anticipated.

Frantic to be dressed and looking extremely attractive when Conrad arrived, she began stripping as soon as she closed the door. By seven-fifteen Micere had showered, reapplied all of her makeup, coaxed her hair into a French twist, and was putting on her earrings when the phone rang. Conrad was in the lobby. After a spritz of perfume and a double check to make sure she had her room key, she rushed out the door.

When Micere stepped off the elevator, her eyes immediately locked with Conrad's. He was waiting for her in front of the doors, holding a bouquet of miniature pink roses. In the space of a few seconds he quickly enfolded her in his arms.

"Well, hello," he said softly, guiding her to a quiet corner, where he kissed her tenderly, on hand at her waist.

His masculine scent filled her head and stirred her heart. She looked him up and down, smiling, appreciating the dark brown suit, tan and white striped shirt, and exotic tie splashed with a melange of orchids, birds of paradise, and palms. His fine dark hair was brushed straight back from his face, the strands of silver at his temples enhancing his sophisticated maturity. The brilliant white smile he flashed at Micere made his eyes crinkle at the corners, reminding her of Billy Dee Williams in *Lady Sings the Blues*.

"Welcome to Dallas," he murmured, handing her the roses. She held the flowers to her nose for a moment, then tucked them into the ring on the side of her blue sequined purse.

"Thanks, they're lovely." Micere turned her face up to his, searching his eyes for a hint of what he was feeling. Tense with anticipation and nervous about the evening, she drew back her shoulders, trying to steady her nerves.

"Sorry I was running a little late," Conrad said, separating from the embrace.

Micere chuckled, falling into step beside him as they walked toward the front of the building. "Truth be told, I was glad you weren't on time," she said. "You won't believe how fast I got dressed."

"Did you accomplish much this afternoon?"

"Oh, yes. NuWay Cookware is going to fund the pilot."

"Congratulations!" Conrad said, holding the door open as they went out onto the sidewalk.

The spring evening was mild, and it was still light

outside. They walked a few blocks, then crossed at the light and entered the lobby of a tall office building. The uniformed security guard on duty at the front desk looked up, waved at Conrad, then resumed watching the bank of monitors on the console that surrounded him.

Micere surveyed the deserted lobby, wondering why they were in the headquarters of the Runyard Corporation. She followed Conrad to a bank of elevators, where he pressed the up button.

He saw her puzzled expression. "Just wait," he cautioned, slipping into the elevator with Micere as soon as the doors whooshed open. He pushed the button for the twenty-seventh floor but said nothing more, standing in silence as the mirrored cubicle zoomed upward.

There must be a private dining room on the twenty-seventh floor, she thought. *Perhaps a secluded, fancy place that requires membership to get in. Or maybe he's rented a private suite, or there's a terrace dining area on the roof,* she calculated, forcing herself to be patient.

But at twenty-seven, when the doors slid open, she saw a dingy, utilitarian-looking passageway that looked as if it might be used by hotel staff to shuttle laundry and cleaning supplies into service. Conrad stepped off first. Micere followed, feeling a little let down and very suspicious about the lack of activity in the area. It was shadowy and eerie, with no signs of life.

"What's up here?" she finally asked, realizing that she knew very little about the man she had willingly followed into this dark, deserted area of the building. *But I trust him,* she told herself, increasing her pace to keep up with him as he strode down the dimly lit hall.

At a dead end, he pushed open a door that led to a narrow staircase. Micere drew back. Conrad turned around.

"Come on. Don't be afraid." He took the steps two at a time and pushed open another door.

A blast of warm air hit Micere in the face, sending her carefully arranged hair flying in all directions. After sweeping several strands from her eyes, she looked around, realizing they were now on the roof of the building. But there was no terrace restaurant or tropical poolside cafe—just a wide expanse of black asphalt dotted with pigeon droppings.

"Over here," Conrad said, tugging her arm. "Come on. Follow me."

They turned a corner, and Micere stopped in her tracks. A gleaming silver helicopter was sitting on the rooftop, its blades spinning, a pilot sitting in the cockpit waiting for them.

"What in the world . . . ?" she shouted over the roar of the engine.

Conrad walked briskly across the rooftop, pulling her along.

"Where are you taking me?" she sputtered, not sure if she should protest or not. Riding in a helicopter was not something she'd ever wanted to do, and now it looked as if she had no choice.

"It's my surprise," he shouted back, jumping in, then reaching back to help her up. "Well, part of my surprise, at least."

As soon as they were safely buckled in, Conrad gave the go-ahead and the pilot took off, heading west, soaring out over tall buildings that were cast in hues of pink and orange as the setting sun spilled over them.

"This is lovely," Micere admitted, relaxing. To still her nerves, she focused on a bank of turquoise clouds stretching languidly across the horizon. Looking down, she was amazed at how dwarflike the tiny cars and people appeared.

"Sunset is the most magical time of the day," Conrad replied, reaching into a built-in cabinet behind them to pull out a bottle of champagne. He popped the cork and filled two crystal glasses, bursting into laughter when one of them overflowed, trailing bubbly onto the floor.

"A toast," he said, handing her a glass, lifting his.

"To. . . ?" Micere prompted.

"To us. To all the wonderful times ahead," he replied, lightly touching her cheek with the cool crystal glass.

The promise in his voice and the sincerity in his eyes drew Micere in. They both took a sip of champagne, and Micere quietly watched as Conrad, with downcast eyes, slid his thumb back and forth along the side of his glass, as if gathering courage to say more.

"I know we haven't known each other long," he finally began, now looking directly into her eyes. "And we haven't had much time together."

"Not much time alone, you mean," Micere added, helping him along. During their spur-of-the-moment encounters in Dallas or Houston, it seemed that either Trina, Yvonne, Jewell, or a crush of customers in either his cafe or her restaurant had always been around. Their "dates" had been trips to the movies, the zoo, an art gallery, or a new eatery they wanted to check out. Quick goodbye kisses at the airport and stolen embraces in the back of taxis had been the norm since the relationship began.

"Right. It's good to have you all to myself for once—though I adore Trina, and envy the friendships you have with your girlfriends. I leased this helicopter—to impress you, of course," he added with a laugh. "But seriously, I wanted your full attention."

"Well, you've certainly got it," she admitted, clutching her glass in anticipation.

"Isn't this fabulous, being high in the clouds, floating free of the troubles and worries and people that occupy our minds and our time? I wanted to be up here, alone with you, when I told you that . . . that I have fallen in love with you." A boyish grin tugged at his lips as he watched for her reaction.

Micere's nervousness melted into joy. Slowly she nodded, then whispered, "Really?"

"Really."

"Oh, Conrad. I . . ." She stopped, swirling the champagne in her glass, thinking, then blurted out, "I'm afraid it's happened to me, too."

"Afraid? Why do you use that word?"

"Because I never believed I'd love again, let alone find someone like you, and I'm so afraid of my feelings. If I'm dreaming . . ."

With a sweep of his arm he encircled her waist, his presence so real and firm. "I assure you, you are not dreaming," he whispered. "I'm the real thing, and so is the way I feel about you."

This time his kiss felt different from all the others they'd shared. It was a kiss of promise, the kind that makes a commitment. It opened the floodgates for Micere's joy to flow right through her soul, chasing away the worries she'd wrestled with so long. The sense of urgency and expectation that Conrad expressed in his embrace made her fears of loving again disappear. When he pulled away, she looked at him in a brand-new light.

He refilled her glass. "Here's another toast," he said. "To the most beautiful, exciting woman I have ever met." Conrad playfully brushed his lips over her nose, remaining close as he whispered, "This is just the beginning of a long, beautiful relationship, Micere. I've waited my entire life for someone like you, and though I don't exactly know what the future holds for us or where we are headed, you must believe that I love you, and my feelings grow stronger each day." With a sigh, he sat back, relaxing, as if a great load had been lifted and everything was right with his world.

Micere took his hand and held on fast, sipping champagne, wondering if he could detect what was racing through her mind. What about Trina? Roger? The restaurant? All the people who would be affected by the slightest change in her current situation? What kind of future could they possibly have with him in

Dallas and her in Houston? One of them would have to make big changes if their love was going to survive. She held the glass at her lips for a moment, unable and unwilling to bring up all the reasons why their love might not survive.

Conrad, sensing her dilemma, brushed a finger over the back of her hand. "I don't expect you to make any promises right now. I just had to let you know how I feel."

The expression of contentment on Conrad's face sent Micere's pulse racing. For so long she'd been unable to think of anything other than the deepening emotional tangle she was helplessly spiraling into, praying that Conrad was falling in love with her, too. But Micere wasn't stupid. Moving their casual relationship to a level of commitment meant upsetting the routine she'd created for herself, her daughter, and her girlfriends. Loving Conrad would make her happy, but she did not want to move too fast and give away too much of herself so soon.

"Conrad," she managed, "I want us to be together, really together, but I have to admit, I think it will be difficult." While speaking those words, her thoughts slipped to the lace nightgown spread across her bed. Yes, she wanted to make love to Conrad that evening, to be with him totally and completely. She shuddered in anticipation.

"It won't be so difficult," he told her. "We have all the time in the world to work out the kinks. You'll see."

It had taken Micere more than a year to shake

the depression that overtook her when Roger walked out. Now it felt good to know that a wonderful man was willing to take a chance at loving her. She was mature enough to know what she wanted, and was perfectly capable of making decisions about her future. And despite Roger's attempts to undermine her self-confidence, Micere had always known what she wanted: to love again someday. Now it seemed that day had come.

Neither the fast-paced singles life nor a lonely future without loving companionship was what she envisioned for herself. Of course, she could manage alone, raising Trina, running her restaurant, and going through life as a single parent, but that was not what she wanted. In a very short time Conrad Winters had managed to ease himself into her mind, her heart, her soul, her life, and she definitely liked having him there.

The sky deepened to a burnt orange as they glided toward their secret destination. Micere watched and listened while Conrad pointed out the State Fair Park with its huge Ferris wheel, and Dealy Plaza, where President Kennedy had been shot. She saw the trendy area where people were shopping, known as Deep Ellum, Dart train stations, and the famous Reunion Center observation tower rising far below them.

What an enchanting way to begin an evening, she thought. For all the money, connections, and power Roger had, he'd never done anything like this for her. She smiled rather smugly, then shifted closer, gently placing her head on Conrad's chest. Reaching up, she gripped his shoulder tightly, letting him know how happy she was to be there with him, zooming high above the gleaming skyscrapers, watching the lights come on as the city got ready for nightfall. The whir of the helicopter made Micere feel as if she were on a private, sacred journey into a future where Conrad would protect and love her with a tenderness she'd never before experienced. She glanced up and captured his lips with hers once again, placing her trust in him. Gently he broke away, then took her glass and set it on the cabinet. He placed both of his hands on either side of her face and drew her lips to his. Micere did not resist, accepting the gentle, urgent press, letting him know that her intentions were as serious as his. She was ready to explore the future with Conrad Winters, the most attractive and romantic man she'd ever met—a man she didn't plan to let slip away.

The helicopter suddenly banked to the south, circling a tall copper-colored building with a blue light blinking on the top. As the helicopter descended, Micere snuggled against Conrad, trying to guess where they were going. When they finally landed, he helped Micere out, then gave the pilot instructions to come back at eleven o'clock. They hurried into a stairwell that led to an elevator, and went down two floors. There they got off and entered a richly paneled room, where an expanse of glass shelving was filled with fresh flowers. An attractive woman wearing an elegant but simple long black dress greeted them. She apparently had been waiting for their arrival, but

Micere thought it odd that no one else was around.

"Good evening, Mr. Winters," the woman said, smiling, as they approached her.

"Hello, Rykia," Conrad replied, using a familiar tone. "Is everything ready?"

"Of course. Come with me," she assured him, opening a set of tall hammered-brass double doors.

The woman stood back. Micere entered first, and drew in her breath when she saw what lay in front of her.

It was a circular room, with gleaming rosewood chairs and tables grouped in clusters near floor-to-ceiling windows that made up the outside walls. The tops of the windows were draped in white gauzy curtains that created the sensation of floating in the clouds. Micere walked to the center of what was obviously a restaurant and twirled around. The place was huge but devoid of customers, and only one table was set with crystal stemware, silver place settings, and a bouquet of red and yellow roses. Dozens of tall white candles twinkled throughout the room, creating a softly lit romantic setting.

Two waiters in cutaway jackets bowed slightly to Micere, and soon piano music filtered into the room from an ebony baby grand in a corner.

"Conrad?" she asked, slipping her arm through his. "Just us?"

"Just us," he agreed, leading her to a wall where an impressive selection of wines was racked. "You choose," he offered as Micere checked the labels.

"Wow. Pretty good stuff," she commented, "but

I don't know what we're having for dinner."

"Doesn't matter. Choose whatever you like."

Thoughtfully, Micere examined bottle after bottle, then decided on a Merlot. A waiter took it from her and disappeared into what she assumed must be the kitchen.

The hostess escorted them to their table, which provided a spectacular view of the brightly lit city. A single yellow rose lay across Micere's plate.

"How lovely," she told Conrad, inhaling the delicate scent of the full-blooming rose.

"So . . . you like it?" Conrad asked, helping her into her seat.

"I love it!" Micere lifted her hands, palms up. "But I can't believe we're the only ones here. And what's the name of this place? I didn't see any sign at the entrance."

"That's because the sign is being made." Leaning over the table toward her, he became serious. "I just bought this place, and when the new sign goes up it will say Skyview by Conrad's."

Shocked, Micere swept the area with an even more appreciative eye, impressed by his recent acquisition. "Yours? Congratulations. This is really first-class."

"You bet it is," he said huskily. "You see, I go first class in everything I do."

CHAPTER 5

Jewell stood at the window and watched Roger get out of his car. *The prick,* she thought, fuming that he would whisk Trina away for the evening, ruining her plans. Trina was pleased about going out with her father but not too happy about missing the hundredth replay of *Toy Story,* her favorite movie.

Jewell had turned Roger's spur-of-the-moment invitation into a special request, assuring Trina that her father was a very busy man and that he was making special arrangements to be with her tonight.

God, I'm a great liar, Jewell thought, listening to Roger's determined footsteps on the hall carpet. The jangle of his keys made Jewell wonder, again, why Micere hadn't changed the locks or asked for his keys back after the divorce. *Well, he can ask all the questions he wants, but I am not about to let him spoil Micere's weekend,* Jewell decided, opening the door before he could use his key.

"Hello, Jewell," Roger said as soon he saw her. "Trina ready?"

"She's putting her toys away," Jewell replied,

annoyed when he simply walked past her and roamed through the apartment, making his usual tour of inspection.

Roger picked up a copy of *Our Texas* magazine, flipped through it, then stuck it back into the magazine rack. Without a second thought he looked closely at the letters on Micere's coffee table and picked up one from a publisher who had turned down the cookbook proposal. Removing it from the envelope, he read it as if it were addressed to him. Jewell wanted to scream, but she swallowed her anger, reminding herself that this was not her house and Roger was not her problem.

"I could have told her that cookbook proposal was done all wrong," he muttered, tossing the letter back on the table. "If Micere would only listen to me, she could save herself a lot of grief." Pacing impatiently, he flexed his fingers, then checked his watch. "And where did you say Micere was staying?" His tone was curt.

"I didn't say," she calmly replied, aware that Micere was at the Fairmont.

"Well, as I told you, she's not at the Hyatt," he tossed back. "I checked."

"You know how conventions can be. Desk clerks get busy. Messages get lost. She'll be back tomorrow night."

His eyes widened, then turned dark with anger. "Don't play dumb with me, Jewell. I know what's going on. You and your love-starved girlfriends have been encouraging Micere to act like a tramp. I know about this guy she's been dating in Dallas. That's where she is, isn't she? Off to see her lover again." Roger spat the words, then stepped closer. "I can find them right now, if I decide to."

Determined to stay calm, Jewell walked to the far side of the room and crossed her arms at her waist. "What's with you, Roger? Micere is free, black, and over twenty-one. Leave her alone."

"Stay out of it, Jewell," he growled, raising his voice. "If you don't want to tell me where Micere's staying, fine. I can call every hotel in Dallas if I want to. And by the way, I'll keep Trina tonight, so you can go on home."

"Roger, it's no problem for me to stay. I told Micere I would. You don't have to keep Trina."

He stared at her as if she had cursed him. "I *know* I don't have to keep her, but I will. And if Micere is going to spend so much time running after her new boyfriend—" He stopped abruptly when Trina came out of her bedroom and gave him a big hug and a kiss. Then she turned to Jewell and pecked her on the cheek.

"Bye-bye, sweetheart," Jewell told her little charge, returning her hug. "You and your daddy have a nice time."

"We'll be fine," Roger said, his demeanor suddenly very sweet. "I have everything she needs at my place, so like I said, you can go on home."

When the door shut behind them, Jewell silently counted to ten. Things were turning ugly. She should have seen this coming. All Micere had done was fall in love, and now Roger was determined to punish her for it.

"That sorry son of a—" She stopped herself, grabbed a duck-shaped cookie, and stuffed it, whole, into her mouth.

Returning to the kitchen, she finished cleaning up the mess they had made and turned off the lights. Next she called the Fairmont and left a message, telling Micere that Trina was spending the night at Roger's. She said nothing about Roger's anger, determined not to spoil her girlfriend's visit or cause unnecessary worry. They'd talk when she returned.

Restless and not really ready to go home, Jewell went down the back stairs and entered the kitchen area of Food for the Soul.

Things were hopping, as always on a Saturday night. The kitchen was crazy, with waiters rushing in and out and Lottie bossing everybody around.

Jewell picked up a strawberry, dipped it in chocolate, and savored its sweetness as she worried about the guilt trip Roger was trying to lay on Micere. With Conrad, Jewell believed, Micere had a second chance at love, an opportunity to build the kind of relationship she deserved. But how could she? Jewell sighed aloud. *We sisters sure have it hard,* she thought, wondering how Roger would feel if the tables were turned. He was dating, too, and even brought his women to the restaurant, showing them off, taunting Micere, who never made a fuss. In fact, Jewell thought, Micere was too damned tolerant of everything Roger did.

"What's up with you?" Yvonne asked Jewell as she came through the swinging doors, a bundle of fresh gladioli in her arms. "Trina asleep already?" She moved aside a jumbo box of plastic gloves, placed the flowers on the counter, and ran cold water into a cut-glass vase.

"No. Trina's gone," Jewell grumbled. "I'm out of a baby-sitting job tonight."

"Gone? Where?" Yvonne eyed Jewell suspiciously.

"Roger's back from LA. Didn't you see him? I'm sure he came right through the dining room and up the front stairs, making sure everyone knew he'd arrived."

"Nope. I've been swamped back here. So he took Trina to his place?"

"You got it," said Jewell. "Damn. You know, that man ought to quit. I don't get it. He's around here all the time. Since his second wife left him, he's determined to make Micere's life as miserable as his own."

Yvonne took exception. "Hmmm . . . I think he's finally realized that Micere was the best thing that ever happened to him. He told me he wants her back."

"Girl, please! I don't think so."

"He came in here looking for Micere that Sunday when Conrad took her and Trina to the zoo. Roger was furious."

"I'm sure he was."

"Personally, I hope they get back together," Yvonne

hedged, aware of their differing opinions of Roger. "For Trina's sake, you know."

"Don't even go there," Jewell warned. "He's so self-involved, he can't see past the solid-gold rims of his glasses. Coming around here, checking things out—you'd think he'd get the message that Micere wants her space. I wish he'd move to Los Angeles. He's got so much important business out there." Irritated by Yvonne's comments, Jewell frowned at her girlfriend, who was fiddling with the tall pink and yellow flowers.

"That will never happen," Yvonne replied, picking up a fern. She clipped the stem and stuck it in the arrangement. "Roger's okay. He's a great father, and remember, he's the reason Micere was able to go into business in the first place. He didn't *have* to finance this place, you know."

"True," Jewell allowed, "but we made this place what it is. Money is tight right now, but we'll survive." Jewell spoke with confidence, but was worried about the forty-five hundred dollars they owed the contractor who had renovated the kitchen.

"You know," Yvonne said, "as long as Micere has custody of Trina, Roger *will* be involved in her life and this business . . . *our* business," she added. "He'll always be around."

The intimate dinner for two at Skyview by Conrad's was a dazzling gastronomic experience of six courses, topped off with fresh blueberry tarts and cream. Micere drank two kinds of wine and more champagne than she'd ever consumed in her life. She was dizzy with joy as they began the helicopter ride back to the top of the Runyard Building.

"Good thing we're not driving," she giggled, settling down beside Conrad. The stars drifted closer and closer as the helicopter rose in the dark blue sky, and she luxuriated in the freedom of soaring into the heavens with Conrad at her side, mentally confirming her decision to invite him to her room.

At dinner they'd laughed and talked about so many things—art, travel, his collection of model trains, and how to make Ruben Wolff mind his manners on the set of her TV show. Conrad had given Micere tips on what dishes to prepare for the pilot, and he'd listened with interest to her ideas on streamlining her kitchen to facilitate filming.

Micere had never had so much fun, and when the helicopter landed, Micere sensed that Conrad wasn't ready for the evening to end, either.

"Let me walk you to your room," he offered as they made their way across the street to her hotel.

"I'd love that," Micere replied, holding tightly to Conrad's arm, feeling young and free and slightly inebriated.

At her door, she waited until he had passed her key card through the lock. Then she turned to him and said the words she hoped he wanted to hear.

"Would you like to come in?"

He smiled his reply, moving with her into the semidark room. Once inside, she waited as Conrad shut and locked the door. At first Micere tensed; then she moved to him, reaching up, anxious to release the emotions she'd felt rising all evening. Filtered city lights shimmered behind the translucent drapes, creating a perfect atmosphere for the lovers.

He kissed her with new passion, indicating his desire, and Micere returned her promise for an evening of love.

Conrad lazily nuzzled the side of her neck. "What time is your flight tomorrow?"

"Five. In the evening," she replied, holding the lapels of his jacket as she walked backward toward the bed.

"We can share breakfast and lunch before you go," he murmured.

"And in between?" she asked.

"I'm sure we'll find something to do." His hands eased up her back to the base of her neck.

Micere smiled, guiding Conrad deeper into the room, her lips only inches from his. When the backs of her legs touched the edge of the bed, she reached down, her fingers searching for the thin spaghetti straps of the lace negligee. Grabbing it, she ducked under Conrad's arm and whirled around.

He stared at her for a moment, then noticed the nightgown. He stepped closer and gathered her to him, resting his chin on her shoulder. "Please, put it on," he murmured, pressing closer, allowing the full length of his body to match hers.

The tenderness in his voice was comforting, easing Micere's fears about moving too fast. They had known each other nearly seven months, though their time together had been limited. And that was the way it would be for a while longer, Micere realized, aching to take advantage of this rare opportunity to be alone with Conrad.

"For you," she whispered, holding the gown to her chest, trying to disguise her nervousness. She slipped into the bathroom, stripped off her clothes, and let the soft ripple of beige lace shimmer over her body. Removing a few pins, she freed her hair from its elegant French twist, letting it fall in dark waves over her shoulders. With a final glance in the mirror, she was ready to give all of her love to Conrad, releasing the pent-up passion that dwelled in her heart.

She entered the bedroom and walked straight into Conrad's muscled arms, sinking down onto the cool white sheets. Touching his smooth, warm skin was like caressing brown satin. Micere slid her cheek along the curve of Conrad's shoulder, letting her tongue trace the length of his neck, tasting the male scent of him. A soft, appreciative moan escaped her lips when he gently turned her onto her back and knelt to look down at her.

"You are beautiful. So beautiful," he whispered, rubbing his hands over her shoulders, along the rounded ridge of her collarbone, down to the rounds of silky flesh rising at the neckline of her gown.

Lifting her hips, Micere pressed her thighs hard against Conrad's, allowing him to slip one arm beneath her arched back. Through half-closed eyes she watched the shadowy outline of his body as it hovered above her like a dark protective angel.

The rustle of stiff hotel sheets was the only sound

she heard as Conrad gently lowered himself close enough to capture her lips with his. Micere entwined both of her hands around his neck, lacing her fingers together, urging him closer. His kiss burned her, branding his taste on her lips, releasing a fire that she wanted to feel forever. As her soul opened up, she eased her hands down Conrad's back and along his spine until she could caress his hard, rounded hips.

Moving together, Conrad and Micere teased and tested places that were new to them, pausing for each other's response. He was patient and sensitive, giving Micere time to adjust, waiting for subtle signals that would help him learn how to pleasure her. When his fingers brushed the curly mound between her thighs, she curved deeper into his embrace, giving him permission to touch, stroke, and bring her to the edge of ecstasy before yielding to him completely.

Micere fell easily into his rhythmic search, joining Conrad in a sensual journey that swept them beyond the moment. She felt herself being lifted, carried by his steady pulse to a place high and far away—as distant as the heavens they'd just soared through, where they'd both confessed their love. When their passion reached its pinnacle, Micere cried out, grasping for those glittering pinpoints of light that were suspended in her mind, entering that enchanted place where nothing mattered but the man she held in her arms.

CHAPTER 6

Two weeks after Micere's introduction to Ruben Wolff, the details of an agreement between NuWay Cookware and the television station had been hammered out. Filming of the pilot program, set in the kitchen of Food for the Soul and featuring Yvonne and Micere as celebrity cooks, was scheduled to begin during the last week of June. Fearful of jinxing the project, Micere swore her partners to secrecy.

Preparations began. Micere worked with the camera crew, set decorators, and food stylists. Yvonne planned the menus and shopped for food with Lottie. Jewell kept a close watch on expenditures.

The hectic days that followed put the women's friendship to the test. Nerves were frayed. Disagreements erupted over simple matters, and issues that had once seemed insignificant took on giant importance. When Yvonne and Jewell got into a screaming match over the five-dollar difference between basic white chef's towels or colorful ethnic prints, Micere just shook her head and walked away, determined to stay calm and rise above the chaos.

In fact, Micere was the only one able to float through this stressful period, hardly showing any strain. She was in love—totally and irrevocably smitten by Conrad Winters, whom she had seen five times during the past four weeks. The future seemed bright, and even Trina looked forward to Conrad's visits, as well as the presents he brought along.

But Trina was not the only one to receive gifts from Conrad. He fueled his long-distance relationship with her mother with a steady supply of surprise packages delivered via UPS two or three times a week. He sent beautifully illustrated cookbooks for Micere to add to her collection, exquisitely framed watercolors to decorate her living area, a silver bracelet to match the earrings he'd given her the morning after they first made love, and fresh flowers that arrived nonstop—so many that they spilled out of Micere's private rooms into the main dining room and the patio. She was overwhelmed by his generosity, his expressions of love, and the fast pace at which their affair was progressing.

The call Micere had been waiting for finally came. The TV pilot would be filmed on the twenty-sixth of June. The evening before the big day, Micere, Yvonne, and Jewell worked late at the restaurant, going over details of the early morning shoot. By midnight the kitchen had been livened up with tropical plants, brightly colored straw mats, and ethnic-theme serving dishes that reflected the variety of foods the restaurant offered. There was so much NuWay cookware scattered around the kitchen, the place resembled the housewares section of a major department store. Ruben Wolff would be on the set, watching the production very closely.

Micere prayed that her generous sponsor would be able to keep his hands to himself, especially around Yvonne, who would not take his chummy, touchy-feely approach lightly. Micere could just imagine what would happen if Ruben Wolff got too familiar with Yvonne, who once had slapped a too-cocky customer in the face with a slice of chocolate pie when his hands "accidentally" brushed across her hips.

"God, I'm exhausted," Yvonne said, going to the coffeemaker on the kitchen counter to pour less than a half cup of coffee in her mug. With a gulp, she drained it and put her cup in the sink. "I think we've done all we can. The show will go on, no matter what. I'm outta here." Grabbing her purse, she waited for Jewell, who was gathering up her books and ledgers.

"Me too," Jewell agreed as she rose. "If I go over these figures one more time, I'll be permanently cross-eyed. The budget for the next three months is truly bare-bones, but we'll be okay."

Micere rubbed the back of her neck, nodding. "Yeah. NuWay may be picking up production costs, but getting ready was more expensive than I thought. We've just got to be careful. No more impulse buying," she said, casting a stern glance at Yvonne, who shrugged innocently and grinned.

"I know, I know," Yvonne admitted. "But you can't tell me those coordinated linens don't set this kitchen off!"

"Right," Micere agreed, admiring the festive atmosphere Yvonne had created. "Well, thanks for staying so late, you guys."

Jewell headed to the back door. "No problem. See you about ten. Can't promise I'll be here any earlier."

"Don't worry," Micere said. "I can handle Trudy and her production crew. They'll be here by seven, I expect."

As soon as Jewell and Yvonne left through the back door, Micere went into the main dining room to recheck the lock on the front door and turn out the lights.

This is it, she told herself. *As of tomorrow, Yvonne and I will be celebrity cooks, and every publisher who ever turned down our cookbook will be clamoring to buy it.* Micere grinned. Food for the Soul was about to become a household name, and she could hardly wait.

Looking out the bay window that faced the street, she was surprised to see a lone car still in the parking lot. Curious, she moved closer to the window, realizing that it was Roger's car. Before she could even blink, he was hurrying toward the front door. She snatched it open and glared at him.

"What are you doing here?" She checked her watch. "It's almost one o'clock."

"I need to talk to you." Roger's tone was rushed. "I was waiting until Yvonne and Jewell left." Ignoring Micere's frown, he pushed past her and entered the hallway, where he stood, hands thrust deep into his pants pockets.

"Talk about what, Roger? It's late. Tomorrow is a really busy day."

"I know. The TV pilot. Sounds like you're about to

start making some real money over here. About time. This place has not been particularly profitable, has it?"

"Please, Roger. Not tonight. And who told you about the show?"

"Yvonne."

Micere was annoyed. Even the regulars knew nothing about the possibility that the restaurant might be featured on TV. "When did she tell you this?"

"I ran into her at the bank last week," Roger replied, pausing to let this information sink in. "In fact, Yvonne had quite a bit of news to share."

A hollow feeling washed through Micere, and she was suddenly angry with Yvonne. Her girlfriend's tongue could be loose, and as much as Micere loved Yvonne, she had learned over the years not to tell her anything that she didn't want spread around the neighborhood like peanut butter on bread.

Roger was acting very smug. "You seem to have a lot of business in Dallas lately, don't you?" His smile became a sneer.

"Yes, I have," she answered forthrightly, offering nothing more. Micere knew Roger was baiting her, and she was not about to play his sick game.

When he finally spoke, he reprimanded her. "The last quarterly report was not so good, Micere. Maybe you ought to spend more time here improving your cash flow and less time running in and out of airports."

"Listen, Roger. I've managed to meet my obligation to the bank every month."

"Yes, you have, but you might try harder to get

your checks in on time. I've been willing to waive late fees and penalties—which, according to our contract, you ought to pay, Micere—but no more."

"You're not losing any money, Roger."

"True, but I'm not making much, either. That remodeling contractor called me. He wants his money. You ought to be able to manage things better. And remember, technically I own this place . . . as long as the note is outstanding. That paltry seven thousand dollars that Yvonne plunked down doesn't give her any clout. I want a better return on my quarter-million-dollar investment, you understand? I've been patient, but this is serious, Micere. Don't expect me to sit by and watch things fall apart. And don't try to turn the management over to someone else."

"Someone else?" Now she was truly in the dark. "What are you talking about?"

"I'm talking about your much-too-intimate relationship with Conrad Winters."

Micere flinched. *Well,* she thought, *it's finally out in the open.* She had wondered when Roger was going to strike. He was such a hard-ass about making money—that was all he cared about—so she was not surprised that his attack was on the financial front.

"Yes, Conrad," she said lightly, breathing his name. "He's a very nice man. I have been dating him for some time."

"I know. I've done some checking. His banker and I are old friends. We've talked . . . several times. Winters is an opportunist. He's scouting locations in Houston to expand; he's set his sights on Food for the Soul, and you don't even know it."

"That's absurd."

"Not really. Winters would love to get his hands on all of this . . . after I've paid for all the renovations and helped you make it a success, that is. Watch out, Micere. If Conrad Winters wants anything, it's most likely your restaurant, not you." Roger jutted out his jaw as he glanced around the elegant dining room. Moving closer to his ex-wife, he grabbed her arm. "That won't happen, I assure you."

Incensed at his implication, she shook him off, rubbing her arm where he'd touched her. "Get out of here. My relationship with Conrad is none of your business. I don't answer to you, and you've no right to pry into my private affairs. Ending our marriage was your idea, and now that I've moved on, you've got some nerve to try to tell me what to do." Micere paused to catch her breath and gather the words she needed to get her message across. "I wish you'd stay away from here, Roger. Stop bringing your women around, flaunting them in my face. In a city the size of Houston, there are certainly other places you can go to eat."

"I *own* this place. You can't keep me out."

"No," Micere relented, "I guess I can't. But unless you've made prior arrangements to pick up Trina, there's no real reason for you to be here, so stop spying on me. Leave me alone and stop pumping my friends for information, too. It's so childish! If you've got questions about my activities, ask me.

What I do on my own time is no concern of yours."

"I beg to differ, sweetheart," Roger growled. "Anything that affects my investment in this place—*and* my daughter—is very much my business. Don't you ever forget that."

Micere balled her fists into two hard knots, itching to punch Roger's face. Bringing Trina into the argument was like a stab wound in her heart. She wondered how he could be so cruel.

"You bastard," she hissed, trembling with rage as Roger calmly opened the front door and left.

It was still dark outside when Micere shut off the alarm clock. Trina was already awake, sensing her mother's excitement. After dressing and preparing a quick breakfast of toast and cereal, Micere and Trina headed downstairs to begin a long, exhausting day.

Trudy Tulane and her production crew arrived promptly at seven, accompanied by Ruben Wolff. The place became a beehive of activity. Cameras were set up, lights were hung, and cables were laid across the tile floors. Micere and Yvonne sat for makeup, rehearsed their scripts, and made practice runs with several of the menu items. Once the cameras rolled, the producer put them through take after take for the next ten hours while Ruben, who was behaving himself, looked on. He was so pleased with the way things went, he decided right then and there to sponsor thirteen shows.

Yvonne, giddy with happiness over this news, crushed Ruben in a great bear hug, thanking him profusely for supporting their show.

"I hear you're the brains behind a cookbook based on Food for the Soul specialties," Ruben told Yvonne when she finally turned him loose. He held on to her arm, making no attempt to disguise his appreciation of her trim, attractive figure.

"I sure am," Yvonne replied, ignoring Ruben's blatant scrutiny.

Ruben thoughtfully cocked his head to one side as Yvonne watched him keenly. "I have a friend at Windell Publishing who would probably take a look at it if I asked her."

"Just wait right there," Yvonne said, crossing the kitchen. She opened a cabinet and removed a thick manila envelope, then handed it to Ruben. "Here it is. Recipes, stories, tips on lightening up southern food, and plenty of photographs, too."

"Let's see what you've got," Ruben suggested, and the two moved into the dining room to go over the manuscript.

Surprised at how well Yvonne and Ruben were getting along, Micere turned her attention to Trudy Tulane. "Now that we've got a commitment from NuWay for thirteen shows, what's next?"

"We'll set up a production schedule. Fax me some program ideas as soon as you can, so we can get together and get things rolling, okay?"

"You bet," Micere replied, her spirits definitely higher than they'd been the night before.

When the crew had packed up and everyone had left, Micere put Trina to bed, then went into her office to call Conrad and tell him the good news. The television show was no longer just a dream; it was really going to happen. She picked up the phone, pressed a few buttons, and then, for some odd reason, put it back down. She paced the room, trying to understand her hesitation to make the call.

I'm exhausted, that's all, she told herself. It was late, and she was entirely too tired to talk to Conrad right then. But as she moved back and forth in front of her cluttered desk, Roger's threatening words returned, filling her mind with worry. Unexpectedly, tears brimmed in her eyes.

"Damn him," she cursed. Roger's financial control of the restaurant was alarming, but what could she do? As long as he held the note, he had the power. She knew Roger could be cut-throat and short-tempered when it came to business dealings, but the sinister way he had brought their daughter into the problem was frightening. Would he try to take Trina away from her if she pursued a relationship with Conrad? Could he? Micere's chest tightened at the thought.

She looked down at the floor, overwhelmed with guilt. Why did she allow Roger to affect her this way? She'd done nothing wrong, and knew exactly what he was trying to do. If she was not careful, he would ruin everything.

Standing, Micere brushed away the tears that filled her eyes and turned off the desk lamp, too tired to wrestle with her problems any longer.

I am not going to give Conrad up, she vowed. *And I'm not going to let Roger control my daughter's future, or mine, even if it means a fight.*

CHAPTER 7

"Things are moving pretty fast," Micere told Yvonne and Jewell once the three of them had settled in her office. "With NuWay behind us, I really think we've got a shot at turning this financial squeeze around. However—"

"The contract with Windell Publishing is looking good," Yvonne interrupted. "You know, Ruben's got serious connections. I'll bet we get an offer this week."

"All right!" Jewell said, giving Yvonne an enthusiastic high five. "Go on, girl! You worked that deal, for sure."

"Damn straight. With this book, we're gonna clean up."

"Well," Micere began, picking up a letter and slowly unfolding it, "as encouraging as that news is, Yvonne, we may have trouble brewing on another front." She glanced at each of her friends, hating to throw cold water on their enthusiasm. "I'm not going to beat around the bush on this, because it's serious."

"Is it that contractor?" Jewell broke in. "He

73

agreed to take installments. That situation is under control."

"No, that's not it," Micere replied, shifting uneasily in her chair. "It's Roger. He's threatening to call in the balance of my loan."

"Roger? What's the deal?" Jewell scooted to the edge of her seat.

"According to this letter, he feels our profits should be higher. If we can't increase them by twenty-five percent by the end of the third quarter, we might be out of business."

"Can he do that?" Jewell asked.

"I'm afraid so," Micere admitted. "There's a clause in our agreement about projected return on his investment, but it's very confusing. I didn't have my own attorney when the loan was drawn up, so I trusted Roger. I never dreamed he'd use the clause to trap me."

"Damn!" Jewell snatched the calendar off Micere's desk. "The third quarter, hmmm? Today's July sixth," she said, flipping pages, counting days. "Twelve weeks from now." Scowling, she tossed the calendar onto Micere's desk. "Let me see that loan agreement."

Swallowing the lump in her throat, Micere handed a thick file to Jewell. "I've read these papers so many times I've practically memorized every line. He does have legal grounds to do this, but I've done all I can to make this venture successful. You know that, Jewell. We just need more time."

Jewell nodded, rubbing her cheek as she read, her

head bent over the legal-size pages. "Let's stay calm. Roger's just flexing his financial muscle, trying to intimidate us."

Micere felt trapped. "I hope you guys realize that this threat has nothing to do with our ability to manage Food for the Soul. This is strictly personal."

"Shit," Yvonne hissed, speaking for the first time since Micere read the letter. She turned her face to the ceiling and exhaled a long, loud sigh. "I didn't think he'd do it. I really thought he was kidding."

Micere's head whipped around. Openmouthed, she stared at Yvonne. "You knew about this?"

Lowering her chin, Yvonne looked trapped. She raised her hands in surrender. "Roger came in Tuesday, while you were picking up Trina's new bicycle."

"What did he want?" asked Micere.

"He was talking all crazy," Yvonne replied. "Ranting and raving about how you were running around, neglecting Trina, jeopardizing his investment. He started asking a lot of questions about how much time you spent in the restaurant—things like that. I told him to talk to you. I didn't know where it was coming from, but he was way out there. He pumped me about Conrad, then told me he had ways to make you do whatever he wanted and he'd make sure things around here changed. Soon."

Micere's lips clamped shut, then she exploded. "Yvonne! Why didn't you tell me before now? Make me do what he wants? I can't believe Roger said that. He must be out of his mind."

"Right. Like I said, I thought he was kidding.

Blowing off steam. I know how he likes to throw his weight around." She reached over and took the letter from Micere's trembling hand and read it. "Damn. This sounds for real." Shaking her head, she passed the letter back to Micere, who slammed it down on the desk. "So, what are we going to do?" Yvonne asked.

"I'm not going to break off with Conrad, that's for sure," Micere said, more determined than ever to show Roger she was not about to buckle under his blustering threats. "This is emotional blackmail, and if I have to go to court to prove it, I will."

Jewell got up and went to stand behind Micere, placing one hand on her girlfriend's shoulder. "We might have to, but remember, Roger hasn't sued yet. This is just his warning shot. Let's get prepared for the fight—if it comes. I'm going to call Jan Brooks and have her look at these papers. You need a good lawyer, Micere."

Micere gazed morosely out the window, unable to respond.

Yvonne looked first at Micere, then at Jewell, propping both hands on the arms of her chair. Visibly shaken by this turn of events, she leaned toward Micere and said, "I think Roger means business, and I see big trouble ahead, girl. I've got seven thousand dollars tied up in this place . . . money I damn sure can't afford to lose." When Micere made no reply, Yvonne plunged ahead. "Don't get me wrong. I understand where you're coming from, but you gotta remember, I put every cent I could scrape together into this restaurant, and I don't plan to blow it. What about the TV pilot? The cookbook? A legal fight with Roger would destroy all of that—destroy everything we're counting on to make this place profitable." Yvonne got up and stalked between the desk and the door two times before turning to Micere. "Honey, you'd better think twice about fighting Roger . . . and maybe you ought to rethink this love thing you've got goin' on with Conrad and concentrate on holding on to Food for the Soul." She stared hard at Micere, then suddenly left the room, slamming the door behind her.

"What's with her?" Micere asked Jewell as soon as the shock of Yvonne's outburst had passed. "Rethink my commitment to Conrad? She's got a lot of nerve." Furious, she crumpled Roger's letter into a tiny ball and dropped it in the wastebasket. "Can you believe that bitch is siding with my ex-husband *against me?* She better get a grip. I'll make sure she gets her measly seven thousand dollars back, if I have to sell my car to pay her. The nerve!"

Jewell calmly retrieved the letter from the wastebasket, then busied herself putting it and the loan papers into her briefcase. Taking her time, she let Micere vent her rage. When Jewell finally faced her friend, it was evident that she, too, knew more than had been said. "Yvonne is just jealous."

"Jealous? Of me?" Micere was shocked.

"Of course she is. Why? Oh, let's see." Jewell's words took on the tone of a wise, interested observer. "You have a thoughtful, handsome man who sends you flowers, lavishes you with gifts, and whisks you away for helicopter rides to rooftop restaurants. She has an on-again, off-again relationship with a man who changes jobs the way most people change clothes. You have a beautiful daughter, while she has no children and time is marching on. She lives with Rufus, or with Bertha or Essie—or out of a suitcase, it seems. You have a beautiful home. Don't you see, Micere? You have everything, and Yvonne feels inferior, left out."

"But she acts like she's happy."

"In her own way she is. But Yvonne's investment in Food for the Soul, and the expectations she has for this place, are the only real things in her life. She can count on the business. She can't count on Rufus. She has girlfriends, but no real family. Now your love affair with Conrad is taking you away from her as well as putting the restaurant at risk."

"Did she tell you that?"

"Not in so many words. Of course she's happy for you, but she doesn't want you to know how deeply your new relationship is affecting her. I've seen the envy on her face when Conrad shows up or you take off to see him. She's scared, Micere. Give her time."

"Time," Micere groaned, considering Jewell's take on the situation. "We don't have very much of that." She went to stand beside the window. "This is a mess, isn't it? Jewell, what should I do? Breaking off with Conrad would certainly solve a lot of problems, but . . ."

"Do you love him?"

"Yes," Micere admitted.

"Do you believe he loves you?"

"Yes. No question."

"Then go for it, girl. Your happiness is more important than this business."

"But I won't be happy if I hurt Yvonne." She turned her back to the window and crossed her arms.

"She'll come around."

Micere fidgeted with the pearl buttons on her jacket. "There is more, Jewell," she started. "I didn't say anything earlier, but Roger is making noises about taking Trina away if I continue with Conrad."

"He wouldn't."

"I think he would." Micere bit her lip as she pondered the situation. "So you see where I'm coming from. I can't be that selfish. I can't risk losing Trina to be with a man."

"He ask you to marry him?"

"It's coming. I feel it, and it's going to be hard to say yes."

"Think he'll ask you to move to Dallas?"

"Could be. So, how can I jeopardize my daughter's security, the restaurant, and Yvonne's investment, all for love?" Her voice cracked, and suddenly the sobs she'd been holding back since that first argument with Roger spilled forth. She covered her face with both hands and cried.

Jewell patted her friend on the back, wishing she had some answers. "It's not going to be easy, but I know you will find a way to hold on to your lover, your child, and this place. I've known you a long time, Micere. You're a fighter, and I'm here for you.

Trust me, Roger will back down and you will never lose Trina."

Micere squeezed Jewell's hand, wanting to believe her. "Oh, God, I hope so. We've all worked too hard to let him rip our dreams, our friendship, our lives apart. I won't let him, Jewell. I just won't!"

"You can say that again, girlfriend," Jewell replied, giving Micere a final hug before snapping her briefcase shut. "I'll call you later," she said as she went out the door, leaving Micere alone in her office, wiping her tears away.

During the days that followed, Micere and Yvonne tried to be civil as they went about the business of running Food for the Soul, never mentioning the argument again. But it wasn't easy. Yvonne adopted a sullen, defensive attitude, while Micere became despondent and wary. They sniped at each other in front of customers and argued over insignificant matters, causing rumors among the staff and the regulars that neither the friendship nor the restaurant would survive this troubling period.

Speculation inched dangerously close to the truth when Roger actually sued Micere for $203,000, the balance of her loan. He charged his ex-wife with neglect of the business and mismanagement of his investment, citing her inability to meet specified quarterly profits and her frequent absences from town.

At first Micere was enraged. She consulted Jan Brooks, her attorney, who immediately began gathering evidence to dispute Roger's charges, in preparation for their appearance before a civil court judge, who would hear the case in thirty days.

In Micere's anger, she blamed herself. She should have been less trusting and more cautious when the original loan papers had been drawn up. She had never questioned the ramifications of the profit margin clause, and now Roger had control. She was beginning to fear that Roger would remain a thorny presence in her life forever.

CHAPTER 8

A week after the lawsuit was filed, Conrad flew to Houston to take Micere to the opening of an August Wilson play at the Ensemble Theater. The evening was strained, and Micere knew Conrad suspected something was terribly wrong. He pressured her to tell him what was going on when they went for a quiet dinner at Club Miranda after the show.

"You've been awfully quiet tonight," he said. "What's wrong?"

Placing her fingertips to her lips, she thought for a moment, then took a deep breath and plunged ahead, unable to put off the discussion any longer.

"Conrad, I think it might be a good idea if we don't see each other for a while. Just to cool things down," she blurted out, unable to ease into the conversation she'd been dreading for weeks. She'd struggled with the tangled issues facing her, desperate to find some peace of mind, and slowing down the relationship with Conrad seemed the only logical thing to do.

"Cool things down?" Conrad was openly hurt.

His dark eyes narrowed as he stared at Micere. "Why? What's happened?"

Her heart ached for him as she watched the expression of disappointment and disbelief that came over his face. She could not look him in the eye. Staring at the crumpled napkin in her lap, she told him, "Nothing has happened. I'm just tired, Conrad. Tired of juggling this long-distance relationship."

His jaw fell slack, but he said nothing, waiting for her to go on.

"We're in the middle of filming three shows back to back right now," she said. "Plus I've got a huge fund-raiser for the Coalition of One Hundred Black Women booked at the restaurant for next Saturday, and Yvonne has been out sick with the flu all week. There's just a lot going on, and I feel as if I'm always trying to fit you in. It shouldn't be like that. Spending time with you should be something I look forward to, not a burden that I can't seem to handle. I'm sorry, Conrad, but I'm exhausted. I can't continue being pulled in so many different directions. Something's got to give."

"I don't want you to put pressure on yourself because of me," he finally said, choosing his words carefully. "I love you, Micere. That's what matters most. Of course, I can't see you as often as I'd like, but that's no reason to cool things off. We'll find other ways to manage, trust me."

"I do, Conrad. But there's Trina to think of, too. As much as I try to justify my time away from her, I feel guilty all the time."

"Ah, so that's what this is about?" His worried expression eased, and the frown that creased his forehead softened. "You have no reason to feel guilty," he said bluntly.

She nodded, unwilling to broach the subject of Roger's veiled threats about filing for full custody of their daughter.

"I understand your situation, but you've got to lighten up, Micere. I adore Trina, and she seems to like me, but she's *your* daughter. You have to feel comfortable with the life you create with her. I never want to be a problem, and I'll never put pressure on you to choose between me and her, but at the same time, you deserve a mature relationship with the man you love, if that's what you want."

"Oh, it is," she said, quickly. Frustrated, she thought for a moment, then added, "I love you, Conrad, I do, but I'm afraid."

"Of what?" he prompted.

"Of making a big mistake. The kind of commitment that loving you requires will change my life so much. Maybe the time isn't right for us."

"The time will never be *right* for us, Micere, not as long as we're separated by hundreds of miles. Sure, you're in Houston and I'm in Dallas, but we can't keep putting our relationship on the back burner, waiting for exactly the right set of circumstances before we claim our happiness. That's foolish. You and I are in a place and time that makes each moment precious. I've tried to do most of the traveling, and you come to Dallas only while

Trina is with her father. What's wrong with that?" he said, evidently puzzled by this sudden change of heart.

"Nothing," she hedged, "but I worry about Trina when I'm with you."

"I understand what you're saying, but don't be so hard on yourself," he said rather sternly. "If Trina sees her mother is happy, she'll be happy, too. This is a time of transition for both of you. We can make it work. I promise."

The confidence in Conrad's voice eased Micere's pain, but she knew happiness would not come easily. Tears crowded in her throat, and she swallowed. "It's just too hard, Conrad," she said. "I'm tired of telling you goodbye almost as soon as we say hello. Just when I get used to being with you, I have to leave. I don't want to continue like this, but I don't know what to do to make it better. You have obligations in Dallas, especially with the new restaurant, and I have obligations that . . ." She drifted off, determined to keep Conrad out of the messy situation she faced.

"But we *can* hold it together. I'll arrange my life to accommodate yours."

"I don't think you'd be happy doing that, at least not for very long," she replied.

"Let me worry about that, okay? Thousands of people manage to have successful long-distance marriages. It's not . . ." He stopped, aware of what he'd just said. Their eyes connected, and his expression froze as he tried to gauge her reaction.

"Marriage?" Micere's heart swelled with joy, but she tensed at hearing the word.

"Well, yes," he admitted. "I guess I'm a little ahead of myself, but please hear me out." Reaching into the side pocket of his jacket, he took out a blue velvet box, then placed it on the table. "This is for you." Watching her closely, he waited for a response. When she said nothing, he rushed on. "I had planned to do this later, after dinner . . . but as I said, we can't wait for the perfect time. It's foolish to put things off when time is so precious, as precious as my love for you." He opened the box and held it under the candlelight for her to see.

Oh, God, she thought, afraid to touch the ring that sparkled inside. *I want nothing more than to slip this ring on my finger, marry this man, and start a new life. But how can I? How can I bring Conrad into Trina's life and expect her to understand? How can I abandon my friends and everything I've worked so hard to build here in Houston and start over in Dallas? Could I expect Conrad to do the same for me?*

Light bounced off the round solitaire diamond shining on its platinum band. The stone's size and brilliance took her breath away. "It's gorgeous," she told Conrad, loving him all the more. He'd taken this step in spite of the complications they faced, determined to believe that their love could survive. "But I can't accept it," she said, staring deep into his eyes.

"Why can't you?" Conrad shoved the ring box to the side, then reached across the table and took both of Micere's hands in his, holding them tightly, as if trying to erase the obstacles they faced. "Is it Trina you're really worried about, Micere, or is it Roger you cannot face?" His jaw tightened, and his lips formed a firm, straight line.

"Roger?" Micere pulled her hands from his, terrified by the tangle of emotions the question brought with it. "Why do you bring him up?"

"Because he's been checking me out. Did you know that?"

"Yes, I knew," she admitted. "And I'm so embarrassed. Roger has no right—"

"Wait a minute," Conrad said, stopping her. "Roger does have every right to know what kind of a man the mother of his child is spending so much time with."

Micere's eyes widened, but she remained silent, curious about Conrad's reaction.

Conrad went on. "I don't blame him for wanting to know who I am and what I'm about, but I do blame him for making you feel as if you don't deserve to be loved. That's cruel, and he can't prevent you from starting over . . . creating a new life with another man." Pulling back his shoulders, Conrad squared himself, as if ready to take Roger on. "In fact, I'd welcome an opportunity to meet him, get to know him, let him get to know me."

"I doubt that's what Roger had in mind when he started poking around in your affairs, believe me. He's not as generous as you. I've tried to keep my problems with Roger separate from our relationship, Conrad, but things have taken a bad turn."

"I sensed as much," he said.

It was time to come clean, Micere knew, but she'd still have to be careful about how much she revealed. "Roger is furious that I am seeing you," she admitted. "He's trying to bully me into giving you up. He can't stand to see me with anyone."

"Then tell me everything. Please, Micere," Conrad urged.

She opened her mouth, paused, then said, "He's filed a lawsuit, charging me with mismanagement of his investment. He's called in his loan to get control of Food for the Soul." Micere went on to explain the details of the suit and her strategy to fight him back. "I can't tell you any more, but I can assure you I am not taking this threat lightly," she said. Closing the lid of the ring box, she slid it back across the table toward Conrad. "So you see why I can't make the kind of commitment you want . . . not right now. I have to concentrate on winning the fight in court, or else risk losing my restaurant."

"Micere, please don't say that. Let me help. My brother has agreed to manage Skyview as soon as it's up and running. I'll be able to spend more time here with you."

"You'd better stay out of this, Conrad. Our relationship only complicates matters. It's best if we don't see each other for a while. Okay?"

"Okay? No, it's not okay! Exactly what do you want me to do? Leave you to go through this alone? I thought we had a whole lot more going for us than just *seeing* each other."

"We do, but I need time to think."

"Then think about the fact that I love you very much, and I want to marry you, not date you. I'm in this for the long haul, Micere, and I thought you were, too."

"I was . . . I am," she managed, wiping a tear. "Oh, please, leave me alone. I've told you I love you, I really do, but . . ."

"But you don't love me enough to confide in me or hang in there with me so we can sort things out?" He stiffened, glaring at her, arms crossed on his chest. Lifting a finger, he signaled the waiter and asked for the check, not looking at Micere. He gazed across the dining room, trying to gain control of his emotions. Finally his eyes met hers, and he stared at her as if she were a stranger. "I guess you're not the woman I thought you were. I'd better get going. I'll miss my plane."

The hurt in his voice and the pain on his face cut through Micere. She'd been deceitful. She'd led him to believe that the financial matter was the heart of her problem, when it really wasn't. The restaurant meant nothing. She could even survive the loss of her friendship with Yvonne. But Trina was her world. She could not risk losing her daughter. Loving and living with Conrad Winters might be a dream that would never come true.

He refused to let her drive him to the airport, so she backed off. When the taxi he'd called pulled up outside Club Miranda, he awkwardly pecked her on the cheek, told her goodbye, and got in the cab, disappearing in the flow of night traffic on the freeway.

Micere watched, silently weeping, feeling abandoned and alone. Conrad had no idea how high the stakes were nor how determined she was to keep him out of a potentially disastrous legal battle. Roger played hardball when it came to protecting what he considered his—the restaurant *and* his daughter. He'd have no qualms about dragging her relationship with Conrad into court or naming Conrad in a custody battle if the situation came to that. He'd take great pleasure in ruining Conrad's reputation, his business, and his personal life. She could not take such a chance.

Micere was trembling as she got in her car and headed home. Driving on autopilot, unable to concentrate, her mind filled with possible questions she'd have to answer in court, questions about her activities for the past seven months. Roger would use every bit of information he could glean from those closest to her to make her look like a bad manager and a bad mother. He'd turn her love for Conrad into a selfish, ugly affair, accusing her of neglect. When she entered the courtroom, she had to be able to truthfully tell the judge that she was not involved in a romantic relationship with *anyone*. That was what she had to do to protect her daughter—and Conrad.

Yvonne opened the door and was shocked to see Roger standing there, looking calm and very sure of himself. She yanked her robe tighter around her body and retied the belt, waiting to hear what he wanted, relieved that Rufus was out of town.

"I need to talk to you, Yvonne." Roger stomped inside, moving to the far side of the living room.

"You shouldn't have come here," Yvonne warned. "I've got the flu, and Rufus will have a fit if he finds—"

"Can the crap, Yvonne. Rufus is in Detroit and you're not sick. You've been hiding out here to avoid going to the restaurant."

"I have not! You're crazy!" Anchoring both hands on her hips, she positioned herself in front of Roger. "Why would I do that? Huh? I own part of that place, remember? Why would I stay away?"

"Because you can't face Micere," Roger said.

"Hmpf!" Yvonne replied, still glaring.

"Don't roll your eyes at me. I know exactly what's going on. You and Jewell and Micere aren't getting along so well these days, are you?"

Stepping closer, Yvonne accepted his challenge. "No, we're not! And it's all your fault, Roger. You're the one who decided to call in Micere's loan. Things were going along fine until you decided to throw your weight around. If you go to court, the cookbook and the television show are ruined. Why? To get back at Micere for falling in love?"

"No, that's not it," Roger said. "I have to protect my investment *and* my daughter. I don't like the way Micere has been handling either one."

"Get out of here, you bastard. I'll lose seven thousand dollars, everything I put into that place, so you can play big shot . . . the *man*. Please!"

Roger crossed the room and sat down in the

armchair beside the sofa, looking up at Yvonne. "You won't lose your money. In fact, if you're willing to help me out, you can see a much faster return, even become rich. How does that sound?" He waited as Yvonne slowly lowered her hands from her hips.

"What do you want from me?" she asked.

"Sit down and listen. I have a proposition that could make you a very wealthy woman."

"What do I have to do?"

"Just tell the truth, that's all," Roger said. "If you're willing to tell the judge everything you know about Micere's affair with Conrad Winters, I'll make you a full partner once I take over Food for the Soul. Fifty-fifty on the profits."

"I'm listening," Yvonne replied, crossing her legs as she sat back on the sofa. "But hurry up. I don't want anybody to know you're here."

CHAPTER 9

The case was set to be heard in civil court on Thursday, and on the preceding Saturday, Jan Brooks and Jewell met with Micere to review the financial records that would be entered into evidence. There were six boxes of papers supporting Micere's business plan, demonstrating how vigilantly she'd watched expenses. Personnel records proved adequate supervision and training of staff, and credit records showed she treated financial obligations in a professional manner. The three women had pulled together every scrap of paper that would help them fight Roger. Bertha, Joan, Precious, and Trudy Tulane agreed to be character witnesses on Micere's behalf.

When the meeting ended and Jan and Jewell left, Micere panicked. She felt herself coming apart. Preparing for the court appearance had taken its toll, making her cranky, withdrawn, and depressed. She placed both arms on the desk, then lowered her head as tears rolled down her cheeks. Insecurity and loneliness had plagued Micere once the finality of the end of her relationship with Conrad set in. He had not called her since she turned down his proposal, and though Jewell had begged Micere to make the first move, she couldn't. As the days passed, she became terrified at the thought of what she'd done. The image of Conrad moving on with his life with another woman at his side brought a stab of pain that cut deep into her heart.

Unable to get a hold on her emotions, she began sobbing loudly, her head still on her desk. She was no longer concerned about being strong, or even about winning the legal fight. All she wanted was Conrad's arms around her once again and to know that their love had a chance.

"Mommy?"

Trina's small voice startled Micere, who immediately raised her head and grabbed a tissue. Ashamed to have been caught crying, she stifled her sobs and dabbed at her face, trying to smile at her daughter, who lingered at the doorway.

"Hello there, sweetheart," Micere said, turning to face Trina.

"Why are you crying?" Trina asked, taking a hesitant step toward her mother.

"Guess I'm a little tired," Micere replied. "Come over here." She held out her arms, and Trina moved quickly to stand near her mother, leaning her head on her shoulder.

"Why doesn't Conrad come to see us anymore?" Trina asked.

Surprised that Trina would bring up Conrad's

name, she stroked her daughter's cheek. "Oh, he's been very busy with his own restaurant, and you know he lives so far away."

Trina nodded, then asked, "Well, is he gone away for good? Is that why you're crying?"

"No," Micere lied. "That's not why."

"But you were always so happy when he was around," Trina said, running her small hand along her mother's arm. "Don't cry anymore, Mommy. Please. Can't you call him and ask him if you can go see him?"

"I don't know about that," Micere hedged, saddened to realize how much her daughter was affected by her miserable state. "I told you he's very busy."

Trina climbed up onto her mother's lap. "Do I have to go live with Daddy?"

Shocked, Micere turned Trina around so she could look closely at her face. "Why did you say that?"

"Because that's what Daddy said might happen."

Fighting to stay calm, Micere probed, "How would you feel if that happened? Would you like to live with your father?"

"No. I love Daddy, but I don't want to live with him. Not all the time. I want to stay here with you."

My God, Micere thought, now enraged at herself as well as Roger. How could she have been so blind? She'd been selfishly concentrating on her own troubles while Roger was filling Trina's head with unfounded fears. There was no telling what else he'd said to Trina in an attempt to bring her over to his side. *The sneaky bastard*, she silently cursed.

"I want you here with me, too," Micere said, then calmly added, "What would you think if I married Conrad? He might move in here with us, or we might have to move to Dallas."

"I think I'd like that! I do like Conrad, and he makes you smile," Trina murmured.

"I'm glad you like him," Micere said softly, hugging Trina close. She'd stupidly shut both Trina and Conrad out of her life just when she needed them most.

"What does Conrad's restaurant look like? Will you take me there someday?" Trina wanted to know.

"Maybe we need to go there so you can see for yourself."

"Great! When?"

"How about right now?"

"Really? Can we?"

"Yes, really." Micere scowled at the stack of legal papers on her desk. Roger be damned! She was going to live her life, and if Roger didn't approve, he could go to hell. There was only one way to find out if she and Conrad had a future together, and that was to go to him and beg his forgiveness. And if she was lucky enough to be offered that diamond ring again, she'd gladly let him put it on her finger. "You bet we can go see Conrad right now," she said, grabbing the phone to call Southwest Airlines.

Once she arrived in Dallas, Micere's courage began to waver. The forty-five-minute flight had given her time to reflect on her impulsive act. She should have phoned Conrad before taking off. Was she acting like a selfish, desperate woman? Would he be annoyed by her unannounced visit, child in tow? Had bringing Trina along been a big mistake? But surely he'd be civil in front of her daughter . . . she hoped. As the taxi sped along the freeway, Micere mentally rehearsed her apology, groping for words to let him know how sorry she was. She should have trusted him to help her deal with Roger.

When the taxi stopped in front of Conrad's Cafe, Micere paid the driver and got out. Standing on the sidewalk, holding Trina's hand, she took a deep breath, then started toward the door. Suddenly, whether or not Conrad would welcome their unexpected arrival was no longer of great concern. One thing was certain: The only way she could be the kind of mother who could raise a happy daughter was to have Conrad at her side.

The hostess recognized Micere immediately and cheerfully escorted her and Trina to a booth at the front of the cafe.

"How you been?" the hostess asked, handing Micere a menu. "Haven't seen you 'round for a while."

"Right," Micere answered. "Just been swamped. Is Conrad here?"

The hostess glanced over her shoulder toward the rear of the cafe. "He oughta be in his office back there. Want me to tell him you're here?"

Micere shook her head. "No, this is a surprise

visit. Would you help Trina order whatever she wants and keep an eye on her for a minute?"

"No problem," the hostess said, alerting one of the waitresses, who hurried over, smiling at Trina. "Glenda, watch the front for a minute, okay?" Then the hostess slipped into the booth beside Trina and they began checking out the menu together.

Micere walked slowly down the long corridor behind the kitchen. She'd been in Conrad's office several times and knew the tiny space would be private. The door was halfway open, and she saw the back of Conrad's head bent over a spreadsheet on his desk. She lingered outside for a moment, her love for him rising to the surface, warming her face. She began to tremble, fearing he might not want to see her, but she knocked lightly, then stood very still until he swung around and scowled.

Startled, she blurted out, "Hello, Conrad."

"What are you doing here?" His tone was terse.

"I came . . ." She took a long breath, then hesitantly stepped forward. "I wanted to tell you—"

"Stop right there!" he ordered, throwing his pen down on his desk.

Micere froze. He was upset. He didn't want to see her. She started backing away, but he rushed at her. "I know I should have called," she began.

But Conrad wasn't listening. He strode past her, slammed the door shut, then leaned against it. When he grabbed her and pulled her to him, crushing her against his chest, Micere let his lips devour hers. She sank into his familiar embrace, kissing him back with all the love and devotion she'd suppressed during the past few lonely weeks.

"I knew you'd come!" he said, burying his face in her hair, which she was wearing free around her face.

"I didn't come alone." Micere gently took Conrad by the hand, leading him to the doorway. "Look out there."

He laughed to see Trina absorbed in a gooey grilled cheese sandwich. "Come on," he said, pulling Micere along.

They sat down opposite Trina, who grinned, then resumed eating. With arms around each other, Conrad and Micere held on as if they were both afraid the other would run off and disappear.

"And what would you like to do after lunch?" Conrad asked Trina when she finished the sandwich.

"Go to Six Flags?" she quickly answered, an eyebrow lifted as she waited for their reaction.

"Six Flags it is!" Conrad agreed, a huge smile on his face.

The rest of the day was spent riding roller coasters, eating peanuts, and buying souvenirs at the amusement park. By the time evening neared, Conrad had listened to the whole story and was not pleased by what he'd heard. Incensed over Roger's maneuvering, Conrad told Micere he was coming to Houston to help her fight for the restaurant and her reputation.

"There is no way I'll stand by and let that man destroy you."

"But what about your obligations here?"

"Jay will be able to manage. As a matter of fact,

I think he'd be kind of glad to have me out of his hair for a while."

"Conrad, this day has been wonderful."

"The first of many more to come," he promised. "But we've got a few things to settle first. Can you two stay overnight?"

"Sure," Micere said.

"Good. You'll stay at my townhouse tonight. I need to square away a few things so I can be free to go with you, and we'll drive back to Houston in the morning."

Micere eased her arm around Conrad's waist, placed her head on his shoulder, and sighed. It felt very good to hold him again and to have him at her side. No matter the outcome of the lawsuit, she knew she'd get through it now that Conrad was back in her life. She never planned to have it any other way.

CHAPTER 10

The interrogation progressed much more quickly than Micere had expected. Judge Pedras, who had studied the documents submitted by both sides, made it clear to everyone involved that he wanted to settle the case that day. He had listened to a representative of the bank, who testified that more than half of Micere's loan payments had been received late, though she'd never missed a payment. With patience and a slight show of boredom, the judge also listened while the remodeling contractor admitted to changing his mind about the installment payments and now wanting the balance of his money. Jan Brooks presented reams of documentation to show that Micere's projections to service her debt were realistic and still on target.

Now the solitaire diamond ring on Micere's left hand glistened under the glare of the fluorescent lights beaming down from the courtroom ceiling. She nervously twisted it, waiting for Judge Pedras's next question. She was agitated and fearful, despite Conrad's comforting presence. The supportive testimony given by Precious, Lottie, and even Ramon portrayed

Micere Sendaba as a professional, a serious entrepreneur. Trudy Tulane told the judge that she was sure the television series would greatly increase revenue for Food for the Soul.

Micere's mouth was dry, but her hands were soaking wet, and nervous tension had settled in her stomach. When the judge finished dissecting her financial arrangement with Roger, her business records, and her management activities, she was not surprised by what came next.

"Are you currently in a business relationship with a man named Conrad Winters?" Judge Pedras asked curtly.

"No, Your Honor," Micere answered.

"Do you have any type of a relationship with him?"

Micere glanced at Conrad, then said, "Yes, Your Honor. He's my fiancé."

"I see." The judge flipped through the stack of papers in front of him. "Mr. Sendaba alleges in his statement of grievances that you are planning to bring in Mr. Winters as a partner. Does Conrad Winters have a financial interest or an investment in Food for the Soul?"

"None."

"Thank you. That's all." He slammed the folder shut and crossed his arms atop the bulky file, looking at Roger with keen interest.

Micere felt light-headed with relief as she sat down, praying that the rest of the inquiry would move as quickly. This judge did not play around. He wanted to be done with this case.

"Yvonne Wilson," Judge Pedras called.

As soon as Yvonne sat down, he asked, "During the past six months, how often was Mrs. Sendaba away from her place of business?"

Giving Micere a smug glance, she sat up straighter, then said, "About fifty percent of the time, I'd guess."

"Your Honor." Jan Brooks stood up to get the judge's attention.

"Yes, Ms. Brooks?" Annoyed, the judge leaned forward, peering over the tops of his glasses.

"I'd like Ms. Wilson to break that percentage down between operating hours and the time that the restaurant was not open for business."

"Very well," the judge replied. "Ms. Wilson, of that fifty percent you mentioned, was this when the restaurant was open or closed for business?"

Now Yvonne looked perplexed and not quite so smug. "Well, she was gone a lot, really. . . ."

"I asked if Mrs. Sendaba was away when the restaurant was open or closed." Judge Pedras's patience was clearly wearing thin.

"She was usually there when the restaurant was open," Yvonne admitted.

"Thank you. Now, to your knowledge, where did Mrs. Sendaba go?"

"She went to Dallas."

"Was this for business or pleasure?"

"She went to see Conrad Winters."

"On business or pleasure, Ms. Wilson? Do you know?"

"Yes, Your Honor. For pleasure, I'm certain."

"And during the time Mrs. Sendaba was away, who managed Food for the Soul?"

"Managed it? I did." Yvonne gave a curt laugh. "Who else? She just dumped everything on me when she took off. I had to make all the decisions about menu changes, handle customer problems, and supervise the staff. But Jewell, our CPA, did help me out. Not often, though, because she had to watch Trina."

"Mrs. Sendaba's daughter?"

"Yes."

Micere's blood boiled to hear that lie. She yanked on Conrad's sleeve. "That's a lie. Trina was with her father every time I was with you, except once."

Conrad covered her hand with his, urging her to calm down. "I know, I know. Don't panic."

The judge went on. "So you are saying that Mrs. Sendaba's personal relationship with Mr. Winters took her away from her responsibilities at the restaurant?"

"Constantly. She abandoned her business *and* her daughter in order to spend time with her lover," Yvonne blurted out. "She didn't care about either. She'd be gone for days at a time, and I'd have to deal with everything—the creditors, the deliveries, the maintenance people. She has no interest in the restaurant anymore. All she's concerned with is this new man in her life."

"That's not true!" Micere burst out, rising to her feet. "How dare you say such—"

The rap of Judge Pedras's gavel and his stern, disapproving look stopped Micere from saying more, and she sank back into her seat, ashamed to have let Yvonne provoke her so easily.

As the judge continued his questions, Micere was forced to endure Yvonne's twisted description of Micere's relationship with Conrad. It sounded tawdry and irresponsible, as if Micere were some self-centered swinger who cared only about having a good time.

"I never thought I'd see the day when Micere Sendaba would put her sexual desires before her business or her daughter," Yvonne finished.

Those words wounded Micere deeply, and the pain that settled over her brought a sting of tears to her eyes. She stared at Yvonne, her girlfriend of thirty-three years. *Who is this stranger?* she wondered.

"I never thought she'd betray me like this. Why?" she whispered to Conrad as Yvonne stepped down from the stand.

Conrad looked over at Micere, raising both eyebrows, as if he was not surprised. "It's obvious. Roger got to her. The question is how," he muttered under his breath.

Micere's confidence fell until Jewell took the stand. Without mincing words, Jewell launched into her version of Micere's lifestyle, insisting that Micere's visits to see Conrad were always carefully arranged and had never affected the operation of the restaurant. She pointed out that Micere had asked her to watch Trina only once, and even then Roger had come by to pick up his daughter. She told the judge that Micere was a devoted mother whose only crime was falling in love—perfectly normal, in her opinion, as it would be with any relationship between mature, responsible adults.

"I'd think a busy man like Roger Sendaba would have more important things to do than try to discredit the mother of his daughter and jeopardize her ability to support herself," Jewell admonished. Surprisingly, the judge didn't interfere when she turned toward Roger and said, "I am ashamed of you, Roger Sendaba. You don't need this money, and you know damn well you don't want the restaurant." Turning back to the judge, she said, "I've known Roger for close to twenty years, Your Honor, and he's the kind of man who wants to own, possess, control, or dominate everybody and everything that comes his way." She sent a cutting look at Roger, who looked stunned. "Isn't that true? And why in the world are you dragging poor Trina into this? You know Micere is a wonderful mother. You know it! And if you'd stop feeling sorry for yourself because you've messed up your life, you might be able to see that Conrad Winters is the best thing that could ever happen to Micere. Just let it go!"

Roger's mouth flew open and he half rose from his chair, but his attorney yanked him back down. Roger squirmed in his seat, frowning, while his attorney sat beside him, stone-faced and grim.

"And you!" Jewell exploded, now directing her anger at Yvonne. "Girlfriend, you know you're wrong, letting Roger use you to punish Micere. I can't believe he got to you. What were you—"

"That's enough." The judge finally had heard

enough. "Just answer my questions, Mrs. Tratt. We don't need your opinions on anything that has transpired here."

Pursing her lips, Jewell sat back and calmed down, adjusting the front of her suit jacket. "Yes, Your Honor," she said, her eyes penetrating Yvonne with daggers.

Judge Pedras concluded by asking Jewell two questions about specific entries in the restaurant's financial records, then said he'd heard enough, and retired to his chambers to make his decision.

The bailiff asked for quiet in the courtroom while waiting for the judge to reappear. Micere embraced Jewell, mouthing her thanks for daring to speak her mind, then latched onto Conrad's arm and clung to him, praying for the horrible ordeal to be over.

When Judge Pedras swept back to his bench, all eyes focused on him. Roger and Micere stood with their attorneys as the judge prepared to render his verdict.

His language was clear and direct. "After reviewing all of the evidence and listening to testimony in this case, I have come to the conclusion that Mrs. Sendaba has done everything in her power to successfully meet the requirements of the loan agreement and has not violated any of the terms. Her business records are in order, her projections for future revenue appear to be accurate, and I am willing to give her time to prove them out." He looked at Roger. "You have no real basis to pull the rug out from under this business at this time, though I understand your concern over past financial performance. My decision, therefore, is to dismiss this case. However"—now he turned to Micere—"I want updated financial records filed with this court again in six months. If your projections are on target, no action will be taken, but if not, you may very well face your ex-husband again in court." He banged his gavel. "Case dismissed." Then he left the room.

"Oh, thank God," Micere said, elated that the nightmare was over. With the support of Conrad and her friends, she had done it—she had shown Roger she meant to hold on to the restaurant and her daughter. When Conrad wrapped his arms around her as they headed to the door, she looked back and saw Yvonne watching her.

"Just a minute," Micere told Conrad, leaving him standing in the aisle as she approached Yvonne.

Micere sat down next to Yvonne and looked into her miserable face. Disappointment in her voice, she asked, "How could you do this to me?"

Yvonne began to cry. "I was so scared of losing my investment in the restaurant. Everything I have is tied up in Food for the Soul. Roger promised me—"

"I can guess what he promised you," Micere interrupted. "Let me tell you something, Yvonne. Of course, I am royally pissed off at you. So mad I could slap your face." Then she took Yvonne's hand, lowering her voice. "But I have no intention of letting Roger's sick maneuvering destroy our friendship. That's exactly what he'd like to see happen. I refuse to give him that satisfaction. Stick with me, girl.

We've got a television show to do, remember?"

Yvonne's face brightened. "Oh, Micere, I was so stupid. I was feeling so low, so desperate, when Roger got to me. It was foolish of me to listen to him."

"Yes, it was." Micere stood, pulling Yvonne to her feet. "Let's go. I don't particularly like the company around here," she muttered, giving Roger a contemptuous look.

Micere linked arms with Yvonne as the two hurried to catch up with Conrad. Jewell, Precious, and Lottie rushed over, hugging Micere, congratulating her on the outcome of the case. Smiling, Micere faced her friends.

"Okay, you guys, we've got some celebrating to do," she told them, realizing that the love and support of her friends was what had pulled her through this crisis. She also knew that the pain Yvonne had caused would fade in time. She was not about to toss away a relationship that had survived three decades, simply because Yvonne had put her trust in the wrong man. All of the experiences, both good and bad, that they'd shared created a bond that could not easily be broken. How could she discard everything they'd meant to each other, done for each other, and expressed to one another, in the aftermath of one tragic day in court?

Micere sighed as she left the court room. *Friendships are just as complicated, stressful, and wonderful as marriages,* she thought, *and just as much work to hold on to.* She knew Conrad would stick by her no matter what Roger tried to do about Trina, and she felt confident that she'd never lose custody of her daughter. And what did it really matter where they finally settled to start their new life together? Houston or Dallas—who cared? Micere was certain about only one thing: At the end of the day, love resided in only one place, and that was in her heart.

◆

FOOD FOR THE SOUL
RECIPES

◆

Crusty Corn Casserole

2 cans corn: 1 creamed, 1 whole kernel
    with juice (16 oz.)
2 beaten eggs
8 oz. sour cream
1 box cornbread mix (8 oz.)
1 stick butter or margarine
Dash of onion powder, 1 tsp. bacon bits,
    or 1 tsp. finely chopped green pepper
    or 1 small jalapeño pepper (optional)

Preheat oven to 350°F. Melt butter in 8"x12" glass baking dish in the oven. Mix all ingredients and pour into hot buttered pan. Bake 1 hour, until crust forms.

Shrimp Jambalaya

¼ c. olive oil
1 c. chopped green pepper
1 c. chopped onion
1 c. chopped celery
2 cloves garlic, minced
2 c. tomato sauce
¼ c. V8 juice
½ tsp. chili powder
¼ tsp. sugar
1 tsp. fresh cilantro leaves, minced
½ c. dry white wine or chicken broth
1 lb. shrimp, cleaned and deveined
½ lb. ham, cooked and diced (use
    cooked chicken or sausage if preferred)
Hot pepper sauce
Hot cooked rice

Heat oil in large, deep skillet at medium-high heat. Add green pepper, onion, celery, and garlic. Saute until tender. Add tomato sauce, V8 juice, chili powder, and sugar. Then add the cilantro and wine/chicken broth. Simmer uncovered for 15 minutes. Add shrimp, ham, or sausage. Add a few drops of hot pepper sauce to taste. Also add 1 tsp. salt or to taste. Cook 10 minutes at medium-high heat to boil. Serve over hot rice.

Quick Kale

2 bunches of kale, tough stems removed,
   picked and washed
2 tsp. olive oil
3 cloves garlic, chopped
2 tbsp. bacon bits
1 c. chicken broth
¼ c. chopped onion
Salt
Pepper
Vinegar or hot pepper sauce (optional)

Heat oil in Dutch oven at medium-high heat. Saute garlic and onion until onion is tender. Add kale, bacon bits, and broth. Reduce heat to a simmer until kale is tender-crisp (about 20 minutes). Add salt and pepper to taste. Sprinkle with vinegar or hot pepper sauce if desired.

THE HEART OF
THE MATTER

◆

SANDRA KITT

◆

PROLOGUE

"Kat, please stop worrying. You haven't forgotten any details, and everything is going to be fine. In any case, it's much too late in the day to start changing your plans. Except for maybe calling the whole thing off . . ."

Katherine forced herself out of her reverie when she caught the note of rising horror in her mother's voice. She turned to the woman standing behind her, who had been unnecessarily twisting curls in the soft gathering of hair at the back of Katherine's head. Katherine cleared her brow and smiled.

"Sorry."

Katherine's mother glanced briefly at her daughter's face as it was reflected in the mirror and continued to smooth her hair upward into the softly twisted knot. "Are you nervous?"

"Not particularly." Katherine shrugged. "I was just thinking I should have heard from Niki by now. She's falling down on her duties as maid of honor," she said dryly. "Well, no matter—there is no way this is not going to happen. I've waited for three years, and I've been planning for the last two. I am ready. And I know you and Daddy are sick of me and want to get me off your hands."

"*Hmpf!*" Elaine Stanley gave her daughter's hairdo a final pat and moved away. "Anyway, I'm glad to hear that you're not having any second thoughts. And you'll put poor Neal out of his misery."

"Oh . . . he didn't exactly suffer," Katherine said slyly. She picked up a necklace, a thin white gold chain with a small heart-shaped diamond positioned in the center, and fastened it around her throat. Katherine tilted her head and admired the look against her caramel-colored skin and the graceful column of her neck. "Do you think I should wear the pearls or this?"

Her mother glanced quickly at her. "No, that's beautiful. Elegant but simple. If you're talking about the fact that Neal moved in with you, I *don't* want to go there. You know very well how your father and I felt about that."

Katherine next picked up a pair of diamond ear studs and began inserting them into her pierced lobes. "I know. But thanks for not getting on my case or harping on it. It just made sense to both of us to—"

"Practice first? Test the waters? You know that's not how folks did it in the past. That's not how your father and I did it. Your nana used to have a saying that goes—"

"I know, I know: 'Why buy the cow if you can get the milk for free?' I'm aware of all that. I only plan on doing this once in my life, and I wanted to make sure the cards were stacked in my favor. I'm sorry, but love just isn't enough anymore. Neal is cute and all that, but he could have been out of his mind. If he was, I wanted to find that out before we took out the mortgage and joint accounts."

Elaine Stanley looked speculatively at her daughter. "Well, if you had changed your mind, I bet there are a few women who would have gladly taken your place."

Katherine pursed her lips and shrugged. "It wouldn't have mattered who else wanted him if he wasn't interested. I didn't have to steal Neal from anyone. He loves me. And I love him."

"Then he's not out of his mind and he shows good taste," Elaine concluded.

"Thanks, Mom, but you're a little bit biased, I think."

"Danika didn't seem all that happy for you when you and Neal announced you were getting married."

Katherine averted her eyes from her mother's inquiring gaze. "That's only because she wanted to be the first of our crowd to get married. You know Niki. She always has to be the first and the best."

"Yes, I know. I love Niki like she's my own, but Lord, her folks have spoiled that girl. I was surprised when she didn't come to the rehearsal last week. The rest of the party was there."

"She said she had a last-minute emergency. Something with work, but nothing serious, I think."

"I see," Elaine Stanley said softly. "I guess you

also didn't think it strange when she didn't come to your shower."

Katherine frowned and hesitated. She glanced covertly at her mother, trying to read her expression. But she wasn't successful at it and never had been. When her mother wanted to mask her feelings, she was very good at appearing calm and in control. Which was how Katherine always knew that her mother was implying something much deeper than her questions sounded.

"What are you saying? That Niki had other reasons for not coming?"

"I'm not suggesting a thing," Katherine's mother said with raised brows and an expression of innocence.

The phone on Elaine Stanley's nightstand rang, and she stepped over the opened boxes on the floor as she went to answer.

"Maybe that's Niki," Katherine said as she began to pull on her pantyhose.

Her mother waded through the white and pink tissue paper spilling from the boxes that had carefully wrapped her daughter's dress, veil, satin shoes, and other accessories. She picked up the phone on the third ring. "I bet it's Neal," Elaine countered. "Hello? Oh, hi, Paula. . . . Yes, she's almost dressed. Where are you?" she beckoned to Katherine to come and take the call. "Wait, you can tell Kat yourself. I'll see you in a little while."

Katherine took the phone from her mother. "Please don't tell me you're going to be late, Paula," she said into the receiver.

"I'm on my way out the door," the voice on the other end responded. "I just wanted to remind you that DeeDee said she will not sit next to Malcolm at the reception. I sure hope you separated them."

"No, I did not. DeeDee gets mad at Malcolm every three and a half minutes. I'm willing to bet that the first thing he'll do is apologize. Then she'll be difficult for a while. And then he'll coo and tease her, and then they'll be tight again before the first dance."

"I just don't want DeeDee to spoil anything," Paula said.

"She won't, 'cause I'm not going to let her. I gotta go."

When Katherine turned around, her mother was holding up layers and folds of creamy white batiste and lace, ready to help her into the delicate garment. Katherine stared at it for a moment, and then sought her mother's gaze. She had a sudden memory of the first time she was preparing to go to school, to kindergarten, and her mother had been in a similar position, holding a new dress for her to wear. She remembered that she'd cried because she hadn't wanted to go, despite the assurances that she would have fun and meet friends, and that her mother would not only take her to school but be there to bring her back home at the end of the morning.

"Now, be careful of your hair," Elaine murmured, positioning the dress over her daughter's head and shoulders.

Katherine silently wriggled into the gown and the fabric dropped into place in layers around her.

Behind her once more, her mother zipped the back and smoothed the soft material, which trailed on the floor. Her mother gently took her arm and guided her in front of the full-length mirror on the inside of the closet door. Katherine stared at her image while her mother fussed with the lines of the dress.

It had not been the wedding dress her mother wanted to see her married in. It lacked the adornment of seed pearls, beads, or Viennese lace. It was not of the traditional stiff white fabrics like satin or organza. Katherine adjusted the narrow shoulder straps of the gown, sighing inwardly with relief and pleasure. This dress gave her exactly the look she wanted: simple, clean, light, and carefree. None of which made any sense to her childhood best friend, Danika, who had all but laughed at her when she'd decided this was the wedding dress she wanted.

"That's not a wedding dress," Niki had derided her. "It looks like a nightgown, for God's sake. There's no waist, no skirt. There's nothing to it, not even a train."

"That's why I like it," Katherine had retorted in her own defense.

She'd learned from early childhood not to let herself be bullied into doing what all her friends were doing. And her taste in clothes had always been simpler than Niki's, whose primary goals were to have the latest in fashion and to get attention. But at nearly five feet nine inches, Katherine knew that too much fuss and detail would not serve her slender, small-breasted figure very well. The creamy off-white dress puddled on the floor at her feet, but would just barely brush it once she put on her shoes. She turned this way and that to see the movement of the gown. She giggled.

"Can you see Niki in this?"

Elaine Stanley chortled and shook her head. "Heavens, no. Danika would look like a child wearing a . . . a . . ."

"Nightgown," Katherine supplied. They both grinned at the image. "What do you think?" Katherine asked her mother, slowly pivoting and holding her arms slightly out from her body.

"Wait a minute," her mother murmured, bending to adjust the hem of the dress.

Katherine heard the funny catch in her mother's voice. She touched her shoulder. "Mom? You're not crying, are you? Don't tell me you're going to miss me. I remember when you used to threaten to sell me to gypsies when I was bad or talked back to you."

When her mother finally looked squarely at Katherine, she was once again composed. If there had been any misting in her eyes suggesting tears or emotion, it was gone. But the replacement was a look of love and tenderness. Of pride and peace.

"I will only say that the gypsies should have been so fortunate. Honey, you look absolutely beautiful."

They hugged, Katherine only an inch or so taller than her mother.

"I had a really great role model. Remember when Eric used to call me a walking stick? And Sky-high?" Katherine mused softly.

"Typical older-brother teasing." Elaine withdrew from her daughter's arms and looked at her watch. "We'd better hurry. We should have left for the church ten minutes ago."

"I'm almost done. Where are my shoes?"

There was a soft knock on the door.

"Danika, come on in," Katherine called out.

The door opened a few inches as Elaine grabbed the handle to pull it further. But then she gasped and began pushing it closed again.

"You can't come in! Go away. You should be at the church with Neal and Eric."

"I'm leaving right now. I just wanted to say something to Kat."

"No, you can't," Elaine said firmly, not letting her husband into their bedroom. "You're not supposed to see the bride until you're both ready to start the ceremony."

"Old wives' tale. Kat, it's Daddy."

"Daddy, I have to finish getting dressed." She searched on her mother's bureau for the delicate and elaborate lace handkerchief that had belonged to her paternal grandmother. It was the "something old" she would have with her throughout the wedding service, due to start in less than an hour. Katherine folded the small square and carefully tucked it into the bodice of her dress, making sure that none of it showed above her neckline. "Could you please call Niki and see if she's left her house yet? And make sure Neal has the rings."

From the other side of the door a deep male voice sighed dramatically. "I was warned that all I'd get to do was run errands and spend money to see my daughter married. . . ."

As the voice faded, Katherine turned and more or less hopped to the door as she attempted to step into her shoes at the same time that her mother was following her, trying to place the flower-covered band with its attached veil atop Katherine's head.

"Daddy, wait!" She peeked out the door, but her father had already descended half way down the staircase to the first floor of her childhood home. "I love you."

Don Stanley blew his daughter a kiss and waved as he hurried to the front door. "I'll see you in church."

Katherine and her mother picked up steam, putting on the last touches for the coming rituals. Elaine hurried her daughter out of the room and down to the waiting limousine. They would be riding with Katherine's maternal grandparents. She was about to step into the backseat of the limo when she hesitated.

"What is it? What did you forget?" her mother asked anxiously.

"Nothing. I just want to call Niki and make sure everything is okay."

"Katherine, get in the car. We have to leave right now or you're going to be late for your own wedding. Niki is either at the church already or she's not."

She wasn't.

Katherine's mother left her daughter to take her

place with the rest of the bride's family in the front three pews of the church. Everyone was where they were supposed to be, including the flower girl, Katherine's niece Kyra, a confident and cute five-year-old in yellow. In the anteroom where the brides-maids had gathered, there was agreement that Danika Evans was going to show off and arrive at the last possible moment.

"I already called her house and there's no answer," Laura Hendricks said.

"Then she's on her way," Katherine affirmed.

"What if she's not?" Eileen Daniels asked.

"See, I *knew* this was going to happen! Niki always has to be the center of attention!" Laura complained.

"Something must have happened to her. Maybe she got sick. Maybe someone in her family got sick," Katherine speculated. "*Something* must have happened. God, I hope Niki didn't get into a car accident. . . ."

There was a moment of stunned silence as the four women, all friends since junior high with the exception of Donna Powers, who was Katherine's former college roommate, each made up a story in their own heads as to why Danika Evans, Katherine's best friend, would be late . . . or not show up.

There was a knock on the door.

"Niki!" four voices said in unison, and everyone rushed to the door.

It opened and the organist, a middle-aged woman, stepped into the room, a little taken aback by the reception she met. "Are you girls ready? Everyone's waiting for you to give the signal, Katherine, so I can begin the processional march."

Four pairs of eyes turned to Katherine as she realized that at this very instant she was going to have to make a critical decision. Her hands began to tremble as she alternated between wondering what had happened to Danika and wanting to proceed with one of the most important moments of her life. Katherine looked into the faces of the four other women in the room. She could feel panic and disbelief spread throughout her body as they all waited for her words. Katherine had believed that, next to her and Neal, Danika was the second most significant person in the ceremony. She was to be more than just the maid of honor. Niki Evans was the symbol of their youth, of their potential and promise . . . of trust. Niki was the proof that they had survived the trials of growing up and that despite the fact that they were so different, they were and would always be girlfriends.

Katherine blinked rapidly and swallowed. She turned to the organist. "Go get my mother. Tell her she's going to be the matron of honor."

The other women exchanged glances.

"Tell her to meet us at the back of the sanctuary and I'll explain."

The organist nodded and left them. Katherine didn't wait for more discussion. She ushered the women from the room, and they went to take up their places for the start of the ceremony. In the corridor the bridesmaids lined up with their escorts. While they waited for Katherine's mother to join them, Katherine hurried to a console table where a large vase of wedding flowers decorated a spot where the guest book lay open.

Katherine quickly pulled out several stems of flowers, quickly fashioning a bouquet. She took one of the ribbons trailing from her own arrangement and used it to tie the bouquet together.

"Katherine, what's the matter? What's going on?"

Katherine turned to her mother. "I need you to be in the party." She thrust the bouquet into her hands, at the same time guiding her to the rear of the bridesmaid line. "You're going to be matron of honor."

Elaine Stanley's mouth dropped open, though she allowed herself to be led. "But . . ."

"Go ahead and start," Katherine firmly directed the organist, who turned and hurried away.

Her father stepped out of another hallway and came to take his place beside her. He displayed only a moment's confusion upon seeing his wife instead of Danika, and then gave his attention to his daughter. He took her hand and placed it on his arm. He patted her hand, gazing into her eyes.

"Neal is a very lucky man."

"Thank you, Daddy."

The chords of the wedding march began with a majesty that sent a chill down Katherine's spine. In the sanctuary the guests all rose to their feet to face the aisle down which she and her father would pass. The groomsmen began their slow walk down the aisle with the bridesmaids, taking up their positions on either side of the minister. Next came Kyra, energetically throwing out fistfuls of rose petals as if she were lobbing snowballs, eliciting amused chuckles from the guests.

Katherine gave a final thought to what might have happened to Danika. She considered her mother's questioning earlier that morning and wondered if there was any validity to the implication that perhaps Niki wasn't happy about her getting married. But why wouldn't she be? Katherine wondered. Danika had *never* not had a boyfriend. She was always being pursued, and always falling in love or breaking up with someone. Katherine, on the other hand, only wanted one man she could love and respect with all her heart.

At the back of the sanctuary Katherine stood alone with her father. She looked around at all the people gathered: friends, family, and acquaintances who, in one way or another, bridged all the years of her life. This was as much a triumph for them as it was for her and Neal and the future they would have together.

The wedding march started with its majestic opening chords. Already the flashes of cameras were going off as heads turned to see her, and a soft collective gasp swept through the room at the picture she made. At the very front of the church, at the altar, Katherine's eyes sought out Neal. He stood tall and handsome next to his brother, the best man, and her brother, Eric, who was one of the groomsmen. Katherine felt palpitations in her heart and a catch in her throat, seeing her future husband as he waited for her. Again she experienced the strength of their conviction that they were meant for each other. It all seemed to be confirmed by the surrounding splendor of the church, the gathering of their loved ones, and the glory of the beautiful spring day. It all seemed perfect and just what she'd always hoped for. The only thing missing was Niki.

Katherine heard movement behind her and glanced over her shoulder. The door of the church was open and sunlight poured in, flooding the floor with a brightness that was nearly blinding. She squinted against it, certain that she'd heard someone come in. Or had someone just gone out?

"We're on," her father whispered in her ear. "You look like a queen, baby. I'm very proud of you. Are you ready?"

There was no time to look around again, no time to wonder or doubt or worry, and no time for regrets. Katherine nodded and squeezed her father's arm as he began to walk her down the aisle.

"I'm ready."

recreation center, she was forty minutes late. She lightly tapped her car horn, hoping the familiar signal would be enough to get her son's attention. But after a minute she found a legitimate space and parked her car at the curb. As she got out and headed for the entrance, Katherine scanned the children leaving with a parent or sibling and the small groups of young teens headed for the local pizza hangout. Some youngsters just milled about the entrance, chatting and socializing. But Scott was not among them. In any case, Katherine had given very clear instructions to him from the beginning that he was not to go wandering off, alone or with anyone else. Not that he didn't sometimes forget. Even then, Katherine knew, she couldn't really fault him. Not after all he'd been through.

Still, the anxiety of not knowing exactly where he was propelled her inside the building. She encountered more children, but none of them was her own. Katherine went to the membership desk.

"Hi, Mrs. Winston," the sixtyish receptionist greeted Katherine as she approached. She was efficiently stuffing envelopes with a folded neon green flyer and occasionally waving to someone or answering the telephone.

"Hello, Mrs. Shapiro. I'm looking for my son. I told him to wait here for me. I'm a little late. Did you get my message?"

The woman scanned a number of Post-it notes stuck to the edge of her desk. She pulled off one and held it up. "Yes, here it is. What did he have today?"

"Swimming."

Mrs. Shapiro sat thoughtfully for a moment. She finally shook her head. "I'm sure that class is over. Why don't you go on back and see if he's in the locker room?"

"Thanks," Katherine said as she headed down the hallway to her left, which led to the lockers, pool, and sauna.

Already she was beginning to panic. The swim class should have ended at five. It was almost six. But there was more than maternal worry fueling her emotions, though Katherine tried to keep it all in check. She didn't have to enter the boys' locker room to know it was empty. There was no response when she called out her son's name from the entrance, and her voice echoed around the room hollowly. Instead Katherine could hear the sound of splashing water and a man's voice giving instructions in a clear, patient cadence. She followed the sounds to the pool. The smell of chlorine was pervasive, as was the odor of wet terry towels. The large tiled room, dominated by the pool, felt humid and airtight. Katherine closely watched two thrashing bodies in the middle of the water, creating geysers and waves with their exuberance. They were like two brown amoebas against the aquamarine of the water. One boy was about fifteen, and the other about Scott's age. Neither of them was Scott. After a quick glance around the pool she spotted her son holding on to the edge as he watched the fearlessness of the other two.

Katherine felt her heart lodge in her throat. Her

son was in the deeper end of the pool. The other two boys confidently roughhoused, easily treading water as they shouted out to Scott to join them. But Katherine knew he couldn't. With a gasp of fear she hurried into the pool area, unmindful of the possibility of slipping on the wet floor in her leather-soled shoes.

"Scott, don't!" she called out, trying to keep her tone from sounding frantic.

Three startled young faces turned to Katherine as she stood poised . . . to do what, she wasn't sure. The pool might as well have been as wide as the ocean.

"He's okay. He's not in any trouble."

Katherine jumped at the sound of the male voice off to the side. She turned to find a man casually sitting in a vinyl lawn chair and watching the action in the pool. He was dressed in swim trunks and a red polo shirt as a cover-up. His sturdy brown legs, peppered with curling dark hair, were bare. Although Katherine had never seen him before, she thought he looked much too old to be a lifeguard. His voice caused her to pause. It was calm and quiet. And the gaze in his eyes clearly communicated that she was to calm down as well, that there was no need for a display of histrionics.

"Mommy, look!"

Katherine came alert again as her son, having spotted her beside the pool, called out. By the time she'd turned her attention back to her son, Scott had left the security of the pool edge and was heading to the center of the pool, his eyes squinched closed.

"Scott," Katherine managed weakly as her son

struck out furiously and with a great deal of turbulence across the width of the pool. His head was thrown back in a futile effort to keep his face above water.

Short of jumping in after him, all Katherine could do was hold her breath and watch, riveted, as her son thrashed his way to the other side. It took a while—though to Katherine it seemed even longer—but he made it. Neither the other two boys nor the man showed any surprise. Katherine followed Scott's every move in wonder. Before she could utter a word of relief or praise, Scott took a deep breath, puffing out his cheeks as he held it in, and started back across the pool.

"He's a little wild, but he's got the general idea."

Katherine followed her son's return. He didn't seem to be making as much progress this time, and in fact seemed to be struggling. About three-fourths of the way across the pool Scott's overhead stroke lost its form and became a flat slapping at the water as his arms flailed. He bobbed under the water, gasping for air as his face barely emerged from the pool.

"Oh, my God! *Scott!*" Katherine said in a strangled voice, covering her mouth. She was about to rush forward when a strong hand on her arm stayed her.

"He's okay," the man said firmly, again with calm assurance.

"Help him! Don't you see he can't make it?" Katherine turned on him furiously. She hurried around the pool to get to the side closest to her son.

"Mrs. Winston, he's doing fine."

"No, he's not! You have to do something *now*."

The man slowly joined Katherine at the edge of the pool. He made no move to jump in the water after Scott or to reach out to him with the lifesaving hook, which was on the floor just a few feet away. Instead he squatted down on his haunches.

"What did I tell you to do if you get tired, Scott? Come on. Think about what you're doing. Get on your back."

Katherine watched as, after a moment, Scott changed his arm motion and leaned back until he was forced onto his back. He stopped kicking and just used his arms to keep himself floating in place.

"That's it. Good!" the man said in approval. "Now relax and try to catch your breath. Take your time. When you're ready, come on back to the side."

Finally Katherine realized that her son was in control again. She watched him closely but could only see that he was not scared or in a panic. And he seemed to know exactly what he was doing. After a moment Scott kicked to right his body in the water, and then dog-paddled to the edge. She went to meet him, picking up a towel along the way. He climbed out of the pool, water dripping from his thin, knobby limbs. She held out the towel to him, prepared to wrap him in it and help dry him off. But Scott ignored her.

Instead he turned to the man. "I wasn't scared," Scott claimed.

"Do you know what happened out there?" the

man asked. Scott shook his head. "You were showing off because your mother is here. When you're in the water you have to pay attention to what you're doing. If you have to listen to anybody, you listen to what I have to tell you." Scott silently nodded. "Go tell your mother you're okay."

The man shouted and beckoned to the other two boys. He went to meet them as they, too, exited the pool at the other end. Katherine gave her attention to her son. Now that he was safe in front of her, she felt foolish about the way she'd carried on. She gave him the towel and watched as he wiped his face with it and placed it around his shoulders.

"I thought your class was over at five," she said.

"It is, but Mrs. Shapiro told me you were going to be late, so I stayed in the water."

Katherine glanced at the man now in conversation with the other boys.

"Is that man one of the instructors, or a lifeguard?"

"That's Brett's father."

"Which one is Brett?"

Scott pointed. "He's the one in the blue trunks."

Katherine watched as the man continued to talk to the handsome boy. Although thin and a bit lanky, he was clearly on the cusp of young adulthood. Katherine could now see the resemblance between father and son, and couldn't help staring somewhat in fascination and regret. There was a closeness between father and son that was obvious even to a casual observer.

"Then he doesn't work here?"

"I don't know. I think so."

"Scott, if you don't know, then you shouldn't be in the pool. What if something had gone wrong?"

"I can swim," Scott informed his mother in a quiet voice. It was clear he didn't want to be disrespectful, but he wanted to convince his mother otherwise. "Mr. Chandler said I'm doing great."

"You're just *learning* to swim. I'm very upset that there's no lifeguard on duty. Anyway, your class is over. Why didn't you get dressed and wait for me at the front desk?"

"Because he wanted to get some practice time in the pool, and I told Scott I could give him some pointers," the man's deep voice explained.

Katherine stared at him as he walked back toward her and Scott.

There wasn't any way Katherine could ignore him, although she wanted to. And she wanted to be angry at him, but found that she couldn't look him in the face. Instead she stared at his long brown legs and the dark swim trunks—which, while not at all revealing, were nevertheless . . . suggestive. Despite the fact that they were standing next to a public pool, Katherine felt that somehow his attire, or lack of, was inappropriate.

He held out his hand to her. She noticed that it was very clean, with a strong wrist and fingers, and veined forearms. For the moment his hand had that peculiar sterile and lifeless look of a limb that had been submerged in water a long time. Katherine

reluctantly took it. It was not only firm, like everything else about him, but warm. And there was
something akin to comfort and reassurance in his
grip, which took her by surprise. It got her attention, and she looked into his face. He didn't squeeze
her hand too hard. But he did hold on. Katherine
stared at him for a moment, tilting her head at an
angle as he reminded her of something from the
past. Then it came to her: This man was the same
height as Neal.

"I'm Brian Chandler."

"Katherine Winston."

"Scott's mother. I know."

She frowned. "Do you work here at the center?"

He smiled. His face was square, and while it was
not exactly good-looking, it had masculine detailing
that gave his features strength and appeal. He looked
solid and dependable. Brian Chandler had the presence of someone you wouldn't necessarily notice the
first time you met him, but after that you'd always be
struck by it.

"I'm a member of the health club. The pool is
ours to use after classes are over each afternoon. I
don't mind Scott using the pool . . . but he is on my
time."

Katherine stiffened, taking his remark as a
rebuff. "You could have told him his time was up and
sent him to get dressed."

"You could have been here on time to get him."

She had a ready response but thought better of it.

Katherine turned to Scott, who stood waiting behind her, seemingly not paying much attention to the adult conversation. "Scott, go and get changed, honey. We're running late."

"Okay." Scott nodded and headed toward the locker room. "Bye, Mr. Chandler."

"See you later, Scott. Don't forget what I told you about keeping your legs straight when you kick."

"I will."

"Meet me by Mrs. Shapiro's desk." Katherine called out one final instruction to her son before facing Brian Chandler again. "Whether or not I'm late is not the issue."

He sighed, crossing his arms. "No. The issue is that you're overprotective of your son." He put up his hand, forestalling her response. "Understandable. But you don't want him to pick up on the panic you feel every time he does something a little risky. That will only make him more afraid to try things. Or he could take chances and not tell you. You don't want him to start keeping secrets, do you?"

The inference was not lost on Katherine, and she had to pay attention to the fact that she had found her son in the pool long after his class had ended. Had he done that before?

"How long have you been helping him? Obviously this isn't the first time."

"This is only the third time." He hesitated, pursing his lips and raising his fine brows. "I have to be honest with you, Mrs. Winston. The first time I saw Scott, he *was* in the pool by himself."

"Oh, no." Katherine closed her eyes, more than aware of the half dozen things that could have gone wrong.

"Now, it's not as bad as it sounds. He was in the shallow end, and the water was only up to his waist. And he was smart enough to have the inflatable buoys on his arms."

"I don't know if that makes me feel a whole lot better."

"It should. I guess he knew what he was doing could get him in trouble. But at least he took measures to protect himself. It's clear that Scott really wants to learn how to swim."

"It was the safest activity I could think of to get him into."

"I'll bet," he murmured wryly.

Katherine looked at him suspiciously. "What do you mean by that?"

Brian Chandler pulled at his earlobe as he quickly considered his answer. "It's safer than, let's say, football."

"That's right. I'd worry about him getting hurt. Football is so rough."

"Probably. But it's a good way for him to learn to work with a team. To learn to be physical and protect himself. And then there's eye-hand coordination. His father probably told him that. It's a man thing," he ended with an apologetic smile.

Katherine stared almost blankly at Brian Chandler for another second before she silently turned away, heading back to the exit. She didn't feel she owed him an answer and was completely unprepared to offer one. She was a little surprised by her reaction to his innocent comments. It wasn't as if she'd never considered such a scene taking place between her son and his father.

"Scott says maybe he can be the first African-American gold-medal winner in swimming or diving," she said, as Brian Chandler fell into step next to her.

"He could be. If he works at it. And if that's what he really wants to do. But he should try out all kinds of things. Basketball is a good choice, too."

They reached the exit to the pool. Katherine faced him once more, surprised that he seemed to be appraising her so thoroughly. And so thoughtfully. She suddenly wondered if he found her unattractive. Or maybe he felt that she was being silly about her son. "Scott's very smart. He can be or do anything he wants."

His brows shot up. "Except play football. And by extension I guess you'd include basketball."

Katherine wasn't going to let herself be baited. She smiled politely but with a veiled dislike. "I'll have a talk with him, but I will appreciate it if you'd make him leave the pool if he shows up again when he's not supposed to be here."

Brian Chandler considered the request for a moment, the slightest frown on his face. "I'm a certified lifesaver, Mrs. Winston. I've never been a lifeguard, but I have taught swimming. I don't mind helping out Scott and giving him extra pointers. If it's okay with you, I can speak to his instructor. My son is in the advanced class, so we're here a lot."

"That's kind of you, but—"

"My son almost drowned when he was seven. It took a long time to get Brett back into the water. His best defense against fear was to learn how to swim."

"And how did his mother feel about that philosophy?"

He glanced down at his bare feet, flexing the toes up and forcing his calf muscles to tighten. "She pretty much lets Brett do what he wants," he responded quietly before suddenly grinning at her, sheepishly but proudly. "He wants to make the Olympic team, too."

He didn't totally redeem himself with his disarming admission, but Katherine was inclined to relax and soften her perception that Brian Chandler was arrogant. She regarded him more closely. His gaze was very direct, disconcertingly so. But his eyes also seemed to fill easily with humor, as they did now in speaking of his son.

"So you don't want your son to play football, either," Katherine commented, somewhat self-righteously.

Brian Chandler shook his head. "It's not about what I want. Brett is on his school's team. But he also plays soccer and tennis, and he's just starting with golf this year."

Katherine nodded. "The Tiger Woods syndrome."

He laughed lightly. "Right. So do you mind if I help Scott out? Even ten extra minutes can make a difference. And as long as you're sometimes late in picking him up . . ."

"I'll talk to him about it tonight. Thanks for the

offer," Katherine said stiffly. His reminder of her tardiness was pointed but not mean. For some reason it annoyed her that Brian Chandler was being so generous and agreeable. She checked the time again, frowning and trying to hurry away. "I really have to go. . . ."

"Mrs. Winston?"

Katherine glanced over her shoulder at him. "Yes?"

"Do you swim?"

"Well . . . no, I don't. Why do you ask?"

"Maybe you'll like to join your son sometime in the pool. I'll be happy to teach you how."

Katherine stared at him, trying to figure out if Brian Chandler was being sarcastic or serious, or whether he was baiting her again. She couldn't tell. She simply rolled her eyes, turned, and walked away. But it was at moments like these that she wished her mother had taught her to be less of a lady.

"Mom, can we get these?"

"Ummm?" Katherine was distracted by the information she was reading on the nutritional value of canned peas. Scott got her attention by pushing a cellophane package of cookies in her face. Katherine focused on the item and quickly shook her head. "No. Put it back."

"But these are my favorites."

She dropped the can of peas in her cart and began pushing it down the aisle slowly as she scanned the shelves. "Scott, just about *everything* is your favorite.

149

But isn't it strange that vegetables and eggs don't make the grade?"

"How about Fig Newtons? Remember the last time we had some and there was only three left? You said I could have them before I went to bed . . . and then you ate them!" Scott said with indignation as the strength of his argument gained momentum.

Katherine shook her head slightly and continued her progress down the aisle. Up ahead a woman with a cart turned into the aisle as well, facing her. Katherine automatically maneuvered her cart to the right to give the woman room to pass on her left.

"I think I should get the Fig Newtons 'cause you owe me, right? You always tell me to be fair."

Katherine suppressed her smile. "Yeah, but I'm bigger than you."

"Mom, that's cold," Scott whined, defeated by his mother's logic even as he giggled at it.

"Okay, you can have the Fig Newtons." Scott did an about-face and scurried off to get his cookies. "Get a box of saltines, too, will you? And please don't run."

Katherine continued her shopping, noticing that the woman approaching was petite and thin. She wore a baseball cap that, considering its size, color, and team symbol, had probably not been chosen as a fashion statement. There was also a haphazard fringe of dark curls poking from beneath the cap over the woman's ears, all in all making it difficult to see her face. She wore jeans and an oversized sweater that even as a style was much too big for her small frame. And she had on dark glasses. To Katherine she seemed oddly enveloped by her clothes, as if she wanted to be lost in them and not noticed.

The female shopper hesitated when she spotted Katherine, staring at her fleetingly through her glasses before averting her gaze and half turning to give her attention to a shelf of salad dressings and oils. Katherine added egg noodles to her groceries, and a box of wild rice. She glanced briefly again at the woman, sensing there was something familiar about her.

They were parallel to one another now. The woman noisily placed a jar of olives and a bottle of ketchup in her cart. The sound of glass against the metal of the cart drew Katherine's attention. She watched the woman fumble as she pulled the cap even lower, if that was possible, over her forehead. She tried to pass Katherine with her cart but in her hurry bumped the front end.

"Sorry," the woman murmured, rushing past.

"That's okay. The carts are too big for the width of these aisles, anyway," Katherine said agreeably.

The other woman didn't respond and kept moving. Katherine glanced at her in curiosity, wondering at her aloofness but certainly not taking it personally. She herself was not inclined to get chatty with strangers in public places. What Katherine saw just in passing however, held her attention. Again she had a feeling of knowing this woman from somewhere. Her profile was partially obscured by the curly hair, but Katherine could see the line of her jaw and cheekbones, as well as her mouth, which was full and beautifully shaped. "Bedroom lips," Katherine's brother would call them, as he'd once described . . .

Katherine stopped all movement to really focus on the woman who was now at the end of the aisle, moving in the opposite direction. She frowned. "It can't be," she said softly to herself as a name came to her mind.

"I didn't know which kind of saltines to get. Which one do you want?" Scott asked his mother as he held up an armful of boxes.

Katherine blinked and gave him her attention. "This one," she said absently, taking one of the boxes from her son's hand. By the time she turned around again, the woman was gone and any lingering curiosity had vanished. Katherine quickly forgot her as she surveyed the items in her cart. "I think that's it for tonight."

"Mommy, I'm hungry," Scott said.

"Yes, I know," she said, checking the time on her watch. "Go put those other boxes of crackers back and meet me at the checkout counter."

"Okay. Can we have pizza tonight? Then you don't have to cook," Scott reasoned.

She sighed, knowing it would be convenient but feeling guilty that she really didn't want to cook. "That's a good idea. But that means we won't have a pizza night on Friday," she warned her son.

"I don't mind," Scott said agreeably as he backed away on his mission.

Katherine wheeled her cart to the front of the

store and the register, picking up two more items along the way. As she waited on line, she thought back over the events of her day. While the grant proposal and its chances of success were certainly of major importance, Katherine found herself recalling her encounter with Brian Chandler. She was still a little concerned that her son had, apparently, been finding ways to use his time without her that she knew nothing about. Scott was not a fresh or disobedient child. She had never before had to worry that he was likely to get into trouble . . . or lie to her. Well, he hadn't exactly lied to her, Katherine decided, but he had been doing something he didn't want her to know about.

The line began to move, and Katherine automatically inched her cart forward while her thoughts shifted to the question of whether or not she was a good mother, and then to her annoyance that a complete stranger like Brian Chandler would dare to imply that he understood her son's actions better than she did. *It's a man thing.* Katherine sniffed as she recalled his comment. It was sexist and arrogant. It was even a little funny. But she also couldn't help but wonder if he was right. *Was* she being overprotective? Was she denying Scott a chance to make friends and participate on teams because she was afraid of his getting hurt? Was she worried that she might lose him? Or that he might develop futile dreams of NBA or NFL superstardom? Katherine began to feel slightly anxious that there were all these decisions about her son's well-being and future that she hadn't considered before, or perhaps was just putting off. Neal had not talked to their son about any of these "man things." But her meeting with Brian Chandler had sparked the realization that there was so much Scott would need to know as he grew into a young man that she would not be able to tell him.

Then how was Scott to learn?

Katherine glanced around with a frown, wondering what was taking her son so long to reshelve a few boxes of crackers. She knew it could be anything. Scott was at that age when he was daydreamy and easily distracted, and he didn't pay much attention to time. She still did not see her son, but two lanes to her right Katherine spotted the woman shopper she'd passed in one of the aisles a little while ago. That sensation of knowing her came back instantly, and stronger this time. Katherine stared at her, more and more certain that the name that had come to her mind earlier was the right one.

Her turn at the checkout counter came up, and Katherine began to place her groceries on the conveyor belt for the cashier.

"Can I get this?" Scott asked, squeezing next to his mother at the counter.

Katherine shook her head even without looking at what her son held up. "If it's not fruit or vegetables or a box of oatmeal, the answer is no." She took the package and gave it to the cashier, even as Scott pouted and sighed in disappointment. "I'm not taking this," Katherine said. Then she turned to Scott again. "Pull the cart through to the end of the check-out so we can use it to get everything to the car."

He silently followed her instructions, waiting at the end of the counter while she prepared to pay. Katherine opened her purse, searching for her wallet. She looked up in time to see the petite woman shopper take up the one bag of groceries she'd purchased and head for the exit. For a fast moment Katherine thought about what to do, and then acted.

"Could you just give me a quick minute?" she said hurriedly to the cashier, and then rushed to catch up to the woman as she was about to exit the store. "Excuse me, but . . . I think I know you."

The woman spared Katherine the briefest of glances and kept walking. "I don't think so," she murmured, not breaking her stride.

Katherine hesitated, feeling foolish now. But as the woman walked away she knew she had to try again.

"You're Danika Evans. Don't you remember who I am? It's Katherine—Kat. I thought I—"

"You've made a mistake," the woman said, shaking her head.

This time she didn't even bother looking at Katherine, who could only stare after the departing woman, sure now that she had *not* made a mistake.

"Mommy . . . the lady is waiting for you to pay."

Her son's entreaty forced Katherine back to the moment. She apologized to the cashier, paid, and piled her bags into the cart. Scott wheeled it next to her through the exit toward the parking lot as Katherine once again looked around for the woman. But she was gone.

"Who was that lady, the one you were talking

to?" her son asked as they loaded the groceries into the trunk of the teal blue Camry.

Katherine frowned as she considered her encounter and compared it with a history that went back nearly twenty-five years. So much had happened in that span of time. *Too* much. Good, bad . . . and tragic. She smiled reflectively at Scott.

"Oh . . . she was someone I used to know a long time ago. We used to be best friends."

CHAPTER 2

"Hello?"

"Hey, it's Eileen. How you doing?"

Katherine frowned and looked at her watch. "Running late. Scott has a dentist appointment, we both have to spend some time at the library, and he has a birthday party to attend this afternoon. Let me call you this evening," Katherine said as she stepped into her brown leather moccasins and tried to put on a pair of gold hoop earrings.

"I'm not going to keep you. Cal is going to drop me off to get my hair done, and we have some shopping to do at Sam's."

"One of these days you should learn how to drive."

"Not as long as Cal doesn't mind acting as chauffeur. And this way I can keep an eye on his whereabouts."

"Eileen, don't you know that if Cal wanted to be out chasing skirts or doing the nasty with someone, he'd do it?"

"Ready," Scott said from the doorway of his mother's bedroom.

Katherine turned her head to peruse what her son was wearing. She wrinkled her nose at his choice of T-shirts and shook her head. Briefly covering the mouthpiece as her friend Eileen continued to chat, Katherine whispered instructions. "You are *not* leaving the house in a shirt that advertises Godzilla stepping on a child!"

"Mom, it's just a T-shirt," Scott said with a shrug of defiance.

Katherine silently mouthed "go" and sent him off with a wave of her hand to change his shirt. Exasperated, Scott trudged off.

". . . but the reason we've been together so long is because Cal knows I will not put up with mess from him."

"What did you say? I'm sorry, I had to say something to Scott."

"I was saying that at least I don't take Cal for granted, and . . ."

"Eileen, this can wait. I *really* have to go."

"No, this will only take a minute. Honey, you will never believe who I heard is back in the area. Danika Evans."

That got Katherine's attention, and she stopped fidgeting impatiently. "Oh, really?"

"She sure is," Eileen said, as if she was privy to a state secret. "Well, it's really Evans-Campbell. You know she got married about ten years ago."

"Yeah, I'd heard."

"I know she didn't invite you to *her* wedding. Probably too embarrassed. Although on second thought, I don't think Niki knows the meaning of the word *embarrassed,* and she'd certainly never attach it to herself. She sure could be a little bitch at times."

"Girls call it being a bitch. My brother, Eric, said she was 'bodacious.'"

Eileen laughed. "There's another term for it, too, usually reserved for men . . . but I won't go there. The other thing is, a friend of my sister saw her and said girlfriend looked *bad*! Now that I found real hard to believe. You remember Niki. Always had seriously cute clothes, and could never let you forget how much she paid for them, either. Or rather, how much she made her folks pay for them."

"I know she's back," Katherine said quietly, remembering the sad figure she'd seen three nights earlier.

"You know? Who called you?"

"Nobody. I'm pretty sure I saw her the other night while Scott and I were doing some marketing. I tried to talk to her, but . . . she told me I'd made a mistake. That she wasn't Niki."

"Get out! Why in the world would she do that? I mean, she lived in this town, and everyone knew her family. Why would she pretend she was a stranger?"

Katherine had been asking that same question for three days. She wasn't sure she'd come any closer to an answer now, and Eileen didn't seem to know any more than she did. "I don't know," she said thoughtfully. "Did you find out why she's back? Is her husband in town with her?"

"Girl, it gets better," Eileen cackled in her best gossip tones. "They're separated."

"Really? Do you know what happened?"

"All I heard was that the man walked out!"

Katherine was about to respond when she saw her son out of the corner of her eye. He'd changed to another T-shirt, which to her way of thinking was only marginally better than the last. Sighing but nodding her approval, Katherine decided she could live with a meteor crashing into the World Trade Center.

"I'm ready," Scott said.

Katherine nodded again and held up a finger to signal for one more minute. "Eileen, I really have to go. Scott is waiting for me."

"All right, but I'll call you later. I want to talk to you about coming over for dinner."

"Not again."

"What do you mean, not again?" Eileen asked.

"I'm not going to come if I'm the evening's entertainment."

Eileen laughed. "Beggars can't be choosers. You can't be trusted to form your own social life. I'm sorry, but a birthday party for eleven-year-olds doesn't cut it."

"Well, sometimes the company of my peers isn't much better!" Katherine retaliated dryly. "Call me tonight."

She hung up on Eileen's continued laughing, but much of their conversation was hardly cause for humor. Katherine was upset for a number of reasons about spotting Niki in the supermarket. But more than that was her surprise and curiosity over

Danika's obvious reluctance to be recognized.

"Mom," Scott called out from the front of the small ranch house.

"I'm coming," Katherine answered, hurrying to once again make up for lost time. She gathered the rest of her things and rushed from the room, her mind still on the conversation.

Eileen and many others, herself included, all had just cause to be angry at Danika, but Katherine had never thought of herself as unforgiving. Anyway, her most prominent feelings, as she hurried to catch up with Scott and get them to his first appointment, were those of great concern.

Katherine drove slowly up to the front of the house and stopped. But she did not park or turn the engine off. She wasn't sure why she'd come, let alone why she might stay. But after that disturbing encounter at the market with Niki, and the call that morning from Eileen, she felt compelled to follow her instincts. And her strongest instincts had told Katherine from the beginning that something was wrong.

She looked over the two-story house, remembering everything about it. From this distance, it looked smaller than she remembered. They used to skip rope in the driveway, and walk the railing of the porch as if it was a balance beam like the one in their gymnastics class. Katherine remembered the one time she and Niki had ventured under the porch, in hot pursuit of a stray cat Niki had decided she would make a pet of. The resulting scratches from the frightened and cornered animal had changed Niki's mind. Lord how she had carried on about being disfigured or dying of blood poisoning . . . and hating cats.

Katherine could no longer remember the last time she'd been to this house. Around the time she was getting married, she thought. But not since then. She knew that Danika's father had developed Alzheimer's and had been put into a nursing home, and that her mother had moved closer to the home to be near her husband and take part in his care. Katherine knew he'd died just two years ago. She knew nothing of the whereabouts of Danika's younger sister, April, only that she'd become involved several years back with a married man nearly fifteen years her senior—a professor at her college.

Katherine shook her head at the mental litany of events in the Evans household, and made the decision to approach the house. Despite some real justification for staying away and turning a deaf ear to the gossip and innuendoes, Katherine remembered above all that she and Danika had been good friends.

There was a Mercedes in the driveway, looking somewhat out of place in front of the small house, which, along with the yard, was showing signs of neglect and age. But Katherine was not surprised. Niki had always had style and class and *very* expensive tastes. And that was what made her oddly unkempt appearance all the more strange.

Katherine approached the door and rang the bell. It sounded exactly the same: loud and kind of grand, as if important people lived here. She half expected to hear Niki's imperial tones from behind the door as she raced through the house to answer. "I'll get it; it's for me" had been her standard announcement when any visitor arrived at her family home. There was no such response now, but Katherine *knew* that Niki was here, quietly hiding.

She persisted, ringing the bell again and then a third time, until finally she heard the slow footsteps coming to the door. Katherine stared at the door as if expecting it to open, while fully aware of the shadow of someone carefully peering through the curtains of the window next to the door. And just to make it clear that she had no intention of walking away, Katherine rang the bell yet again. She had learned tunnel vision from Danika.

The door opened slowly and a small face, hidden under the bill of a baseball cap, appeared in the small crack of the opening. Katherine had had days to imagine this moment, and she did not let one iota of shock show in her face or voice. She smiled genuinely.

"Hello, Danika. Surprised to see me?" Katherine was pretty sure her question took care of everything. And it left little room for Danika to offer excuses. But she said nothing as she silently waited for Katherine to say something else, to state her purpose in coming. "I knew it was you I saw the other night. Eileen called to tell me you were in town. You remember Eileen Daniels? She got married, but she's still Daniels."

The small woman on the other side of the door said nothing. But more than ever Katherine was prepared to stand her ground. She thought back to the foundation of her relationship with Danika Evans, established when they were twelve years old and had discovered that they shared a common birthday.

"I'm here to see you, Danika," Katherine said softly, in a nonthreatening voice. "You don't have to pretend you don't remember me, and I'm not going to leave unless you close the door in my face."

For a moment Katherine thought Danika would do just that. She would certainly not have been afraid to. But it would have been silly now that they weren't adolescents anymore.

The cap and face withdrew behind the door. But the door opened wider, silently inviting Katherine to enter. The first thing she noticed was how dark the house was. All the curtains were drawn. The last bit of natural light was cut off when the door closed and was locked behind her. She looked around quickly, seeing furnishings she remembered and the familiar layout of the first floor of the house, which stimulated memories.

"I didn't think anyone would notice me," the voice said behind Katherine.

She turned and faced Danika, her smile still in place. She would have recognized that voice anywhere. It was forthright and deep for so small a woman. Sexy, men had always thought.

"Obviously you didn't want anyone to. But maybe I know you a little better than a lot of people."

The head shook from side to side. "No, you don't. We haven't seen each other since . . ." She stopped. "We're not twelve years old anymore."

Her tone was flat. Resigned. It made Katherine curious and nervous. "Or even twenty-five, unfortunately," she said in an attempt at a bit of humor. It did not go over well. "But I *wanted* to be right that it was you in the market the other night."

"Couldn't you see that I didn't want to talk?"

"Oh, you made that clear. But you should have known I wasn't going to let it drop there, Danika. One thing I learned from you was that *no* often means *maybe*. I haven't seen you in nearly fifteen years. But I'm here now."

Danika spread her arms a short distance from her body before letting them drop to her sides again. "Well, now you see me. I told you I'm not what you remembered."

Katherine swallowed. That was very evident. And it all began to fall into place for her, with a realization that sent a chill through her body. The change was too drastic. She did remember enough of Danika Evans to know that her vanity, if nothing else, would never allow her to let herself go. Unless something else was interfering with her decisions.

"Well, neither am I. I've gained a few pounds, but I still have my own teeth, and so far I'm winning the war against gravity," Katherine said with a slight self-deprecating shrug. She was rewarded with a facial movement that, while not exactly a smile, was at least a reaction.

"If you've gained weight, you carry it well, damn you. I like your hair shorter. When you wore it long it made your face look long as well."

"Thank you." Katherine acknowledged the observations without rancor. When they were teenagers Danika's comments often had come across as pure catty criticism.

For a moment they just stared at each other. Katherine figured it was Danika's turn to say something, *anything,* and she was prepared to just stand there until it happened. But she could see that her friend was struggling with what to do next. Finally Danika shrugged and turned toward the den. It was an automatic reflex. The den was where they'd held their most secretive discussions and made their most important decisions together.

"Well, we might as well sit down. I'm getting bored with standing in the hall."

She led the way into the small room. Everything there was the same as well, except that the small love seat looked like it had been made up as a temporary bed, with linens bunched at one end. Without explanation Danika climbed back onto the love seat, fully clothed in her unattractive camouflage getup. Even the cap remained in place, but a closer look began to confirm Katherine's growing suspicions. She sat in the Queen Anne wing chair opposite Danika and pulled one leg up under her, just as she used to do when they were young.

"I heard about your father's illness and his passing. I sent condolences to your mother."

Danika lowered her gaze, busying herself with spreading the light wool blanket across her lap and thighs. "I know. She told me," she murmured indifferently.

"How's your mother?"

"She decided to stay in the Camden area, even after my father died. You know my sister lives in Philadelphia. They're close to each other."

"No, I didn't know that."

"April finally got that fool to divorce his wife and marry her. But I don't think that's any great victory."

"Well . . . they must really love each other," Katherine offered awkwardly. She'd never known April very well.

"I think it was the only way for either of them to save face, after the scandal they caused. Who knows, maybe they're happy. People do such stupid things. . . ." Her voice trailed off.

"Speaking from experience?" Katherine dared to challenge.

"Why not? You used to tell me all the time that I never thought about what I was doing. I just threw myself into the middle of a situation and let the dust settle wherever." She let her head drop back against the sofa and closed her eyes. "If the gossip mill still works around here . . . and you know I'm talking about Eileen, who could never keep her mouth shut or mind her own business . . . I guess you heard that I've separated from my husband."

"Yes, I heard."

"Actually . . . he left me," Danika said. "It was probably my fault. I was difficult and demanding, and . . . and said some terrible things."

"Well, that certainly sounds like you."

There was a ghost of a smile on Danika's face. Her closed eyes opened just a fraction, and Katherine knew that she was being appraised through Niki's thin lashes.

"Holly is with her grandparents for the moment."

"Holly?"

She nodded. "My daughter. She's seven." She tilted her face more toward Katherine. "Was that your son? The boy in the market?"

Katherine nodded. "Scott. He'll be twelve in September."

"You and I met when we were twelve. Just in time for junior high."

"There's no junior high school anymore in most places. It's just seventh grade, in middle school. Ninth grade begins high school."

"You just told me more than I ever wanted to know about it."

Katherine grinned sheepishly.

"Your son looks exactly like Neal."

Katherine blinked. "Yes, he does."

"He's a handsome boy."

"Thank you."

"I heard about what happened to Neal. I know I should have written or something. . . ."

"You had your own life to live. And it's not as if we had kept in touch all those years," Katherine said.

Danika sighed heavily and closed her eyes. "My fault again. When things went wrong between us, it was usually my fault, wasn't it?"

"You're being hard on yourself. I don't remember you being so bad."

"And you were the nice one. Don't be nice. Let's just call it for what it was. I was a bitch sometimes, and we all knew it."

"You could be difficult," Katherine conceded.

Danika nodded and accepted the observation. "Does your son . . ."

"Scott."

"Does Scott remember his father? Does he know what happened?"

"He was there when his father was killed," Katherine said. It felt strange to be talking so aloofly about her husband's death. There had been a very long time after that when the mere sight of her son caused her to cry in despair and memory. Scott did look exactly like his father. The physical reminder was both a blessing and a trial. But after a while Katherine had become grateful that she had been given so much of Neal in Scott.

"What happened exactly?"

"It was a hit-and-run. He and Scott were in the park and they were playing catch. On the walk back Scott dropped the ball and it bounced into traffic. He would have run after it but Neal made an attempt to catch it instead. He never saw the car, never knew what hit him. He was killed on impact. The driver was never found."

Danika stared at Katherine for a long moment, stunned by the random horror of the accident. "What about your son? I guess he freaked out."

Katherine shifted in her chair. She cleared her throat. "He was in shock for almost a week. For a year afterward he had nightmares and couldn't sleep alone. Then Scott began to get over witnessing his father's death, and *I* fell apart."

"I'm sorry," Danika said in her aloof tone, making it hard to know if she was sincere or not.

"In answer to your unasked questions, yes, I loved him very much. Yes, I miss him desperately. We were trying to get pregnant again when he died."

"That was a long time ago. Are you seeing anyone?"

Katherine was shaken at the idea, even though an unexpected image of Brian Chandler came instantly to mind. "Oh, no. I'm not interested. Scott and I have a great relationship, and I don't need—"

"Bullshit," Danika muttered succinctly.

Katherine was so taken aback she couldn't respond right away. And she wasn't even sure that she could—at least, not convincingly. That was a surprise to her as well.

"It's not really an issue. I stay busy and spend so much time getting Scott from one activity to another—"

"You're using that poor kid as an excuse. You can't tell me you *never* think about sex and making love or having a man take you out."

Katherine took the defensive. "Is that what's happening with you now that you're separated from your husband?"

Danika frowned. "That's different. We had a

choice about being together or apart. And we blew it. That's our fault, mine and Rodney's."

"So what happened between you?"

A stubborn look came across Danika's thin face. "Like I said, stupid stuff. All my fault."

"Does it have anything to do with why you're here in your parents' house again? Or the way you look?"

"What do you mean? What's wrong with the way I look?"

Katherine raised her brows, incredulous. "Are you serious? You look terrible. I have never seen you without manicured nails, a beautiful outfit, or makeup. You spent more time on your hair than any female in the history of the species, Niki, even without the black-woman hair thing. Now, you may not think you look bad, but you can't tell me you aren't aware of what you're putting on."

Danika shrugged, pulling the blanket up to her chest and hugging it close. "I just slapped something together. I had something to take care of for my mother."

"So for the last three days at least, or even longer, you've been just slapping together your outfits, not caring what you look like or who you'll see . . . or who will talk about it? Don't expect me to believe that. You grew up in this area. What made you think people wouldn't notice?"

"And talk about it, it seems."

"Like I said, you don't look like the Niki we remember."

"Like I said, I'm not."

"Why not?"

She grew impatient and huffy. Danika sucked her teeth. "Well, why do you care? We haven't seen each other since . . ." She gestured vaguely with her hand. "Since when you got married. You do remember I didn't show up at the service, right? Don't tell me you weren't mad as hell and wouldn't have killed me if you'd run into me afterward."

"Okay, I won't." Danika's mouth twisted skeptically. "Everything worked out fine. I made my mother the matron of honor, and after a while I stopped wondering if you were all right. I figured that if you were dead, I'd hear about that. But since I didn't, I realized you must have had another reason for not coming to my wedding and not telling anyone why. That's on you, Niki. But you missed a great party."

Danika stared at her for a moment. "Yeah, I heard."

"What happened to you?" Katherine asked in almost a whisper—carefully, as if the very question might send Danika into flight again.

Under the baseball cap Danika's eyes grew furtive, her gaze indirect. Her beautiful mouth tightened as she seemed to withdraw right before Katherine's eyes.

"And I'm not talking about back then. That's over. I mean right now."

"I don't want to talk about it, okay?" Danika said in her curiously deep voice.

"Niki, we all have bad times. But you never used to let anything get you down. DeeDee used to say you had ice water in your veins."

"Yeah. All my so-called girlfriends didn't think I had any feelings. Well, ask me if I care what they think," Danika muttered. "Nobody knows anything."

"You're the only person who can set them straight. We used to be best friends, Niki. Why can't you talk to me? I'll stay as long as it takes."

Niki scoffed. "What are you going to do? Stay here all day and night until I break down and talk?"

But Katherine had a better idea, and it was going to take only a few seconds. She uncurled herself from the chair and leaned forward. Danika seemed to realize too late what Katherine had in mind and pulled back, shrinking from the outstretched hand, putting up her own arms to ward off the advance.

"No! Stop it! Leave me alone, Kat. *Don't touch my hat!*"

She made a futile attempt to slap Katherine's hands away, but Danika didn't have enough strength to succeed, and her blows were weak and glanced off Katherine's arms. She cowered, trying to cover her head with her hands and arms.

"Give me my hat!" Niki said in a furious and emotional voice.

Katherine made no move to do so. She was riveted in place by what she saw. Lying in Danika's lap was a dark, curling mass of hair, like a mop head. It was a wig of unrealistic quantity and style. It was like something dead—or, worse, a harbinger of death. What little hair Niki had left made her look like a shiny brown cue ball with ears and a little fuzz on top. It was both comical and so painfully sad that Katherine felt her throat close over with the need to burst into tears.

"Niki. . . ," Katherine managed to say. She stopped there, not wanting to add anything that even remotely sounded like pity or even sympathy.

"Give me my hat," Danika demanded again, but the fury was gone. "I'll never forgive you, Katherine. I hope you're satisfied. You got your payback for my not showing up at your wedding."

"Feeling sorry for yourself isn't your style, Niki. This isn't revenge for anything you did. This is a disease. I would never wish this on anyone. Even a girl-friend who's a pain in the ass sometimes," Katherine said in a clear voice. "And I'm telling you right now that if I had that kind of power, I would make it go away."

Cautiously Katherine approached Danika and sat next to her on the love seat. She didn't give her back the absurd hat, but dropped it to the floor. She swept the wig to the floor as well. Niki was still curled up, fetuslike, in the far corner. She made no sound, and Katherine knew she wasn't crying. She couldn't recall ever seeing Niki cry about anything.

Katherine offered no words of hope. She didn't cluck and tsk and fuss, as if Niki was a child. And she herself didn't cry, although she felt the need so much that her heart literally ached.

"Cancer," Katherine stated rather than asked. She could see the signs of chemotherapy. Niki barely moved her head in answer. "What kind?"

"What does it matter?" Niki asked wearily.

"It's about time. You either have it on your side . . . or you don't. Is it . . . ovarian?"

"No. My breast."

Katherine didn't move, didn't utter a sound. She let her eyes drift close. Niki was right. What was the difference?

Katherine gently touched Niki's arm, half expecting her to jerk away. When Niki didn't react, she curled her fingers around the thin limb and pulled the arm away from her head. She wanted to see Niki's face and eyes. She wanted her friend to see, too, that this didn't matter one bit. Their friendship had been founded long before either of them even had breasts. They had always been different, and that was precisely what had always held them together. They'd fought, broken up, made up, and done the whole thing over and over again until they'd grown up.

"When did you find out?" Katherine asked.

"Just after my father died. I didn't tell my mother for a long time. She didn't need to worry."

"And your husband? Rodney?"

Danika shrugged. She smoothed her hand over the globe of her head, as if testing the surface. "I drove him away. I wasn't going to wait around for him to leave me. I was sick all the time. I had to have a million tests, and then the therapy. My hair fell out. I couldn't even think about making love."

Katherine frowned. "How do you know he was going to leave? Did he tell you so?"

"He didn't have to. I looked like hell, Kat. I lost weight and none of my clothes fit. All I wanted to do after my therapy was stay in bed and sleep."

"So you're saying that just because you felt lousy about yourself, you blamed him for what you were thinking? That doesn't make sense, Niki."

She grimaced and pouted. "You know how men are. Always want you to look like you just stepped out of Neiman Marcus."

Katherine shook her head at the absurdity and the vanity. "You sent him away because you believed your husband loved you only for your hair and the way you dress? Niki, even *you* couldn't have been so shallow as to marry someone like that."

"I'm not the woman he married," Niki said poignantly.

"I hope not. He must have seen you when you didn't have makeup on. And what about when you got pregnant and were sick for months? Was he repulsed when you couldn't walk without waddling and looked like you'd swallowed a bowling ball? Did he watch you give birth? That's the acid test. Neal swore he would never let me get pregnant again after that experience." She peered into her friend's face. "Just what did you say to him to make him leave?"

Niki sighed, her gaze tired and reflective. "I told him I was going to die. I told him that if he was going to leave and find another woman, then he'd better do it now."

Katherine groaned in disbelief. "For God's sake, Niki!"

Danika turned to regard her. "You can think I was foolish if you want, but he left."

"You hardly made it easy for him to stay."

"Well . . . it's done. It's over."

"It's not over. You're here. Okay, so your hair is gone. It will grow back."

"My breasts are gone, too," Danika said flatly. "They won't grow back. If they do, I'll make medical history."

Katherine stared at her with her mouth open. Her gaze went to Danika's chest.

"I could have had reconstruction, but . . . they wouldn't feel like mine."

Katherine shook her head as she stared at her childhood friend. "You've been through all of this alone and never said anything. Never called me."

Danika looked at her directly, and for the first time Katherine saw the loss and fear in her eyes. "Not after what I did. What could I say? 'Kat, my breasts fell off and I look like Gandhi'?"

Katherine struggled not to laugh. She was stunned that she even wanted to. It reminded her of all those stories of people who suddenly started laughing at someone's funeral. "Well . . . it could be worse."

"Oh, yeah? How?"

"At least you don't look like Yoda."

Danika snorted. "I thought he was sort of cute, with his green self."

Katherine chuckled. "You're cuter . . . but he has more hair!"

That did it. They howled with laughter, collapsing against one another in a fit of hysteria. Katherine was relieved. It seemed a very good way to say hello, forgive the past, hope for the future . . . and hide the fall of their tears.

"Hi, Katherine." The woman beamed.

Katherine was so deep in thought that when the door opened and a smiling white woman appeared, she didn't remember where she was or why. She was more aware that the woman had a full, healthy head of light brown hair. Everything about her was in stark contrast to the woman she'd just left. Katherine could still see Danika—small, thin, and bald, yet oddly beautiful—and felt somewhat disoriented by the unexpected events in both their lives. Death, separation, aging parents, cancer—these things had *not* been on the agenda when they'd been fourteen and made plans for their future.

"Hi, Alice. How's it going?" Katherine asked as she stepped into the house. In the background could be heard the voices and laughter of adolescent boys having a boisterous good time.

"Well, it hasn't come to threats or body blows. The boys are actually pretty well behaved," she explained, leading the way to the rear of the house. "They're having a good time . . . but I'm worn out! There was less work and noise when Emily had a birthday gathering a few years ago."

They passed through the kitchen, which looked as though some destructive force had been let loose and had emptied out the cabinets and refrigerator. There seemed to be hundreds of plastic cups and plates with leftover food piled on every surface.

"How did it go at the library? Did you get your research done?" Alice asked as they headed not to the family room, where some of the noise was coming from, but the backyard.

Katherine recalled her change of plans after she'd dropped Scott off for his classmate's birthday party. Instead of returning to the library, she had gone to see Danika. It had been a good trade-off and a much more important use of her time. "I still have some work to do, but I might do a Net search."

There was the sound of a basketball bouncing on cement and occasionally hitting the backboard of a netted basket before glancing off and dropping through the hoop. As Alice slid open the kitchen doors to pass through, Katherine caught a glimpse of a few boys and a man in a game of hoops. One of them was her son.

A phone rang somewhere behind them. Alice turned back to find the cordless phone, which was buried somewhere on the kitchen counter. As she answered she waved her hand at Katherine, indicating that she was to continue out into the yard.

Katherine stood just inside the door, however, watching the action. Scott did not notice her presence right away, and she was able to witness his playing without the self-consciousness that might have made him hold back. Right now Scott was skinny, all big

179

feet, knees, and elbows, and already more teenager than kid. Already tall for his age. It hit her full force how much he resembled his father, but the resemblance did not end there. Watching him play, she also saw a youthful fearlessness and confidence. And it was clear to Katherine that her son was very talented.

Scott got possession of the ball after it was banked on the last shot from the father of one of the boys. He bounced and dribbled, controlling ownership as he tried to set himself to take a shot. Scott twisted, looking for an opening. He pivoted and planted his feet. Another boy trying to guard him jumped to block the shot, but Scott ducked to fake a move. He sprang up on the balls of his feet. In what seemed to Katherine like slow motion, her son released the ball into the air. It rolled off the end of his fingers, rotating as it headed for the basket. The ball never touched the board or the rim, but dropped cleanly through the net.

There were shouts of approval from the others in the yard. Katherine felt not only great pride, but also regret that Neal could not see his son's development. It had been a long time since she'd thought of the loss or felt the loneliness. She had been left with the gift of her son, but for the first time she could see how she'd been holding him back from his full range of possibilities. She might fear for his safety, but she couldn't protect him, and it would be criminal not to allow him to test himself.

When Scott saw his mother he waved sheepishly to her. Katherine smiled at him and made note of the way he quickly suppressed the graceful athlete of a moment ago and became the quiet, thoughtful, and polite little boy she knew. He became engaged in a knowledgeable discussion of the merits of Phil Jackson's coaching, Dennis Rodman's hair, and Shaq's acting abilities.

"He's good. Very smooth."

Katherine turned to the man standing at her shoulder. She kept surprise out of her eyes and voice as she met the gaze of Brian Chandler.

"Who?"

"Your son."

"Are you still trying to convince me that I should let him play?"

Brian slipped his hands into the pockets of his dark slacks and shook his head. "I don't think I have to. You saw him. He moves well, and he's comfortable with his body. He likes sports." He slowly smiled. "It's nice to see you."

Katherine didn't respond directly to his greeting. She hadn't expected one. She felt stunned by his admission but was more disturbed by not being able to tell if he was being sarcastic or polite.

"What are you doing here? You're a little old for this crowd, aren't you?"

"My son and I were invited. Brett goes to school with the Adamsons' daughter, Emily. They're somewhere inside watching a video on the big-screen TV. You know it's not cool for them to hang out at a kids' party, but there was lots of food."

Katherine grinned.

"But to answer your *real* question about how I know the Adamsons, Mike and I work at the same company. I was hired almost a year ago."

"I wasn't trying to be nosy."

"Not nosy. Curious."

"Oh, good. You've already introduced yourselves," Alice said as she joined them. "I've been wanting to have a dinner and invite everyone. We'll have to do that sometime . . . after I've recovered from today." She turned to Katherine. "That was a great gift Scott gave to Mike junior. He said it was awesome. Thank you."

"I'm glad he liked it." Katherine glanced at her watch. "I'm sorry, but Scott and I really have to go."

"If you let him stay, I'll be happy to drop him home afterward," Brian offered.

"That's a great idea," Alice said enthusiastically.

Katherine shook her head, already turning to walk back into the house. "I appreciate what you're trying to do, but Scott has a school project due on Monday and he has a lot of work to do on it still." She signaled to her son that they were leaving, and he began saying goodbye to his friends.

"I'll call soon and try to arrange dinner with all of us," Alice said to Katherine.

Katherine made a general farewell, avoiding any direct comments to Brian and not even looking at him again as she turned away to enter the house. Only then did the uncomfortable sensation in her stomach, a combination of tension and excitement mixed together, begin to disappear. Only then did she feel back in control and grounded.

Scott caught up to her as they reached the front door.

"So, did you have a good time?"

"Yeah, it was fun," Scott said casually.

Katherine had to smile to herself. She knew it wouldn't have been cool for him to show a *lot* of excitement. "I'm sorry I have to pull you away, but . . ."

"I know," he said with a sigh. "I got that stupid thing to finish for my science teacher."

"You mean you *have* an *assignment* you have to finish," she corrected.

Scott looked at his mother with patience and forbearance. "That's what I said."

"Mrs. Winston, wait up a minute. . . ."

"Go get in the car. I'll be right there," Katherine instructed Scott. But he stood leaning against the side of the car waiting for her, absently using his hands to slap a drumbeat on the roof in time with some music he could hear in his head.

Katherine reluctantly turned as Brian came toward her. She kept her expression blank, but she was prepared for him.

"I wondered if we could get together sometime. . . ."

She was shaking her head before he'd finished. "No, I don't think so."

He raised his brows, puzzled. "I had some things I wanted to say to you about Scott. What did you think I was asking?"

Katherine found herself caught with her mouth open and her foot in it. She quickly tried to compose herself, hoping she didn't look as foolish as she felt. "Oh . . . I thought . . . I . . ."

Brian watched her face, seeing the way her guard had suddenly slipped. "I know you're concerned about Scott's activities, and I thought perhaps I could offer some advice," he said smoothly. "And I'd like you to meet my son. Maybe the four of us can do pizza or burgers some Saturday afternoon."

"I don't know. I . . ." Katherine continued to fumble. She took a deep breath in an effort to suppress her confusion. "I appreciate your offer, but . . ."

"Look, I'm not trying to interfere with your parenting. I just thought maybe I could ease your mind and give you some insights about what's okay for Scott to try at his age." Brian paused, as if he could see he wasn't making any headway. "If it's okay. I don't want to do or say anything that makes you uncomfortable."

Katherine shook her head. "No, that's fine. I just . . ." She shrugged, struggling to make sense. She looked at him openly. "I think I should have a talk with Scott first. See what he wants to do."

"Then is it okay if I call you?"

He looked at her, his eyes appraising and warm. His face had a masculine maturity that Katherine felt gave him the appearance of a man who wasn't to be crossed. Not mean or hard, but strong and persistent. She hesitated, still looking for the land mine, still feeling a bit cornered. Still realizing how unprepared she felt for someone like Brian Chandler. But she also knew that now was as good a time as any to get over it.

Finally Katherine shrugged. "Sure. Why not?"

He smiled warmly. "Exactly. Why not?"

CHAPTER 3

"Mom, are you awake yet?"

No, she wasn't awake yet. Nor did she want to be.

"Almost," Katherine murmured in a sleep-thickened voice, and with some regret.

She'd been having a dream in which she was sitting in her office. The door was open onto a mazelike corridor of other open office doors and hallways. She'd glanced up from her desk to see a man standing in the middle of the corridor, casually and silently regarding her. It was as if he'd been waiting to get her attention. Something about him was not only familiar but startling in the instant fascination he created in her. Katherine had felt drawn to him and stood up from behind her desk to get a closer look.

"It's Neal," she said breathlessly to herself. Part of her knew it wasn't true. But there was another belief that compelled her. Maybe there had been a mistake. Maybe Neal hadn't died after all. She called out his name, but he turned away, walking toward an adjacent hallway.

Katherine had gotten up from her desk and

rushed into the hallway after him. "Wait!" she called out, but he didn't respond. When she reached the second hallway, she caught a glimpse of him turning into an office. But he didn't look the same. In fact, it was harder to see him clearly, as if he was fading. When she got to the doorway, Katherine called out his name again. But the man who responded and turned around to face her looked like Brian Chandler.

Katherine had recoiled. "Where's my husband?" she asked him angrily, as if it was his fault that she couldn't find Neal. Brian had smiled and was about to say something.

But she heard only her son's voice.

Katherine groaned as she rolled over and forced her eyes open. What had Brian been going to say? "Are we late?"

Scott was standing at the side of her bed in his sleep attire, cotton knit pajamas with printed images of Michael Jordan on the fabric. The ribbed cuffs at the wrists and ankles exposed too much arm and too much leg. He had outgrown them, Katherine noted, and wondered when that had happened.

"No, we're not late, but . . . can I stay home today? I don't feel good," Scott muttered in a little-boy voice.

Katherine watched him closely—the way he didn't really look her in the face and stood twisting his body nervously. She moved over on her bed and patted the space next to her. Scott climbed on top of the comforter on the bed and lay next to his mother with his head on her arm.

"What's the matter?" she asked, tilting her head against his, experiencing again, as she sometimes did, the wonder that she had given birth to this child, who would one day become a man. Katherine felt him shrug.

"I don't know. My stomach hurts, and I feel funny inside."

Katherine sighed and thought about it. "Mmm. Sounds to me like a case of the willies."

Scott looked at her and squinched up his face in puzzlement. "The willies? What's that?"

"Well, it's this thing that attacks boys and girls when they're afraid to do something. They worry about it because they think they're going to fail. And before you know it, all that worry makes your insides shake like crazy. It feels like butterflies. When your uncle and I were kids, our father used to call it having the willies." Katherine absently lifted one of his arms and stretched it out. The cuff of the pajama top was a good three inches above his wrist. Scott *definitely* had outgrown this pair. "Is that what it feels like?" she asked.

"I don't know. Maybe I have a fever. It could be serious, you know," Scott said, sounding much too reasonable for someone who was supposed to be sick.

Katherine shook him gently. "I think it's the willies. You know, if you tell me about it, maybe we can make them go away."

He was silent for a second. "Well . . . my teacher, Ms. Stewart, said she wanted the class to write about

187

what makes our father a great person. And . . . I didn't know what to write. And then she said she wanted us to bring in pictures of us with our dad."

"What is this for?" Katherine asked quietly.

"For Father's Day. We're doing a special project in school."

"That's easy," Katherine said smoothly, playfully rubbing her son's head. "What do you remember about him?"

"I think I remember when he showed me how to tie my sneakers. And when he and Uncle Eric took me fishing and I caught something."

"Good! What else?"

Scott shrugged. "When I had bad dreams and he came into my room and stayed so I wouldn't be scared."

"He made you feel safe?" she asked.

He merely nodded. He tilted his head back and looked wide-eyed at his mother. "Was it you or my father who taught me to ride my bike?"

"That was me. But your father taught you how to whistle, and showed you how to draw Woody Woodpecker. Do you still remember how?"

"I don't know."

"You see? There's lots of things you can write about," Katherine assured him, warmed by the memories Scott still had of his father.

He was thoughtful for a long moment. "Yeah, but . . . all of that stuff was when I was a little kid. Kenny Nicholls's father is teaching him how to sail. There's this girl in my class, and her father was in the Olympics once."

"Scott, you know that everybody is not the same and everybody can do different things. Your father was a smart man. And he did something that I bet hasn't happened to anyone else in your class. Maybe even in the whole school."

He sat up, interested. "Yeah? What?"

Katherine smiled at him and lightly pinched his chin. "He saved your life." She hesitated, wondering briefly about the wisdom of reminding her son of that day. "In that moment he thought more of you than he did of himself. That's pretty special, don't you think?"

"Yeah," Scott breathed out, his brows raised in appreciation.

"So you see, you have a lot you can write about. Maybe the other kids still have fathers, but—"

"But my father was a hero," Scott piped up firmly.

Katherine grinned. "That's right," she whispered. He thoughtfully nodded his head, thinking the whole thing over. "While you get dressed I'll pull out that box of photographs, and we'll pick out some of you and me and your father for class. How's that?"

"Okay," he said agreeably, getting off the bed.

"Do you still feel like you want to stay home? I can call Dr. Cannon and make an appointment for this afternoon to check you out."

"No, that's okay."

"Good. How about some pancakes for breakfast? Do you think that will calm down those willies?"

"Pancakes! *Yeah!* That's phat, Mom."

"What?"

"Phat. That's cool." He snorted, heading for the bedroom door and shaking his head. "Man, you don't know anything."

Katherine smiled peacefully. "I know. That's why I'm glad I have you."

"Kat, Kat, wait . . . look at that. That is *gorgeous*!"

Katherine responded to the urgent yanking on her arm. She turned to see what Denise Markham was so excited about. In the display window of This and That, the chic boutique a few blocks from their place of employment, were three mannequins, each wearing a different sample of the styles for the upcoming summer. The outfits were brightly colored: orange and yellow, pink and lilac, blue and green. They were contemporary, without fuss or details. But also very unforgiving on the wrong body.

"I like that one," DeeDee said, tapping her manicured nail against the window glass. Her choice was a pink and lilac sheath dress with front patch pockets at hip level, a V neckline, and a hem that stopped about three inches above the knee.

"It's cute," Katherine conceded. "But where would you wear something like that? It's not right for work."

DeeDee sighed longingly, and they turned away to continue their walk. "I didn't say I would buy it. I just said it was cute. I also know it wouldn't look good on me. And you're right, I don't have anyplace to wear it,"

assuming anything," Katherine said carefully. "There could be lots of reasons why Niki's keeping to herself."

DeeDee looked skeptical. "Like what? We've known that girl most of her life. She too good to remember us?"

Katherine looked her friend squarely in the face. "Then why don't you give her a call? Ask her yourself."

"Not me," DeeDee haughtily, as if such a thing were beneath her. "Eileen said she's probably hiding 'cause her husband left her. I know you were her best friend and all that, but I *swear* Danika used to get on my nerves. Don't you think there's something really weird about her?"

Katherine took advantage of the opening DeeDee provided. She glanced at her watch. "What I think is we'd better get back to work before we get fired."

"Let's meet for lunch again on Friday."

"Call me Friday morning and we'll talk about it," Katherine said, beginning to back away.

"Want to take Scott and Nathan to the rink to try out their in-line skates?"

"Maybe." Katherine waved as she turned to go.

"Want to meet my boss? He's not my type, but he's available."

"*No!*" Katherine said emphatically, walking away.

"Picky, picky, picky," she heard DeeDee complain behind her.

Although Katherine was amused by Denise's comments and observations, she also found herself mildly annoyed for a number of reasons. One was the unkind and catty way in which her girlfriends were attacking someone they'd all known since childhood. It was true that Niki had been difficult to be friends with: sometimes imperious and immature when they were adolescents and teens, and other times needy and demanding. Katherine had always found it bewildering that she was the only one who could see through Niki's veneer of ego and see a girl who had been adored but pressured to be perfect and to be all things to all people.

Katherine was surprised that no one else had figured out that something had to be terribly wrong for Danika to be behaving as she was right now. But Katherine knew it was not her place to give away secrets. Niki had her own reasons for keeping silent on her illness, and Katherine had to respect that.

But the other thing that touched a nerve with Katherine was DeeDee's continual harping on her single state. It wasn't as if it was a disease, but DeeDee certainly made it seem that not being interested in a man after six years of being a widow was somehow abnormal. Katherine frowned as she entered the municipal building where she worked for the state arts council. Was she?

In all honesty she *hadn't* given much thought to dating and being with a man or even marrying again. Being a single mother and giving her attention to Scott had taken up almost all of her time. She didn't begrudge any of it and was confident and pleased about the relationship between her and her son. Or at least she had been. Maybe if DeeDee had never said anything . . . or if she hadn't had that talk with Scott . . . or if she'd never met Brian Chandler . . .

Anyway, from what she remembered about dating rituals, they weren't all that much fun.

When Katherine entered her department, she waved to let the receptionist know she'd returned from lunch. She continued on to her office, hearing the ringing of her telephone as she approached. She was inclined to let it ring until her voice mail responded, but then reasoned that it could be the school calling about Scott. Or another family member. Or even Danika. Katherine reached across her desk and picked up the phone.

"Council on the Arts."

"Katherine Winston."

"Yes, speaking."

"I know," a voice said, amused. "That wasn't a question, it was recognition. Hi. Brian Chandler."

Katherine felt disoriented. The fact that they were merely talking by telephone did nothing to change her reaction to his voice or name. It was just disturbing that she had a reaction at all. "Mr. . . . Chandler . . ."

"Brian. You sound different on the phone."

"I guess I do. More formal, perhaps."

"Just the opposite," he countered. "More spontaneous and comfortable."

"Oh," she murmured at his assessment.

"I think I took you by surprise. Good."

"What do you meant by that?" she asked cautiously.

"Only that I'm beginning to know and understand you."

That made her nervous. "What can I do for you?" she asked smoothly.

He chuckled. "Okay. Is this Katherine asking, or Mrs. Winston? Don't answer. I'm only teasing. I hope it's okay to call you at work."

She wondered how he'd gotten the number. "Sure."

"I'm sure that I'll see your son this afternoon when he comes in for his lesson. How about we get something to eat afterward? I know it's a school night, but it doesn't have to be late."

"Actually, Scott won't have a lesson today. There's a class trip tomorrow and he's staying over tonight with a classmate whose mother is one of the trip's chaperones," she informed him, unreasonably relieved that she had a legitimate excuse to squelch his suggestion.

"That's okay," Brian said smoothly. "Then it can just be you and me."

Katherine opened her mouth to give him another excuse . . . and didn't have one ready. She struggled and searched and couldn't think of a thing, and knew immediately it was a tactical error. There was no way anything said after such a long pause could be honestly perceived as an excuse. "But . . . well . . . I thought you wanted to talk about Scott's swimming?"

"I do, but he doesn't have to be there for that. What time do you get off work?"

"Depends. About four, four-thirty," she informed him weakly. *Coward,* she berated herself.

"Shall I pick you up at your office or at home?"

"But I didn't say—"

"If you have another night in mind, tell me. I can adjust my calendar."

Katherine knew she didn't have the same flexibility. And she wanted to get this over with. If she just let the man have his say about her son's progress, then he would see that was all they had to talk about, that they had nothing else in common. Katherine sighed in relief. She'd figured it out.

"No, I guess tonight is fine. Why don't you pick me up at my house? Five-thirty?"

"That's good. I'll see you there."

He hung up, and Katherine felt a wave of panic rush through her body. Why had she given in? Why hadn't she told Brian Chandler that while she appreciated his interest in her son's progress with sports, she could handle and guide Scott by herself? Besides being a bald-faced lie, it made Katherine feel stubborn and childish. And defensive.

She decided it was a miserable sensation, this subtle dance of notice and interest, the advance and retreat as they stepped into each other's space. She wasn't used to sharing hers with anyone else but Scott. And she was not so unreasonable as to recognize that her son being her sole focus had its limitations. But perhaps her occassional loneliness wouldn't have mattered so much for a longer time if she hadn't met Brian Chandler and known from their second meeting that he was pursuing her. And she wasn't sure how to behave or what to feel.

The sensation was like when she was thirteen and wondered if any of the boys liked her. Was she too skinny or too tall . . . or too flat-chested? The answer had been yes to all of those. But it hadn't mattered one bit.

Katherine sat on the edge of her desk and mulled over the situation. On the other hand, she could be reading the whole thing wrong. Which was an indication of something else altogether: insecurity, curiosity, maybe wishful thinking.

This is embarrassing, Katherine thought as her phone rang again and she got up. What if it was the other way around? What if the heart of the matter was that Brian Chandler was picking up on vibes from her?

Katherine sent the last e-mail and sat back in her chair. She checked through the letters and applications for grants on her desk and picked up the ones that needed to be photocopied and sent to various council members. Leaving her office, she walked to the copy machine, located in a cluttered little room next to the equally small staff lounge at the back of the complex of offices. Methodically Katherine made her copies, enjoying the relative quiet of the office now that most people had left for the day. The sound the copier made as it did its magic, duplicating almost anything fed into it, was soothing and hypnotic.

It wasn't often that her son spent the night away from home. She knew it was something she would have to get used to more and more as Scott became less dependent on her and more involved with his friends. It had to be that way. But it came with the almost painful realization that her son was growing up, and one day he would leave, more or less forever. He'd have his own life to live. College. A career. A wife and children. And she would be left a widow.

A spinster . . .

Katherine took her pile of copies and thoughtfully headed back to her office. She was in bad shape, she decided, when a five-minute walk to make photocopies became a therapy session. She walked into her office and stopped short at the figure seated in her chair. It was a very thin woman in a black jumpsuit that made her appear even thinner, even more waif-like. Katherine was sure that a whispered breath could knock her over. The attempt at a little makeup was largely a failure, mostly because it looked so garish against the tan skin and fright wig.

"Danika," she uttered in surprise. "What are you doing here?"

"I shouldn't have come," Danika said flatly. Nevertheless, she stared at Katherine with a kind of wide-eyed appeal that was all the more wrenching because Katherine recalled so vividly what their mutual friends were saying about Danika.

"Maybe it was a mistake to come here. My mother told me a few years ago that you worked here." She scanned the office quickly.

"It's not a mistake, but . . . why didn't you call me?"

Danika looked both defiant and bewildered for a moment. "To tell you the truth, I thought you'd put me off if you knew it was me—make up some kind of reason not to have anything to do with me."

"Niki," Katherine intoned with genuine surprise. "For God's sake, why would you think that? Did you forget I was the one who came to see you last week?"

Danika closed her eyes wearily. "I've burned so many bridges. . . ."

Katherine came a little closer. "Bridges can be rebuilt. Why are you here? You look like you should be in bed. Niki, are you okay?"

She nodded. "I . . . I just . . ." She opened her eyes and regarded Katherine. "I was supposed to drop by the hospital for a quick checkup and to have some blood drawn to see how effective the chemo is but . . ."

"You mean you haven't done it?"

Niki clasped her hands together in her lap and leaned forward, almost hunching over, as though she was drawing into herself. "I'm afraid they're going to keep me and I'll never leave again."

The honesty of her fear and feelings, the possibility of that really happening, tore at Katherine's heart. She knew very little about the disease that was attacking her friend, and she hadn't bothered to find out. But Katherine *did* understand the isolation and helplessness. Her life had never been at risk the way her girlfriend's was right now. But one tremendous loss most definitely had made her appreciate and hold much more dear all that she still had. She reached for one of Danika's bone-thin hands and was surprised at the strength with which Danika held on.

"Come on. First I'm taking you to your appointment. And I'm going to tell them that if they hurt you, I'll have to kill them." Danika managed an appreciative chuckle and obediently stood up. "Do you feel like getting something to eat afterward?" Katherine went on.

"Anything I can get my hands on. But I'll throw it all up in the morning. That's what the chemo does to you."

"That's okay. After we finish at the hospital, let's go get all our favorite junk foods." Katherine picked up her phone and called a coworker to say she was leaving for the day. She briefly remembered all she was supposed to do before her day was over, and made the decision it could all wait. Katherine turned to Danika. "Let's go. We'll do the doctor thing, and then we'll go celebrate."

"Kat, what is there to celebrate?"

"Life," Katherine said as she and Danika left her office. She linked her arm with Danika's, subtly giving her physical support without appearing to coddle her too much. "Don't play dead until you have to. Tonight there is a piece of KFC that has your name on it."

"Girl, you're crazy," Niki murmured.

But Katherine could already feel and see the difference in Danika. Maybe it was just knowing she wasn't alone and there were people she could depend on. But Katherine understood her girlfriend enough to know that it had been hard enough for Danika to come to her. She had certainly never forgotten some of the things Niki had done over the years to hurt her and others. But when it came right down to it, their friendship was enduring because they both had survived the testing of it.

Katherine felt a strange honor that, of anyone she might have turned to, Danika came to her. That was proof enough for her that they were still tight. Not like when they were kids. The criteria had been different then. Now as adults, they had both history and experience to draw on, as well as lessons from their past hurts and disappointments. It made no sense to hold a grudge.

Forgiveness was much easier . . . and more gratifying.

For a moment Katherine thought her son had decided to come back home for the night. But then it quickly became obvious that the dark figure sitting on the top step leading to the front of her house was too big to be Scott. She drove slowly to her driveway, and when she turned into it, her headlights briefly flashed over Brian Chandler as he watched her approach.

Katherine methodically went about the business of parking her car for the night and gathering all of her totes, bags, and packages. She got out of the car, locking it, and went to the front of the house to let herself in. Silently she walked up the three steps. She was glad that Brian could not possibly see her face or expression in the dark, but she knew he was looking directly at her. In a way Katherine was not surprised to see him. He was the kind of man who would see things through until the end. And he was a man who kept his part of a bargain.

She carefully sat next to him, not touching him. After perhaps half a minute of absolute silence between them, Brian turned his head in her direction. Katherine could feel his gaze. She could imagine his questions. She could hear his calm breathing. But she also didn't sense that he was angry.

"I have to tell you this is a first," he began in quiet admission.

"What?" she asked just as quietly.

"Being stood up."

"Oh," she acknowledged. That certainly was one way of looking at it.

"Crisis at the office?"

She shook her head. "If it had been, I would have called you back. It was . . . personal. Very unexpected. I . . ."

He touched her hand briefly and released it. "You don't have to explain. You've just said it was personal. Is Scott okay?"

"Yes. And Brett?"

"He got a bad case of the urry-ups, so I made sure he ate and was home before I came over tonight."

Katherine hesitated, nervously gnawing on the corner of her lip. "How long have you been waiting?"

"Since I was supposed to meet you. About . . ." He

examined the LCD numbers on his watch. "About three hours."

Katherine cringed inwardly, sighing outwardly. "So you never got anything to eat?"

"Well . . . I found a couple of breath mints in my pocket."

She couldn't help chuckling. She knew he was still watching her. Suddenly Katherine wished she could see his face. "I can put together something for you. Why don't you come inside?"

"Thank you. I appreciate the offer. But I think we should call it a night and take a rain check. Come on, it's late. You better go inside . . . and I better go."

Together they got up, but Brian just stood on the top step watching as Katherine unlocked her front door and stepped into the house. She looked in his direction. She didn't know what to say. For some reason she didn't apologize, and she wondered if Brian would think that that was rude of her. Probably not. So far Katherine had decided that his ego was rock solid but not overbearing. He could express concern and interest without being intrusively nosy. He wasn't pushy. He was understanding and forgiving.

"Would you want to give it another try sometime?" he asked.

She was not unaware that the choice was hers. Now was her chance to let him down easily. Now was her chance to discourage his interest in her son's welfare. To go back to a comfortable routine of daily life that only in the past month could she begin to admit left much to be desired.

And then there was Neal.

Guilt racked Katherine. There was not a single day that she did not think about him and wonder how their lives might have grown and been different if he had not died. There were still times when she missed him terribly. But mostly he was a warm memory permanently locked in her past.

And she considered all the men she'd met since his passing to whom saying "no, thank you" had been easy and painless and without second thoughts or regrets. Already Katherine knew this was different. She'd known that when she met Brian Chandler in the steamy pool room of the local recreation center. Should they try again? What were they going to try?

"Yes," she answered softly.

"Good," Brian said casually. "I'll give you a call. Good night, Katherine."

She stood watching until he reached his car and opened the door. The interior lights of the Lexus detailed him briefly before he started the engine, closed his door, and pulled away from the curb.

Katherine closed her door and locked it.

To be continued, she thought.

CHAPTER 4

"Kat, look what I found."

Katherine got up from her knees and dusted her hands. She adjusted the bandanna and used her forearm to wipe the sticky mixture of dust and moisture from her cheek. "I'm coming," she called out, leaving the den on the first floor where she'd been pulling file boxes and other stored items from a small closet.

She walked into the living room, where Danika was ensconced in a chair surrounded by boxes and files taken from other parts of the house. There were stacks of papers and garbage bags filled with more papers all around her. On the coffee table were vials of medication, a pitcher of iced tea, and a barely touched box of Godiva chocolates. Katherine had given them to Niki. Predictably, they were her favorite candies: expensive and rich. The deal was that she could have a piece of candy for each filled bag of garbage that resulted from going through years of records and receipts.

On Danika's lap was an open yearbook from the

graduating class of Randolph High School. She was slowly leafing through the pages.

"Oh, my God," Katherine groaned as she bent over Niki's chair and peered at the pages with a wry grin.

"Look at Denise's hair. That is awful!"

"Yeah, but it was the fashion back then." She pointed to a figure in a group photo of girls from the tennis club. "I hear Sylvia married some rich man from California."

"Mmm-hmmm," Niki confirmed as she turned the page. She got excited when something else caught her attention. "Whatever happened to Mr. Fisher? Remember when people started saying he was messing around with Terry what's-her-face? You know which girl I mean. . . ."

"No, I don't," Katherine murmured, shaking her head.

"Yes, you do," Danika insisted. "She had big breasts from the time she was thirteen, and she used to go around in those tight sweaters. Didn't she and Mr. Fisher get married when she finished school?"

"Oh, right," Katherine recalled. "Well, I guess she got the last laugh. I remember now that Eileen did mention they're still together, with two kids and a huge house in Sparta."

Danika returned to examining the pages of the book but had fallen silent. Katherine frowned at her, wondering what had happened now. She acknowledged that Niki was given to mood swings, but she knew that much of that could also be due to her being tired and weak at times, to stress and anxiety, and to the frustration of not being in control of her life. Katherine touched her shoulder.

"You all right? Can I get you anything?"

Danika shook her head. "Not right now."

"What's the matter?"

Danika snorted. "Everything. But I'm trying not to complain, Kat. I'm sick of being sick. I'm tired of being alone. I want my life back. I want my child."

Katherine moved several boxes from the coffee table and sat on the top of it, next to her. "I didn't hear you mention your husband."

Niki made a gesture of indifference. "It's too late. He's not going to forgive me, Kat. I was a real bitch to him, and he didn't deserve it. He worshiped me."

"I don't know why," Katherine interjected dryly.

"Me either," Danika whispered.

Katherine put an arm around her friend's shoulder. "Is this the same person who told all the girlfriends that she was who she was and didn't have to apologize for that?"

"I'm eating those words as fast as I can. No wonder nobody liked me. I was *so* conceited."

"You certainly had your share of self-confidence."

"Well, look at me now. No husband. Not much family to speak of. No friends . . . and I have cancer. I have been put in my place."

"Feeling sorry for yourself again?" Katherine said bluntly.

"Just facing the facts."

"*Your* facts. First off, you could call your husband if you really wanted to. Second of all, you do have a mother, a sister, a daughter, and some nieces. And you do have friends."

"Yeah, and not one of them has called me. I know they're all talking about me."

Katherine sighed patiently. "Niki, of course they're all talking about you. You haven't called them, either. You've been hiding in this house by yourself like a leper. Okay, so you have cancer. It's not contagious. And it's not a punishment from God. You said yourself your tests look good and the chemotherapy is working. What else can you possibly want?"

Danika looked at her with her oversized eyes. "I want my life back, Kat. I want a chance to say I'm sorry to everyone. A chance to start over."

"You have it. Anytime you want to use it."

Danika blinked at her strangely for a moment and then frowned. "How come you're not mad at me, Kat? Don't you remember what I did at your wedding?"

"You mean when you stood me up and left me without a maid of honor? It was too bad you decided not to come, but I still got married, Niki." Katherine leaned toward her and spoke earnestly. "You're my best friend, but I wasn't going to let you ruin the most important day of my life just because you decided to throw a serious hissy fit."

"But don't you know why?"

Katherine picked a dust ball from the knee of her jeans and nodded. "Yeah, I thought about it. Denise sort of told me what might have been going on in your mind but I didn't really believe it. She said it's because Neal married me and not you. Because you thought I had taken him from you. You forget one thing: He wasn't in love with you. Yeah, he thought you were fun and sexy. I know you met him first and had a few dates. But quite honestly, Niki, I thought you were acting like a spoiled brat when you didn't show up. I was disappointed, but you didn't hurt *my* feelings."

Niki looked taken aback. "So you're telling me that all I did by not showing up was make a fool of myself?"

"That's about it," Katherine confirmed.

Niki sputtered and suddenly burst out laughing. She doubled over with it, slapping her leg. "Girl, *please* don't make me laugh. It hurts."

Katherine grinned at her. "You know what else? When the minister asked if there was anyone who objected to me and Neal getting married, we *all* looked around to see if you were hiding and were going to jump out at us!"

Danika was laughing so hard she couldn't catch her breath. Tears of mirth rolled down her cheeks. It was so contagious that Katherine finally joined in, seeing in hindsight the funny side of that day.

Katherine gasped for air as she wiped tears away. "DeeDee said that if you'd shown up at the reception, she'd have stabbed you through the heart with one of these cocktail stirrers . . . with Neal's and my name on it!"

That image sent Danika off into a fresh spasm of laughter. They laughed until after a while they didn't know what was so funny. Danika was practically sliding off her chair, and Katherine developed a stitch in her side. She pressed her hand to it until the laughter finally died down. They looked at each other with girlish smiles, the way they'd done as adolescents when they told secrets or self-consciously used foul words in an attempt to act grown-up.

Danika held out her hand, and Katherine took it without hesitation.

"I'm so glad we're friends. I'm so glad you're here."

Katherine squeezed the delicate hand gently. "You're not going to get all mushy, are you?"

Danika just chuckled, this time too worn out to succumb to full-throttle hysteria. "We used to have so much fun when we were kids."

"Haven't you noticed, Niki? We're having fun right now," Katherine said.

"You know what I mean."

Katherine stood up suddenly. "You know . . . I think we should have a party."

"What?"

"I'm going to call up everybody—well, at least everybody who's still around—and invite them over to my place."

"I can't come. I—"

"Take it easy, it's not for you," Katherine quickly said. "This is just going to be a girl thing. We'll sit around and drink wine, and tell everyone's secrets, and laugh at how we've all changed for the worse."

"I can't—"

Katherine ignored her. "I'll have everybody bring something. You know, like a potluck lunch. I'll do my famous chicken salad with mandarin oranges and pine nuts. What do you want to fix?"

"Katherine, I *cannot* go to some party with all those people," Danika whined.

Katherine could hear the genuine fear in her voice. She sat down again and faced her. "Niki, they are not 'those people.' We're talking about folks you've known most of your life. Friends."

Danika was shaking her head stubbornly. "They won't come. I'm telling you."

"You're wrong. Want to bet?" Katherine asked, holding out her hand. It was loosely curled into a fist with the pinky finger extended outward.

"Get out of here!" Danika admonished her, pushing her hand away. "I'm not going to bet you anything."

"'Fraid to lose? Let's bet, and I'll shoot you for it. I call even."

Evidently Danika's imagination was engaged by the familiar ritual they'd used since childhood for settling disputes. She put her hand in the same position. They hooked their little finger and used the pressure of their knuckles and thumbs to pull the fingers apart. Then, using only their middle and index fingers, they counted to three, and each of them put out either one or two fingers. If an odd number of fingers was counted at the end of three attempts, it would be Niki's win. But if the number was even, the victory went to Katherine.

Katherine made sure she won.

"You cheated!" Niki accused her.

"Prove it."

Niki sucked her teeth. "I'm not coming to no party." She nervously plucked at the wig and sat way back in her chair, as if she were trying to disappear into the cushions.

"You'll be there."

"How can you be so sure?"

All of Katherine's teasing vanished. She stood towering over her childhood friend. It wasn't a form of intimidation so much as a dare. "Because if you don't, they'll all know you were afraid. If you don't show up, they will never let you forget it, and neither will I."

Katherine smiled as she witnessed what a difference a month or so could make. On the other side of the viewing partition she could clearly see what was going on in the pool. Scott, standing in the shallow end with the water at chest level, was nodding, acknowledging the instructions he was getting from Brian Chandler. She watched everything carefully, noticing how closely her son paid attention. And she was very aware of how thorough Brian was in his instructions. Instead of witnessing the spectacle of a whirling dervish with windmill arms splashing his way through the water, she was actually able to see that Scott's strokes were a little smoother and better coordinated.

Brian Chandler was a good teacher, she thought.

Watching him with her son, Katherine suddenly could get a better idea of the kind of man he was. He was patient, obviously. And attentive. He knew how to give information, how to listen and watch. He knew when to praise and when to get tough if Scott repeated his mistakes.

Katherine watched him as much as she watched her son. She couldn't help but be fully aware of Brian Chandler as a man. He was well proportioned and fit. Athletic, but not a jock. Muscled, but not buffed. She acknowledged that he had all the right stuff, as her friend Eileen would say, and gave him his due as a man. But Katherine found herself paying attention to much more.

And that's how she knew she was in trouble.

She wasn't sure if it was the way he had of giving his undivided attention to a person or the quiet confidence with which he seemed to do things. It could be that he seemed also to know what he was talking about, and could back it up. For sure it was because he was good with her son. Scott responded naturally to Brian Chandler and clearly was inspired by his fifteen-year-old son.

But he had other qualities as well that she'd made note of. Like how he'd behaved the night two weeks earlier, when she stood him up to be with Danika. No anger or accusations. No ego bent out of shape. Just an acceptance that something had gone wrong. It wasn't the end of the world. And there would be other opportunities. But he hadn't pushed it. She wondered if he would again.

Through the Plexiglas partition she watched as Brian demonstrated with his arms the correct stroke. Then it was Scott's turn to try the movement out of the water while Brian talked to him all the while, occasionally guiding Scott's arm in the right motion so he could feel how it was supposed to be. Next Brian indicated he wanted to see Scott try it in the water, coordinating with his leg movements as well. Brian climbed out of the pool, smoothly leveraging himself out of the water by bracing his hands along the edge of the deck and springing up. Katherine admired his easy grace.

Scott took in a deep breath, held it, and, throwing his body forward, tried out his technique. As Scott swam Brian monitored his progress by pacing him alongside. Scott's arm-over-head motion caused his body to twist from side to side, and he still tried to keep his face and head above the water. But overall Scott's movement through the water was less wild and more efficient. He made it the length of the pool easily. When he reached the other end, Katherine wanted to applaud.

Brian said something else to Scott, who nodded vigorously. They stood together at the end of the pool, and Katherine realized that they were going to race. At the count of three Scott took off. Brian allowed him about ten feet before he dived in himself, and there was no question that for a while he tempered his stroke to stay just a bit behind her son. Then Brian pulled ahead slightly as they neared the end of the pool. He won, but it wasn't a slaughter. And Katherine suspected that the finish was deliberately orchestrated that way, not to defeat her son but to make him work so that one day the outcome of another race would really be in doubt.

They both climbed out of the pool, grabbed their towels, and headed into the locker room. Katherine left the viewing stand and went to wait for her son by the receptionist's desk. She had been waiting just a few minutes when she spotted not only her son but Brian and Brett as well.

Katherine stood transfixed for a moment as she watched them approach. Her son was in animated conversation with Brett Chandler, a tall, lanky teenager still in braces, which seemed incongruous when everything else about him indicated he was in the midst of the physical passage from teen to young man. But Katherine was really paying attention to the fact that with Brian Chandler and his son, Scott seemed much more open and relaxed—just like at the birthday party for Michael Adamson a few weeks back, and unaware of her presence. He seemed much less a little boy who needed to be protected. And what he needed, she realized with a jolt, she could not give him.

When she caught Brian's gaze upon her, Katherine smiled politely, not giving anything away.

"Mom, did you see me?" Scott asked, coming to his mother's side.

Katherine resisted touching him—another indicator of change. Just recently she had noticed that Scott pulled away from public displays of affection, as if it was embarrassing that his mother hugged him the way she'd done when he was a kid.

"I sure did. You were really good," she complimented him, proud but not gushing.

"Mr. Chandler says that now I have to learn how to breathe."

Katherine looked at Brian. She felt the urge to avert her gaze, certain that he was staring at her because he was looking for a particular reaction from her. To what, she wasn't sure. Although her imagination actively invented a lot of things, she didn't want to go there.

"I think he's got a point," she answered wryly.

"He'll pick it up in no time. Scott's a fast learner," Brian said, stopping in front of her. He turned to the other boy, putting his arm around the boy's shoulder. "This is my son, Brett. Brett, Mrs. Winston."

"Hi, Mrs. Winston," Brett said, sticking out a long, thin arm with long, skinny fingers.

Katherine noticed the way his voice hovered between two octaves, but with already enough bass in it to show he was going to sound a lot like his father. She took the offered hand and smiled warmly at him.

"Hi, Brett. I have to thank you and your father for all the work you've been doing with Scott. He's having a great time."

"That's okay, I don't mind," Brett said with a shrug. "It's kind of fun showing him stuff that I know. He's like a little brother."

Katherine didn't know why it happened just at that moment, but she and Brian exchanged glances that held a lot of silent questions.

"Brett knows how to in-line skate and he said he'd show me." Scott turned to his newfound friend and spoke in a stage whisper, as if his mother was invisible. "She doesn't know how. Anyway, she'd probably fall and hurt herself."

"Thanks a lot," Katherine said to her son with mock indignation. She could sense Brian's attempt to hide his amusement. "You go ahead and make fun of me, then tell me who's going to take you to Great Adventure for your graduation."

Scott looked stricken by his mother's words. "Mom," he murmured, trying hard not to whine, "I was only teasing. . . ."

"Now that you can swim, you think you're so grown-up. Don't forget I'm still bigger than you."

Brett got a kick out of that and playfully rubbed Scott's head. He cackled. "Your mom just snapped on you, man."

"Maybe we can all go together," Brian suggested, again looking at Katherine for a reaction.

Katherine frowned. "To Scott's graduation? It's just sixth grade."

"I meant to Great Adventure. The four of us. Think you can put up with a little kid and two old folks for a day?" Brian asked his son.

"Yeah, that's cool," Brett agreed with great restraint. "I'd like to see the little guy here upchuck on one of those rides that turn you upside down."

Brett tried to evade Scott's attempt to grab him, chuckling with the peculiar air-horn sound of a changing voice. They briefly roughhoused.

"Okay, okay, calm down," Brian said, taking control. "You two have energy to spare . . . you must be hungry, so why don't we use some of it up to have dinner?" He looked directly at Katherine, his gaze communicating silently with her. "I've been wanting to fill Scott's mother in on his progress, make a few suggestions. Do you have to rush off right away?"

Katherine opened her mouth to say yes, she did have things to do and people to see . . . and then she couldn't think of a single thing that was really that urgent. And she couldn't lie. "Well . . . no, not really. How does that sound to you, Scott? Want to have dinner with the Chandlers?"

His eyes lit up. "Yeah!"

"All right, then," Brian said, ushering the four of them to the door of the rec center. "Why don't you and Scott follow us, Mrs. Winston? Brett and I have a favorite place we go to about three miles from here."

"Call me Katherine," she said boldly, without too much thought. *Mrs. Winston* suddenly made her sound not only old, but like someone she no longer was.

As they all filed out the door, Brian stood back to let her go ahead of him, and his eyes held a surprised but pleased look. He grinned almost boyishly, and it gave his face a vulnerable quality that Katherine found appealing.

"I'm going to turn onto Teaneck Road," Brian informed Katherine as he pointed in the direction he'd take. He waved briefly, turning to his car.

"Scott and I will be right behind you."

"Mom, can I ride with Brett?"

Katherine stopped in her tracks and turned around to her son. He stood some ten feet behind her, next to Brett. She blinked as she once again viewed the three males together. There was clearly a bond between them that seemed natural. And it occurred to Katherine that her son needed this: the psychic connection to other males with the same interests and inclinations, a chance to do "man things," as Brian had joked many weeks earlier.

Brian could see the ambivalence in her. He put a hand on her son's shoulder. "I'll keep an eye on him," he promised.

Katherine finally nodded, giving her permission. "Fine," she said quietly. "I'll see you all at the restaurant."

Scott was having a great time.

They all seemed to be, Katherine had to admit, and that included herself. Once they were seated in the casual restaurant she found herself relaxing. Soon there was zero time for her to think about the moment. She only had to just do it. In truth, there was constant conversation, especially the unique teenage language and observations going back and forth between Brett and Scott. It was an instant education for Katherine to find out what her son knew that she didn't know he knew, and once again the experience pointed out to her that he was very much developing a peer group that had nothing to do with her. In an interesting insight, she could see that Scott needed and enjoyed the company of his own kind—the male of the species.

But she didn't feel threatened by what she saw as Scott's attention to and affection for the Chandlers. Rather, what she felt was just a calm acceptance of the changes. The heart of the matter was that Scott was growing up.

"Would you care for another iced tea?"

Katherine smiled absently at Brian and shook her head. "No, thanks." He signaled the passing waiter for their check. Automatically she reached for her purse.

Brian briefly shook his head. "I'll get it," he said, pulling out his wallet.

"I really think I should. It's the least I can do, what with all the help you've given my son," Katherine said.

He didn't respond right away, taking his time to extract a credit card and hand it with the bill back to their waiter. "I coach Scott because I want to, and because I like him very much. But if you feel that strongly about it, you can get the next one."

She was clueless. "The next what?"

A slow smile curved his mouth and warmed his

gaze. "If we go out together again . . . the four of us."

His inference was not lost on Katherine, and it finally dawned on her that Brian Chandler had expectations. Not unreasonable ones, and not even particularly personal ones, but just a natural sense that things should continue. She didn't agree or disagree with his suggestion for a future outing, but let the idea hang in the air, not committing to it. It was something she was going to have to think about.

She looked not at Brian but at her son. "I think we'd better be going, Scott. I *know* you have homework, and I *know* you haven't done it yet."

"I don't have that much," Scott was quick to point out.

"That's good, but we still should leave now."

Brian turned to his own son. "I didn't hear you make the same claim. Do you have homework?"

Brett shrugged nonchalantly. "I just have to print out an essay I had to write for my history class, that's all. And I have a practice tomorrow after school."

"Want me to pick you up?"

"Naw, that's all right," Brett said as they all began to stand up. "I'll walk home with some of the guys."

They slowly made their way to the parking lot exit and their respective cars. At the door Scott pointed to another side room to the restaurant he hadn't noticed before. There was a lot of noise and activity coming from the room, and the sound of adolescent voices.

"What's in there?" Scott asked, pointing.

"That's the arcade," Brett responded. "They have some cool video games. Wanna see?"

"Can I, Mom?"

"Well . . ." Katherine hesitated, looking at the time.

"It won't take long, Katherine. There's only four games and an air hockey table," Brett assured her.

"Ten minutes?" Brian suggested as a compromise.

"Okay," she agreed, and quickly got her son's attention before he dashed off to the game room. "Ten minutes," she reminded him.

"We'll be in the parking lot," Brian also called after them as he held the door for Katherine to pass through.

Leisurely Katherine and Brian walked through the lot in the direction of their cars. It was just after twilight, and the air had that calm, warm feel of late spring. She took in a deep breath, smelling the freshness of the trees and shrubbery. This was her favorite time of year. Autumn was her least favorite; Neal had been killed in October.

Katherine was very conscious of Brian next to her. It was the kind of awareness women had when they were with a man, as opposed to being with a girlfriend. She could feel the physical differences. The imbalance of physical power and presence. She felt the kind of security and vulnerability that came with it, as their roles seemed defined in terms of their gender and not their individual personalities. Male, female. Couple.

She glanced at his profile. Brian too seemed to be

deep in his own thoughts. She wondered for a moment what they were.

"Do you think Scott should really pursue Olympic swimming as a goal?"

"Why not? I wouldn't discourage him if I were you. I don't know enough about the requirements for the U.S. team or the past records of earlier medal winners to know how he should be trained. But it's easy enough to find out. Right now I believe he should not even think about competition, but just have fun learning to swim." He stopped at her car and turned to lean back against the door on the driver's side. "Let's face it. Swimming is not even on the short list of sports most black youngsters want to do. If Scott goes all the way, and no one gets there before him, he could make history."

She looked quizzically at him. "If that's the case, how come you learned to swim so well?"

He became reflective. "Peer pressure. My father was in the air force, and we were stationed sometimes on bases where there weren't a lot of other black families or kids. It seemed like *all* the white kids knew how to swim. A lot of parties and socializing took place around backyard pools. I had to learn, but I've also always loved it. I started teaching Brett almost before he could walk."

The reference to his son's development brought a thought to Katherine. Not that it hadn't been there before, but it had never seemed relevant, and it certainly hadn't been any of her business. Brett's mother. Brian's wife. Or whatever. He was suddenly staring at her, and Katherine wondered if he could possibly be reading her mind. Was she giving off signals? Had anything she said or not said alerted him?

"I'm divorced," he calmly and quietly stated.

Her stomach roiled with the implications of his admission. As though it was important to get that out in the open, important for her to know.

"Oh." She nodded foolishly

"I'm sure you know what that's like. You get a little nuts, always wondering if you did the right thing by getting a divorce."

She blinked at him, shaking her head. "No, I don't."

He frowned, clearly confused. "Excuse me?"

"I'm not divorced. My husband's dead." Brian's surprise was evident in his eyes and stunned expression. "Didn't Scott tell you?"

Still intently regarding her, Brian shook his head. "No. He never said anything, and I wouldn't have pumped him for information about his father. I could just tell there wasn't one in the picture. If you don't mind me asking," he began carefully, "was he sick?"

She shook her head. "No, it was a hit-and-run. It was a while ago. Almost seven years now." She realized that openly talking about it was easier than she would have imagined. People didn't ever ask, and she'd had years of practice getting over the fact of it.

"Sorry to hear that," Brian said sincerely.

Katherine acknowledged his sympathy but didn't pursue it any more.

Neither did Brian.

"Moving right along," he murmured, stroking his chin thoughtfully, "I'd like to get together again, soon. Not with the boys, but just you and me."

Katherine noticed the size of his hands. She'd always been attracted to the size of a man's hands.

Don't go there. A warning bell went off in her head as her mind drifted. She was horrified to realize that Danika had been right about her needs.

"Well . . ."

"You do owe me, you know. Remember, you stood me up."

"I had a good reason," Katherine defended herself calmly. "And you told me I didn't have to explain."

He nodded readily enough. "That's true. But I didn't say I was going to let you forget about it. If you want, I'll spell it out. I'm interested. I like you. I like your son. How do you feel about that?"

Katherine stared silently at him, knowing that she would be able to see and read a lot in his expression. He was serious, and Brian Chandler did expect an answer from her. No games, no frills, no manipulation. He wasn't going to try to play her. She either knew what she wanted to do or didn't. She needed to make a grown-up decision that had absolutely nothing to do with Neal.

"I . . . it's just that . . ."

He stepped away from the car and was no more than six inches from her. He looked down on her without attitude or posturing. A realization seemed to brighten his eyes for a moment, and there was a quiet sound of acknowledgment from the back of his throat. His gaze was both gentle and understanding—a powerful combination.

"I'm sorry. I shouldn't have put it like that. It's been a long time, hasn't it?"

His voice was a velvet whisper. The kindness in his question rocked her, dug deep, but didn't hurt. It was the truth, after all. She was no longer ashamed to admit that there hadn't been anyone else since Neal. She'd not thought that much about it . . . until now. Katherine didn't answer but continued to search out his intent in what he said, how he responded.

Brian sighed and reached for her hand. He surprised her by lifting it and kissing the back of her fingers with a soft touch. "There's no hurry," he said. "There's lots of time."

She felt relief. He wasn't going to pressure her. She looked at him and then quickly realized that he was bending toward her. She had no time to say anything and was too slow in trying to move away. The pressure of his mouth was soft, sensual, and fleeting. She didn't even have a chance to fully register what he'd done, to repulse it or enjoy it or question it.

"The way I look at it, we had to get that out of the way, too. Next time you won't have to worry if that's going to happen. I'm here to tell you flat out that it will. Are you free the Saturday after next? Brett's off to his grandparents' in Sacramento for a month."

She tried to think. "Scott goes away to camp for two weeks."

"Fine. How about meeting me at the club? It's time you learned how to swim."

"No, thanks. I'm very happy not knowing. I have no desire to make the Olympic swim team," she said dryly.

He grinned broadly. "I own a small boat. If you can't swim, Scott, Brett, and I can't take you with us when we go cruising on the Hudson or Long Island Sound. Don't worry, I won't embarrass you, and I'll make sure we have the pool to ourselves. Then maybe we can just take a long drive. Stop somewhere to eat and talk. Get to know each other."

Katherine had to admit it sounded very appealing, fun, and relatively safe. "We'll talk about the swimming lessons. Otherwise, I'd like that."

This time when he lightly kissed her she was prepared. And again it was quick. Just an indication of Brian's interest . . . and perhaps a hint of things to come. Katherine unconsciously touched her fingers to her mouth. That made him smile at her. Brian let her hand go.

"Here come the boys. They're right on time," he said wryly, discreetly moving a little away from her.

Katherine couldn't have agreed more.

CHAPTER 5

Katherine carefully placed the four glasses of iced tea on the wood serving tray and added the small dish of sliced lemons and limes. From the living room came the voices of women. Sometimes it was quiet as one of them related a story or secret and the others listened intently, occasionally acknowledging with little murmurs and comments like "Girl, I heard that," or "Get out!" if it was something unbelievable. And "Lord have mercy" if it was sad. There were still a few friends who had not arrived yet, including Danika, and when the doorbell rang, Katherine sighed in relief and rushed for the door.

"I'll get it," she said, meeting DeeDee, who was already on her way there.

But instead of Danika, it was her next-door neighbor, the talkative Mrs. Crockett, a retired nurse whose favorite pastime was everyone else's business.

"Hi, Isabel. Oh, I guess the mailman left some of my things in your box again. I'm sorry you had to go to the trouble," Katherine said, taking the envelopes.

"Oh, I don't mind bringing them over." The

older woman smiled, flashing a set of improbably perfect teeth that were dazzling white in her oak brown face. "I see you got a letter from the IRS. Did you forget to file this year?"

Katherine smiled patiently but didn't answer directly. "Thanks for bringing them back," she replied, smoothly deflecting the query.

"I was about to go for a little walk, but I have time to sit awhile. I *love* that little apple tree in your yard. Gives good shade," Mrs. Crockett hinted.

"I don't want to keep you from your walk. Actually, I have company at the moment, and—"

"Oh, how nice. Family? Friends?"

"Ah . . . it's an . . . an association I belong to," Katherine improvised. "Thank you Mrs. Crockett."

Katherine watched her neighbor turn away as she closed the door. Her guilt at being less than hospitable was eased immediately when the phone rang behind her. She dashed back to the kitchen.

"I'll get it!"

"Kat, will you please stop flying through the house like the Road Runner and come sit down with us? You're missing all the news."

"I'll be right there," she told DeeDee, then picked up the receiver. "Hello?"

"Hey, Kat. It's me."

"Paula, where are you?"

"I got off at the wrong exit, but I'm straight now. I'll be there in about fifteen minutes."

"Good. I was beginning to worry."

"Is everyone else there?"

"Just about."

"Don't tell me you got Danika to come."

Katherine laughed lightly. "I'll see you soon." She hung up.

She took the tray of drinks and finally joined her friends in the living room. DeeDee and Eileen were on the sofa, and her mother was in the recliner. There was a chair for Paula, when she arrived, as well as a rocker and ottoman.

"Katherine, this is such a great idea," Eileen said, accepting a glass of tea. "We should do this more often, you know?"

"I don't know if I can stand seeing you all *that* much," DeeDee cracked, and everyone got on her case.

"Well, I think it's lovely that you ladies have remained friends over the years," Elaine Stanley said.

DeeDee squinted at Katherine's mother. "I swear, Mrs. Stanley, you look exactly the same as when Kat got married all those years ago. I don't know what you're doing, but can I borrow some of it from you?"

The women laughed lightly at the compliment to Elaine Stanley, who did indeed look youthful and fit.

"Well, it's no secret. First, you get rid of your kids when they go away to college, and you change all the locks on the doors so they can't come back!"

"Four more years," Eileen moaned, which was the amount of time before her daughter finished high school.

"And then you have a husband who appreciates

you, loves and respects you, and stays out of your kitchen," Katherine's mother continued.

"Well, so much for that," DeeDee chuckled.

"And you remember to always take as good care of yourself as you do everyone else. Finally, you love God, from whom all blessings flow."

They were reflecting on that when the doorbell rang again. Katherine excused herself and went to open it. She knew it could be Paula, who should be arriving about now. But she was hoping for someone else. However, when she opened the door Katherine was stunned to find Brian Chandler there, whom she hadn't been expecting at all. She stared blankly at him. And then it hit her.

"Brian . . . oh, no . . ."

He appraised her silently. His gaze was speculative and searching. Not angry, but clearly somewhat curious. "Hi," he drawled smoothly.

Katherine closed her eyes in disbelief and pressed her hand against her face. "Don't tell me I did it again."

"You did. You know, this is very bad for my self-esteem."

She touched his arm and quickly withdrew. "Brian, I'm so sorry. I'm so embarrassed."

"That's a good start." He nodded, but again didn't appear in the least put out. "I figured maybe it was my brand of toothpaste, or you *really* don't want to learn how to swim."

"No, no, it's none of that."

"Was it because I kissed you? Was it too soon?"

Now he was serious. Katherine blinked at him.

He was casually dressed in jeans, with loafers instead of sneakers, and a simple black T-shirt that did him justice. His sunglasses hung carefully from a hand that was posed against a hip.

"No. It wasn't that, either." Katherine glanced back into the house, where the party was continuing without her. She stepped out the door and partially closed it, facing Brian again.

"But I am interrupting something."

"The truth is, I've been very distracted. I have a friend—my best friend from when we were little girls—who's been ill. And I'm having a luncheon for her. You know . . . girlfriend stuff."

He silently nodded, understanding brightening his eyes. "Got it."

"She's not even here yet, though, and I'm a little concerned."

"That something's wrong?"

"Or that she won't show up. She's been known to do that."

"Then you don't need me to add to your worry." He checked his watch. "I think I'll do some laps at the club anyway. Maybe catch a movie."

"I really am sorry. Please don't take this person-ally. I was looking forward to . . . to . . ."

He lightly gripped her shoulder. "I'm really glad to hear that. Let's plan something a little less athletic. Swim lessons can wait a few weeks. There are a couple of concerts coming up. Luther or Patti, your choice."

"Oh, Luther," Katherine said without hesitation.

He slowly smiled. "I'll get the tickets." He briefly clasped her hand, squeezing it before releasing it and turning away. "I hope your friend shows up."

But even as he uttered the words a car pulled up slowly and parked in front of his. It was Paula. And right behind her came yet another car. This time it was Danika. Katherine stood in her door and from a distance watched as Paula and Danika alighted from their cars, exclaimed over each other's presence, and stood talking for a quick moment. Brian said something to them, causing both Paula and Danika to laugh. Katherine smiled at the moment, grateful to Brian and relieved at the arrival of the last of the guests.

Brian put on his sunglasses and waved to her before getting back into his car and driving away.

Katherine hugged Paula and Danika, whispering in the latter's ear, "Girl, you had me worried. Are you okay?"

"Scared to death," Danika muttered.

Paula went past them both into the house, and the sounds of greeting raised the noise level once more.

Katherine looked over Danika. She was dressed very simply in silk pants and a coordinated silk tunic top. She looked lovely, if painfully thin. She wore a little makeup today. And her baseball cap, sans wig underneath, was black velvet covered with little round gold rivets for a slightly jeweled look. Her appearance suggested short hair but was ambiguous as to a style. Actually, the cap was rather attractive, and Katherine felt it would deflect undue curiosity.

"Do I look okay?" Danika asked Katherine. Her

tone, however, wasn't so much nervous as impatient, as if she just wanted to get this over with.

"Stop fishing," Katherine said. "You look fabulous."

"You're a liar, but thank you. Who was that man?"

"Oh . . . Scott's swim coach."

Niki peered closely at her. "Oh, yeah? I thought Scott was at camp. What aren't you telling me, Kat? You been holding out?"

Katherine urged Danika through the open door. "There's nothing to tell, Niki."

"Hmpf! There will be."

It was only as the two of them neared the living room that Danika held back, grabbing the back of Katherine's summer dress to prevent her from entering the room.

"Kat, wait," she hissed. "I can't go in there yet."

"What's the matter? Are you feeling sick or something?"

"I . . . I just need to catch my breath."

"Do you want to go to my room? Should I call your doctor?"

Danika blinked at her. "You didn't tell them anything, did you? About what's happening with me, I mean."

"No, I didn't. I know all of us are friends, but . . . I didn't think I should be the one to give that information. Anyway, you look fine. Why should they even think anything's wrong?"

About that Katherine was wrong.

As soon as she and Danika entered the living room all conversation stopped, and four pairs of eyes turned to watch them. Katherine could have killed them all. They were all staring at Danika as if they were expecting to see a tail or to hear her speak in tongues. It was rude, Katherine thought. But why shouldn't they have been as curious as she had been when she'd first seen Danika in that supermarket? She'd looked positively awful that night. She looked much better now. But anyone who'd known Danika a long time would notice that something was definitely different about her.

Katherine had no idea what to say that would stop their intense scrutiny.

Danika finally broke the silence. "Well, I made it. Late as usual, of course."

DeeDee shook her head. "Had to make the grand entrance. Just like always," she said dryly.

Katherine sighed in relief.

"Danika, I heard you were back and staying at your folks' place. Now, why haven't you called me?" Mrs. Stanley admonished easily in her best mother voice.

Eileen added her two cents. "I wondered if you were going to surface."

Danika carefully made her way to the rocking chair, which Katherine had deliberately left empty for her. She sat and arranged herself in regal fashion. This they were *all* used to. Niki always came late, and always got the best seat, and always gathered folks around her like a queen holding court.

And she hadn't forgotten how to behave imperially.

"That's the cutest cap," DeeDee observed. "And it looks so good on you, Niki."

"Thank you," Niki said graciously but quietly. "A friend of mine gave it to me."

"How nice. Any special reason?" Mrs. Stanley asked.

"Yes. It was . . . a going-away present."

The conversation picked up from there, and before long there was a comfortable give-and-take, with fussing and complaining, laughter, and jokes—just as they'd been doing since junior high. Katherine let it go on for another twenty minutes before calling everyone to the dining table, where they could help themselves to the potluck buffet lunch.

"Niki, what did you bring? I don't see your famous blueberry cobbler, or even your chocolate bourbon pecan pie. One thing I'll give you, you sure could bake some mean desserts," Eileen said, loading her plate with a little of everything.

Katherine looked anxiously at Niki. Even though she'd asked Niki to bring something, she hadn't insisted because of the time and effort involved. But everyone had always looked forward to Niki's desserts.

"I already had dessert," Katherine put in, thinking quickly. "An ice cream roll. Not very exciting, but cool."

"I'm buying drinks later," Danika said unexpectedly, making Katherine frown at her. "Champagne."

"Really? That's a special-occasion drink. What are we celebrating?" Mrs. Stanley asked.

Danika exchanged glances with Katherine. "Life."

Katherine sat next to Danika, trying to gauge how she was doing, whether she was getting tired or feeling ill. But Niki assured her that she was fine.

They ate and talked and laughed a lot. They were almost through the meal when Paula leaned closer to Danika and said to her, loud enough so that everyone else was able to hear, "You know, I wasn't going to say anything, but you've lost a lot of weight, Niki. Not that you needed to. And you never had to worry about it. But I'll tell you quite honestly, you do look a little too thin."

"Well, I'd sure like to know the diet she's on. From what I can see, we could all use to lose a few pounds," Eileen said.

"Speak for yourself," Mrs. Stanley said.

"Cancer," Danika said clearly into the teasing atmosphere.

All conversation stopped cold again. Katherine's gaze swept quickly around the room. Danika had everyone's attention.

"Excuse me, but . . . what did you say?" DeeDee ventured.

"I said cancer. The big C."

Everyone had stopped eating, some with forks poised and mouths open, and just stared at her.

"Breast cancer. Did anyone notice that my boobs are a lot smaller?"

The silence continued as everyone stared at Danika, trying to figure out if she was teasing or not.

"But Niki is really fine," Katherine said cheerfully, hoping to wipe the stunned expression from everyone's face and to keep the mood light. She looked to Danika for guidance. How much did she want to explain?

"Oh, my God, she's not kidding," DeeDee said.

Niki shook her head. "No, I'm not. I sincerely wish I was, but . . ." Slowly Danika put her fork down. She looked to Katherine as if to say, *This is it. This is the moment.* She reached for the bill of her cap and pulled it off. An audible gasp went around the gathered women, and the room fell silent again. But this time it was filled with shock, surprise, and disbelief.

Danika now appeared like a tiny hairless doll, her ears sticking out. She looked thinner, and her skin carried a peculiar ashen tone under the brown. Her eyes were huge in her small face. Her hair was beginning to grow back, though, and she now had very short, very fine hair covering her scalp and defining the shape of her head.

"I've lost about twenty pounds, my breasts, and my hair. But I'm still here, folks, so please don't feel sorry for me."

"Oh, for heaven's sake," Mrs. Stanley said quietly. "When did you find out, Danika? How long has it been?"

"Almost two years since I was first diagnosed. Then there was surgery . . . the Big M. Then there was radiation and chemo. . . ."

"Oh, Niki," Dee Dee murmured in horror.

"But you never said anything. You never told any of us," Paula said.

"What was I supposed to say? That I found lumps and they were probably going to kill me?"

"You could have told us, Niki. Why didn't you?"

"Because of the conversation we're having right

now," Danika said. "I didn't want to have to deal with your feelings about it, or your guilt because I have it and you don't. And I sure as hell didn't need anyone's pity."

"I wouldn't have given you any pity, anyway," DeeDee said, not mincing words. "You just would have cursed me out."

"So what happened?" Paula asked. "I mean . . . did they just take your breasts and that's it? Are you going to be okay?"

Everyone waited for her answer, and Katherine realized that she herself had been afraid to ask about Danika's chances. Even using the word *cure* seemed too ambitious.

"For now," Danika said easily. "I've been having chemotherapy. It seems to be doing the trick. I'm in remission."

"But that's great," Paula exclaimed. "That means the cancer is not growing."

"But it doesn't mean it's not there. This is the second time," Danika said. She absently rubbed her hand over her nearly bald pate. "Right now I'm waiting for my hair to grow back and I need to put on some weight. Other than that, I'm fine."

"What about your husband? Your daughter?"

Niki kept her composure. "My daughter has been with my mother for a while. I have had to deal with a lot of changes and decisions recently. And my mother decided to clear the house and rent it. A lot of things. I didn't want Holly to see me sad or crying. I did quite a bit of that. As for my husband . . . he needed some time to himself, too."

Clearly no one really knew what to say or how to behave, so Katherine stood up, only half finished with her lunch. "I have something for Niki. I saw it a few weeks ago and thought it was just right for you."

Katherine retrieved a small package wrapped in bright paper with a springlike floral design. Katherine handed the gift to Niki. "Here's hoping that you won't have to use it for very long."

Danika stared at the offering suspiciously. "What is it? I don't need another wig. You hate the one I have, anyway."

"It's not a wig. Go ahead, open it."

Everyone quietly watched Danika rip the wrapping away. The meal was largely forgotten, and Katherine was glad that everyone was watching Niki. Slowly the gift revealed itself, and it was clear that most of them had no idea what to make of it. It was a strip of bright yellow and orange kente cloth sewn together to make a band. Part of the material had been fashioned into a flower.

"What is it?" Niki asked, turning it this way and that.

"Oh! I know what it is," Paula said, getting up from her chair and coming around to Niki. She took the item from her hands and held it up, showing the large circle that it formed. "This is for her head," Paula informed them. "Like the ones mothers put on bald-headed babies!"

"Oh," Eileen murmured in recognition. "What a clever idea."

Paula carefully fitted the headband on Danika's head. Together they tugged it into place and put the flower at an angle.

Niki turned her head back and forth. "What do you think?" she asked no one in particular.

It was very becoming, and everyone seated at the table knew it. Danika turned to Katherine.

"Thank you," she said softly. "Thank you for the wonderful headband, and for the luncheon, and for bringing us all together again."

"I wish I could say that it was just for you," DeeDee said. "Katherine suggested a luncheon as a reunion. We need to keep in touch. We need to put our baggage behind us and remember that we go way back."

"Then this is as good a time as any to say how much you all mean to me," Danika said. She turned to Katherine and smiled at her. "And I especially want to thank Kat for reminding us of that. Husbands come and go . . . half of them ain't no good, anyhow. Your children will grow up and leave you. But we stay together no matter what other changes are going on in our lives. We weather them. We support each other." Niki glanced around the room. "Having my childhood friends around me is the best gift I've had in a long time."

"Niki . . . are you going to die?" Paula asked bluntly.

"Yes." Everyone gasped. "But not this year, or even next. Sooner or later. I've come to accept that, because I know it's true of all of us. The doctor says my prognosis is good. I hate that word. Why can't he just say, 'Live long and prosper', like Spock? Why can't they say, 'Go home and don't come back unless you have to'?"

That finally got a quiet chuckle of amusement and agreement from the women. Everyone had questions, and Katherine was relieved to see that they held nothing back. The curiosity was understandable and real. Danika's answers were honest and generous. She wasn't afraid to talk about her experience, the good and the bad.

Katherine slipped away to open the champagne that Danika had paid for, her contribution to the luncheon, and poured half a dozen glasses of it. She again put everything on a tray and took it into the dining area.

"This is Niki's bubbly," she said as everyone held a glass.

"I propose a toast," Eileen said, standing up and raising up her glass. "Here's to Danika's good health—and to her hair growing back."

Slowly Danika came to her feet. "No. I think we should toast each other and our friendship. To girl-friends everywhere."

"To the future," Mrs. Stanley added.

"And to the many blessings we have, even when we don't think so."

DeeDee put her arms in the air, the way Pastor Monroe used to do on Sundays at church service. "Can I get an amen?" she asked with closed eyes. The women chuckled warmly.

"Amen," they said in unison.

CHOICES

◆

EVA RUTLAND

CHAPTER 1

"He makes over half a million a year," Millie said.

Becky almost dropped the phone. "Half a million! How much is that a week?"

"Oh, for God's sake, Becky! Come out of the 'hood!"

"What?"

"How much a week! That's project thinking. Jesus, Becky, you're eighty miles and ten years away from that slum."

"Old habits die hard." Becky chuckled. "Did I hear 'the 'hood'?" This was terminology Millie would never use around her more classy friends, Becky thought. Nor would she be likely to refer to their old neighborhood at all, preferring to keep her past as distant and as dark as possible. "Better watch it," she quipped. "Many a slip 'twixt the tongue and the lip!"

"Oh, shut up and listen. Becky, this guy is—"

"Hold it!" Becky released the phone and grabbed her son in the nick of time.

"You talking to me or Tommy? What's he yelling about?"

Becky wrapped one arm tightly around Tommy, who was protesting with all the vigor of his four years, and clutched the phone with one hand. "I'm trying to talk to you, and he's yelling because I won't let him splash through the water."

"What water?"

"A leak in the . . . Oh, for goodness' sake, talk to Tommy. See if you can shut him up." Becky set Tommy on the kitchen counter and handed him the phone. "Tell Millie what happened to your dinosaur." After Tommy had been appeased by a few soothing words and a cookie, she recaptured the phone. "That's why I called you. I don't think I can make it to your dinner tonight."

"Are you crazy?" Millie's words exploded in her ear. "You have to come. The only reason—"

"But this leak . . . I've got water all over the place."

"Call a plumber."

"I did." She had called one recommended by her neighbor. "I don't know how soon he'll get here." *Nor how much he'll charge,* she thought. *Probably an arm and a leg.*

"So? Your baby-sitter can let him in."

"Millie, you don't understand." She'd have to leave a blank check. Risky.

"I set up this whole thing for you, and I'm not about to let you muff it. Samuel Hendricks is the guy, Becky. He's got class. Black as the ace of spades, but real good-looking. And smart as a whip! Had to be to get where he is."

"I know," Becky said, remembering. "Harvard MBA, West Coast vice president for DT Corporation . . ."

"Then you know these women are on him like white on rice."

Becky smiled. "And I'm to join the crowd?"

"Darn right. With your looks, you've got an edge on most. Tonight's your chance to bowl him over. A quiet, intimate dinner, just the four of us—Hal and me, you and Hendricks."

"All right, all right," Becky said, laughing. "I'll be there. That is, if the plumber gets here in time."

"He will. Just pay him and come on. And wear that black dress with the slit. Shows off your to-die-for legs. Want to borrow my pearls?"

"That's my doorbell. Probably the plumber."

"Good. Problem solved. Be ready at six. I'll have Hal pick you up. That way I can ask Hendricks to take you home."

"Okay. Gotta go." Becky replaced the phone, scooped up Tommy, and raced to the door.

"Saunders Plumbing," he said.

"Thank goodness," she said, hardly glancing at him. "Back here. A leak." It suddenly occurred to her that it might be the machine itself. Should she have called the Sears repair service? Darn. If she had to buy a new washing machine—

"Well, let's take a look." There was something in the way he said it, some calm assurance, that, surprisingly, transmitted itself to her.

She thought she should move the towels she had

placed around to soak up the water, and put Tommy down so she could do that. Of course he moved eagerly toward the mess. She was about to stop him, but the plumber spoke first. "Stand back, sonny. I need your help."

That stopped Tommy in his tracks. Becky, as surprised as he, looked up to see the man take a small tool from his pocket. "Hold this for me," he said, handing it to Tommy. "Keep it away from the water. Can't afford to let my tools get wet."

She was also surprised that Tommy obeyed, keeping a tight hold on the tool while the man wrung out the towels and cleared up most of the water. Then, with careless ease, he pulled out the washing machine and made a short inspection.

"Not bad. Just a leak in the connecting pipe. We can take care of that, can't we, buddy?"

Tommy, wide-eyed, nodded.

"What's your name?"

"Tommy."

"I'm Carl. Okay, Tommy. You keep an eye on things here while I get something from the truck." He returned with the part and started to replace the PVC tubing, managing to engage Tommy in the task. "Hold this . . . hand me that . . . hold this pipe steady while I tighten this over here . . . this look okay to you?"

She smiled when Tommy, looking helpful and very important, peered closely and announced, "It's okay." He was now at ease and bombarding the man with questions: "What does this thing do? Why are you doing that?"

There were things she should be doing, but she found herself listening, intrigued by their banter. And now she did look at . . . had he said his name was Carl? He was really quite good-looking. Or maybe she was just partial to dark reddish brown skin and coal-black curly hair. That was what had first attracted her to her deceased husband, Tom. Same dark, deep-set eyes, too, only Tom's eyes had had a dreamy but serious look. This man's eyes were alert and lively with a hint of laughter, as if . . .

"Thanks, Tommy. Really appreciate your help."

Realizing he was packing up his tools, she reached for her checkbook. "Thank you," she said as she handed him the check for $59.85. "You don't know how glad I am to have that mess cleaned up."

"Could have been worse. If you'd had a full flow . . ." He hesitated. "There's not much pressure."

"I know."

"These steel pipes are old and corroded," he said. "You might want to think about replacing them."

"Yes, but not just now," she said as she saw him out. This was not news to her. Everything in this house needed replacing. Maybe she and Tom should have bought one of those tract houses with brand-new plumbing and wiring.

She thought back to when they had found the house; she had been pregnant at the time. They'd looked at new houses, but Tom had dismissed them. "Pocket-size lawn and paper-thin walls," he'd said. "A good strong wind would knock it down, not to mention a rough and tough boy," he added as he caressed her swollen belly.

So they had bought this sixty-year-old Victorian with lots of space and a big yard for the large family they planned to have. They knew it needed a lot of fixing up, but if it hadn't been in such bad shape, they couldn't have afforded it. And Tom was handy with repairs. If he hadn't died soon after little Tommy's second birthday . . .

Becky would not look back. The present was all she could manage. It was hard on her substitute teacher's fluctuating salary, which was on the low side now that the flu season was over and fewer teachers were calling in sick. But she meant to hold on to the house. After twenty-two years of apartment dwelling, this was the first single-family house she had ever lived in. She loved it. And, on the practical side, it had its pluses. It wasn't in a prestigious neighborhood, but the area was a lovely, quiet one of beautiful curving hills with big old houses that had been grand in their day. Good neighbors, too, with families moving in and refurbishing the old. Folk who could not afford a new upscale house like Millie's.

Thinking of Millie's house in fashionable Oakland Hills, she smiled. Millie had always craved the biggest, brightest, and best. Acted like she had it even when she didn't. She had been as poor, as needful as any of the rest of them, but she would walk through that project with her head so high that the gang dubbed her "Madame Queen." The pose may have been a bolster against the shame she must have felt about her pa and his drunken, abusive rampages. It had been a blessing for both Millie and her mother when the old man died.

But, she thought, Millie's Madame Queen stance had been more than a bolster. It was also a banner, Millie proclaiming what she meant to be. Always. In school, the blacks had a tendency to hang together, regardless of class, and the poorer ones among them got a glance at how the other half lived. Even now she could see Millie at the home of one of their more affluent friends, her eyes wide open, watchful, taking in every detail. She'd been defiant, determined, signaling the message *I'm going to have all this. And more.*

And now she has it, Becky thought with a touch of pride. Not only was Millie an attorney herself, she was married to Harold Banks, the junior partner in the old prestigious family law firm of Banks, Burroughs, and Banks. As the saying goes, she was living high on the hog. *Well, nobody deserves it more than Millie,* Becky thought. *She worked hard to become—*

"It's Cindy!" Tommy cried, racing to the door even before the bell rang. He had been watching from the window for his favorite baby-sitter's arrival while she'd been daydreaming, her mind in the past. It was almost five. Leaving Cindy on the floor with Tommy and his jigsaw puzzle, the television blaring, Becky raced upstairs to dress. She was glad that the plumbing problem had been taken care of and that Cindy was available, so she wouldn't have to disappoint Millie. Some people might call Millie a conniving social climber who had wormed her way into the tight, exclusive circle of Oakland's black elite, but Becky was not among them. It was true that Millie loved position and prestige, true that Millie had achieved both and now moved in a different circle than she. But though the social gap between them had widened greatly, Millie had remained her truly loyal best friend.

Standing by the big bay window that fronted her Oakland Hills home, Mildred Banks switched her gaze from the diamond-encrusted watch on her wrist to the sloping driveway outside. It was five-thirty and Hal wasn't home yet. He'd race in at the very last minute, she thought, grubby from golf, with no time to dress and pick up Becky. Then suddenly she saw his car.

She rushed to the hall and called sharply down as he entered from the garage. "You're late! I told you Sam Hendricks is coming to dinner, and you've got to—"

"I know. Pick up Becky." Harold Banks bounded up from the lower floor and kissed his wife on the nose. "Told you I'd be here."

"You haven't even dressed. I told her you'd be there at six, and it's almost that now. You get on that darn golf course and nothing else matters! Honestly, Hal—"

"Cool it. I'll make it." Whistling, he mounted the stairs to the upper level.

"In a pig's eye you will. I laid your clothes out. Try to hurry. And try not to make a mess!" she snapped.

Not that he was listening, and she knew he would leave a trail like a snail from bedroom to shower. Thank God Sam Hendricks wouldn't see it. She gazed with smug satisfaction at the perfection of her spacious living room. The rich colors of autumn were subtly blended in the soft cushions of chairs and sofas, cleverly arranged in conversational groupings. It was still cool enough for a fire, and logs blazed in the massive stone fireplace. There was not a footprint on the plush carpet, the leaves of her potted plants glistened, and the chrysanthemum arrangement on the coffee table was the perfect bright touch. This room and the dining room beyond, mainly used for formal entertaining, were isolated from the bedrooms and family living quarters upstairs and from the large recreation room on the bottom level, with its easy access to the grounds and swimming pool. The privacy of each area was what she liked, Millie reflected as she adjusted the switch on each lamp for the correct soft glow. She had practically designed the split-level house herself—*though you'd never know it from the size of the bill the architect submitted,* she thought with a wry smile.

"I'm off!" Hal shouted as he ran downstairs.

Millie glanced again at her watch and sighed. Hendricks would probably get here before Hal and Becky did, so she'd have no chance to give Becky the once-over. Becky was apt to be careless with her appearance, a failing common among women who were born good-looking. Becky never spent one dime at the beauty parlor. She still wore her hair in an old-fashioned Afro—so, as she said, she could just wash it and let it go. Lucky for her, the short cut accentuated her perfect features, and those dark copper curls were enhanced by her golden tan complexion.

He won't even notice what she has on, Millie decided as she walked through the dining room and gave the table a last inspection. The china and silver gleamed, the linen was spotless, the napkins lay crisp in their silver napkin rings. From the dark and distant past lingered an image of cracked and mismatched plates, heavy mugs on a stained and battered table. With a flush of pride, Millie touched a finger to the flower arrangement, then moved one candle a fraction of an inch. Perfect.

The table was not extended, but cozily set for four. She had purposely not invited a crowd. With a large group of people Becky had a way of fading into the background and quietly listening, just as she'd done at the Circlets' tea, when she should have extended herself to be particularly charming.

Of course, Becky had had no idea that she was under inspection as a prospective member of that exclusive club. *Doesn't even know that I have twice submitted her name—and that she has been twice rejected by those bitchy snobs!* Millie sighed. Those women were suckers for a little flattery, and if Becky had just put herself out a bit . . . But she wasn't the type, Millie told herself, and anyway, it probably wouldn't have made a difference even if she had made the effort. There had been only two openings this year. Of course they'd taken Lois Coleman, whose grand new house overlooked the bay. And Jessie Taylor, whose husband had just been elected to the California Assembly. Yes, those were the tickets to the tight little circle of Oakland's black elite: a big fancy house or marriage to a prominent man, preferably both.

And this ain't handed to you on a silver platter, Millie thought. *You gotta work for it. And plan. Shoot! I took one look at Hal, got myself hired in that stuffy old Banks law firm, and was married to him before he knew what hit him—and before the Lord and his ma got the news! Lord, was old Mrs. High-and-Mighty burned up! Her darling Hal married to this social-climbing bitch from the wrong side of the tracks.*

Oh, yes, I know what she and those high-society witches thought of me. But I was Mrs. Harold Banks by then, and that alone pushed me down their throats even though they choked on it!

Well, the hell with that! Nobody can deny that I've been good for the firm. I guess being old and prestigious tends to make you too complacent or too proud to grovel for the bucks. But I'm used to groveling. And even old Mamie Banks has mellowed, seeing the new business the green lady lawyer is bringing in.

I've been good for Hal, too. He might laugh at me for, as he puts it, "getting all hot and bothered about doing things right for the right people." But that's good business, too. Sam Hendricks might be a catch for Becky, but he's also a potential contract for Banks, Burroughs, and Banks. DT Corporation is set for a lot of new projects in this area.

And a union between my best friend and the new VP for DT is just icing on the cake. Now, Becky, if you just play your cards right . . .

At that thought, Millie sighed again. Becky didn't play the people game. And as for pursuing a man . . . Millie considered that Becky had just drifted into that marriage with Tom.

Drifted, nothing. He pursued her like crazy, worse luck, she corrected herself. Then Millie crossed her heart, meaning no disrespect to the dead. Tom had been a nice man. A nice ordinary elementary-school teacher . . . going nowhere.

To tell the truth, Becky didn't care all that much about getting somewhere, either.

But I care, Millie thought. *I'm tired of seeing her scraping to hold Tommy and herself together on a meager salary, and that old house practically falling down on them. And I want my best friend right here in the in crowd with me.*

Millie had never forgotten that Becky and her mother's nearby apartment had been a safe haven whenever Pa got abusive. There was no mean, abusive pa in that household; Becky's father had died in Viet Nam when she was a baby. Becky had often laid an ice pack on a swollen jaw or a black eye. And afterward she'd never breathed a word about it. When some other kid would start to smart off about the ruckus the night before in number eighteen, Becky had a neat way of turning the conversation to a different topic.

Oh, for goodness' sake! Why am I thinking about those days and that dump? Millie walked into the kitchen to check on Cora, her part-time maid, who had come in to serve the meal.

"Don't forget," she told her. "I've already boiled these beans just enough, and rinsed them with cold water. When you get ready to serve them, put them in with these ingredients that I've sauteed, just long enough to heat them up. Do you have the dip ready? Now, before dinner, when you serve the drinks . . ."

CHAPTER 2

Becky was ready when Hal arrived.

"Hello, beautiful!" he said, giving her a brotherly kiss on the cheek. Hal was short for a man, about her height, and a full inch shorter than his wife. He had pale skin, sandy hair, and the most constantly cheerful disposition she had ever encountered in anyone. He was late, but seemed in no hurry.

"Where's my main man?" he demanded.

"Here's me!" Tommy cried, kicking over his jigsaw puzzle in his hurry to get to him.

Becky, watching them go through their usual handshake and what's-happening routine, wondered, not for the first time, why Hal and Millie had no children of their own. No room on their crowded calendar, she supposed, what with their busy business and social life.

"You're looking luscious and lovely as usual, lady," he said as he helped her into the car. "You'll knock him out!"

"I'll be at my seductive best," she said, laughing.

"You do that. We wouldn't want Millie to knock *you* out."

He was teasing, but just barely, she thought. Millie had not taken kindly to Becky's failure to seal any one of the previous "connections" Millie had so carefully set up.

The trouble was, Millie's conception of Mr. Right was not always hers.

"What do you think of the imminent Mr. Hendricks?" she asked Hal, wondering why she felt his assessment was more valid than Millie's.

"Seems like a pretty decent guy."

That was it, she thought. Hal's assessment was of the man himself, not his position and prosperity.

Still, there's nothing wrong with a little prosperity, she thought as they approached the Bankses' house. She was impressed, as usual, by its grandeur, the big bay windows and the fourteen-foot-high double entry doors. The expansive lawn was well tended, the shrubs neatly clipped. No faulty wiring, corroded pipes, or leaking roof.

Must be nice.

"Uh-oh! I'll catch hell," Hal said. "He beat us here."

Becky looked at the sleek, expensive sports car parked in the driveway. *Maybe this one* is *the right mister,* she speculated to herself.

"What's so funny?" Hal asked.

"Nothing." She coughed, smothering the chuckle. She sure wasn't going to tell Hal she was thinking of making a play for Mr. Moneybags when all she had seen was his car!

How did one go about making a play? Her

thoughts were running riot by the time they entered the living room.

Hal was right about catching hell . . . quietly. The look Millie gave him was as sharp as a whip. But her smile was warm and gracious when she turned to the man standing by the fireplace and drew Becky forward. "Sam, this is my friend, Becky Smart. Becky, Sam Hendricks."

Becky swallowed the gulp. Millie hadn't mentioned the man himself. Not a word about tall, rather fair, and undeniably handsome. Sam had keen patrician features, and the eyes looking down at her were hazel with flecks of gold.

"I've been looking forward to this," he said, taking her hand in a warm grasp. "I've heard so much about you."

"I too." Thoughts of things like cars and money faded in his overwhelming physical presence. She found herself gabbing. "That is, I've also heard a great deal about you, Mr. Hendricks, and I'm delighted to—"

"Now, now, none of that Mr. Hendricks stuff. We're all on a first-name basis here. Right, Hal?"

"Right. Here you are, Becky." Hal said.

"Thank you." She took the tall glass, glad of the distraction. Self-conscious under Hendricks's steady gaze, she took a sip. Just as she liked it—lots of orange juice and very little vodka.

"A refill, Sam?" Hal asked. "Scotch and soda?"

The men moved to the bar, and Millie moved close to Becky, a definite question in the surreptitious lift of her brow.

Becky cast a covert and approving glance at Hendricks. The Armani suit of lightweight wool fit as if especially tailored for his tall, slender frame, and the Bally loafers of soft leather seemed quite at home on Millie's plush carpet.

"So you've known Millie a long time?" Hendricks was again beside her.

She nodded, hoping the hot flush evoked by his continued appraisal didn't show.

"Forever," Millie answered for her. "We grew up in the same neighborhood, about a half block between us, huh, Becky?"

"About." Becky smiled. He probably thought, as Millie intended, that the "block" consisted of houses rather than rows of brick apartment buildings, all the same shape. Before he could zero in on details, Millie skipped to their college years.

"That was an exciting time," she said.

Exciting? Maybe, Becky thought, looking back. Her mom and Millie's pa had died, and Millie's ma had been relegated to that nursing home. She and Millie, at seventeen and eighteen, were alone and on their own. They should have been scared, but what they really felt was a sense of freedom for the first time in their lives.

"Oh, yes, we roomed together during the whole four years," she heard Millie say.

Becky thought of the crummy studio apartment, long shifts at fast-food stands, classes crammed between treks to the financial aid office, and dutiful visits to Millie's mother at that pitiful nursing home.

It hadn't been easy. Had it not been for affirmative action and Millie's determination, they'd never have made it.

The way Millie was talking, it sounded like a happy four-year romp through one of those fancy universities.

But Sam Hendricks was eating it up. "I know what you mean," he said. "Those are the happy, carefree years. At least mine were."

"You were at Yale, weren't you?" Millie asked. "Did you like it?"

"Enjoyed every minute. Especially the fights."

"Fights?" Becky asked, puzzled.

"No strong-arm stuff," he said, laughing. "Skirmishes for position. Head of the debate team, class president, and so on. You know."

She didn't know. They had had no time for extracurricular activities.

"Yes, we certainly do know," Millie said. "I take it you were quite involved. Did you—" She paused when Cora appeared at the dining room entrance and glanced nervously at her. Millie stood and put down her glass. "I think Cora is ready for us. Come along," she said, taking Hendricks's arm and leading him to the table.

"Everything is lovely, as usual, Millie," Becky said, looking at the crystal wineglasses, the shining silver, and those beautiful plates that cost a hundred dollars each. Millie had bought a dozen full place settings, Becky recalled, trying to calculate her friend's total expenditure. *That must have been enough to re-tile my whole roof.*

The oh-this-is-nothing wave of Millie's hand reminded Becky that she should act as if she took such things for granted. She concentrated on her salad, an unusual mixture. Tiny shrimp and slivers of . . . pineapple? Whatever it was, it gave a sweet tang to the crisp greenery and was incredibly delicious.

Millie lifted her wineglass as she addressed Sam Hendricks. "Now, tell us. Where were you in these exciting skirmishes?"

"Right in the middle, I'm afraid. I thrive on competition. Keeps the juices going."

"Oh? And which of the prizes did you compete for?"

"Pardon?"

"Class president, head of the debating team, or editor of the campus paper?"

"Oh. Well . . ." He chuckled and shrugged, as if in modest apology. "I must admit I gave them all a shot."

"All?" Even Millie was awestruck.

"Oh, not all at once," he said. "Though I was class president and head of the debating team simultaneously during my last two years. But only associate editor of the school paper."

"Busy man." Hal's dry comment was his first in some time.

"You could say that. But I guess once you start, you just keep running. And, to tell the truth, I enjoyed the hassle. It was fun."

"Speaking of fun, did you join a fraternity?" Hal asked. Hal had been a staunch member of Kappa Alpha Psi, which he termed the "good-time guys," since his college years at Morehouse in Atlanta.

"Oh, yes, as a matter of fact, I did," Hendricks said, naming a fraternity none of them had ever heard of. "And perhaps that was the greatest hurdle of all."

"Why so?" Millie asked.

"Well . . ." He hesitated. "Actually, everything was quite open at Yale. But face it—we haven't rid ourselves of all traces of racial barriers yet. This was the most prestigious fraternity on campus, and no black had ever been admitted." He held up a hand. "You know how it is."

"I'm sure there was some opposition," Millie said.

"Oh, yes. Quite a few sons of fathers from the old school. To tell the truth, I wasn't all that interested, but Bill Traylor, my tennis partner, was determined to get me in."

"Traylor? Of the brokerage firm?" Millie asked, eyes wide.

"Yes, that's his family. Bill and I were old buddies from all our summers at the Vineyard."

"Martha's Vineyard?" Millie asked, as if to pin it down.

Hendricks nodded, and Hal chuckled. "You and the president. Were you with his party last August?"

"Nope. I wasn't invited," he said, smiling. "But I did drop in on the folks for a couple of days while they were there. Played a round of golf with Vernon. I'm seldom there now, though. Too busy."

"But you do have a place there?" Millie persisted.

"My folks do. That's where they hauled us kids as soon as school was out. Mom said it was better than the streets of Philly."

Or the projects, Becky thought, remembering long hot days of stickball in the narrow lanes between apartment buildings. She tried to imagine what it was like to spend summers on an island, with sandy beaches, cool breezes, and an ocean at your feet.

"It must be lovely there," she mused.

"Yes." He cut into the tender slice of prime rib. "Of course, it's getting pretty touristy now, and—"

"So you did get in?" Millie, on another track, interrupted. "Into the fraternity, I mean."

"Oh, yes. Those who were opposed to my membership were greatly outnumbered. Many of the guys were already my friends."

"Good friends—and good business contacts, it seems," Millie said.

"That's my wife!" Hal said, grinning. "Business first."

"At least there's more on my mind than golf," Millie snapped.

Hal's face sobered, and Becky, seeing Millie was on the verge of a flare-up, hastened to intervene. "I take it you play a bit of golf yourself," she said to Hendricks.

"Indeed I do. Nothing wrong with golf," he added, smiling at Millie. "Nothing wrong with business, either. Great combination, as a matter of fact. Many a deal has been signed and sealed on a golf course."

That's diplomacy, Becky thought. Neither Hal nor Millie had lost face, and the tension was broken. Or so Becky thought.

But Millie was not an easy loser, and Hal's long hours at golf were a sore point with her. "That depends," she said. "Not everybody plays golf with the likes of Vernon Jordan—oh!" She concealed the grunt from Becky's kick with a cough. "Too much pepper," she apologized, with a sidelong glance at Becky.

Becky didn't care. She didn't like the way Millie was always putting Hal down, and Millie should know it didn't make her look good, either. She searched her mind for a safe topic. Weather. "You must find California a pleasant change after Philadelphia's rough winters," she said to Hendricks.

"Quite a change. Quite a state! Warm sand and sun in the south, and snowy mountains in the north—great, I understand, for skiing."

Becky was about to ask if he skied, but Millie, she of the one-track mind, spoke first. "Great state for business, too."

"Oh, yes, I'm finding that out. I talked with Ray Samples yesterday, and he told me his company is in hot pursuit of the state's RFP for a new sewer development project."

"Oh, yes," Millie said, and launched into details about which company was likely to make a counter-bid.

From then on, the conversation was strictly on business, and dominated by Millie and Hendricks.

Millie urged him to tell of his astounding accomplishments in various areas of the country. It was quite a list, but Hal seemed hard pressed to keep from yawning.

Becky was impressed, though. She was on unfamiliar ground, but gathered from the big names and big deals he mentioned that he was quite a wheeler-dealer.

"I suppose you have great plans for this area," Millie prompted.

"Oh, yes. But that's enough about me. I want to know more about this pretty lady who has kept so quiet the entire evening," Hendricks said, and turned a questioning look toward Becky.

"Oh. Th-There's not much to tell," she stammered. Thrown so suddenly into the spotlight, she felt quite insignificant after Hendricks's awe-inspiring recital. "I'm a schoolteacher, and a single mother," she said, wondering if Millie had told him she had a child.

"Yes, Millie said you had a son. He is how old?"

"Almost four, going on fourteen." On safe ground now, she talked about Tommy, her heart. She wished she had brought snapshots.

Hendricks said he must be a handful, and he was looking forward to meeting him—as if he intended to see more of her, Becky thought, pleased.

The evening ended on this note, and Millie, as planned, asked Hendricks to see Becky home.

"I'll be delighted," he said, smiling at Becky. "I want to be sure of the way to your house."

Snuggled in the soft leather seat of the Mercedes,

Becky felt surrounded by luxury . . . and a bit uncomfortable. Should she ask him in when they reached her house? He would find it pretty different from—

"Tell me, Becky Smart, what do you do with yourself?"

"Do? I . . . not much." She shouldn't ask him in. The house would be a mess.

"A pretty lady like you? I can't believe that."

"Believe it." She almost laughed. "Between Tommy and work, I stay pretty busy."

"Not too busy, I hope."

"Oh. W-Well, I . . . ," she stuttered, suffused by a prickle of pleasure. He meant to see more of her! Well, that settled it. She wasn't going to spoil her chances by bringing him into all that clutter.

"I'd better see you safely in."

Darn!

It must have hit him full in the face. His polished loafers were definitely out of place among the toys, crayons, and puzzles scattered on the floor. She turned off the television and roused Cindy, who was asleep on the couch.

"Cindy is Tommy's favorite baby-sitter," she explained.

"I am glad to meet you, Cindy," he said to the girl, who was putting on her shoes. "Would you like me to take her home?" he asked Becky.

"No, she lives next door. That's why she's my favorite sitter, too. I just watch her in from my doorway."

He watched with her as Cindy ran across the yard and into her own house. "Could I offer you . . . ?" she began, then hesitated. She didn't have any liqueurs. "Coffee?" That was a stupid question, anyway. They'd had both liqueur and coffee at Millie's.

"Nothing . . . except your telephone number." He bent to kiss her full on the lips. "I plan to see more of you, lovely lady."

Becky watched him go, her fingertips pressed to her mouth. How, she wondered, could a kiss be so possessive, yet at the same time so impersonal?

And why was she standing there, analyzing a kiss, when she should be going into raptures? This absolutely fantastic, once-in-a-lifetime man wanted to see her again!

CHAPTER 3

Millie was on the phone early the next day. "Well?"

"He . . . he's nice."

"Nice? Is that all you've got to say? He's it! Perfect for you."

"Oh, sure. And all I have to do is—"

"Play your cards right. He's digging on you, girl! Couldn't take his coveting eyes off you!"

Coveting? More like judging, she thought, remembering his continued appraisal. But . . . "He did take my phone number."

"Fantastic! Now, when he calls—"

"*If* he calls." She'd thought about that. "Might just be a polite gesture. I'm sure he doesn't call every woman he meets."

"'Course not. Only those of his choice."

"And there must be plenty. Why he'd choose me is beyond—"

"Damn it, Becky! You never did know what a prize you are!"

"Your opinion," Becky said, laughing. "We'll see what Mr. Right thinks. *If* he calls."

"If, if, if! Get it through your thick skull that *you* make the choice!"

"Me?"

"And you gotta move quick. Lots of hungry women out there, especially when it comes to a man like Sam Hendricks! You gotta take quick action, honey."

"Oh, Millie, you talk like the poor guy has no say-so at all!"

"Not much. Okay, laugh if you want. But you know I'm right. Heck, if I'd left things to Hal, he'd still be a bachelor, swinging a golf club, occasionally sitting on his backside at that stuffy old law firm, getting nowhere!"

Becky was still laughing. But hadn't she watched Millie go after Hal, tooth and nail? And the new glass-clad Banks Building in Jack London Square, which housed not only their law offices but those of several tenants, was, Becky thought, a shining symbol of progress directly attributable to Millie's five years with the family firm. "I'm not like you, Millie," Becky said.

"And that's a pity. With your looks . . . well, never mind about that. If Sam doesn't call, you should . . ." The strategic planning continued.

As it turned out, however, Becky had no need for the strategies outlined by Millie. Sam Hendricks called that same evening. "Short notice, I know. But I wondered if you'd accompany me to the mayor's birthday dinner Friday evening."

"I . . ." She blinked. The day after next. Black tie. What on earth would she wear? "I'd love to," she said. Millie would kill her if she refused.

She searched through her closet. She couldn't wear the black dress again. Besides, it wasn't dressy enough. The blue silk was kind of cocktailish, but a bit long for the current fashion. It would have to do. That meant she'd have to shorten it and get it to the cleaners in time.

She had almost finished turning up the hem by noon the next day when Millie bounced in.

"After you called, I thought about this!" she announced, holding up a fabulous sequined cocktail dress that threw the blue into darkest shade. "It's been hanging in my closet for a month!"

Becky stared at the dress. At Millie.

"I knew it was too little when I bought it," Millie hastened to explain. "But I couldn't resist. Been dieting like crazy and still can't get my butt into it. It should be a perfect fit for—"

"You're lying, Millie." It had been a long time since Millie fit into a size six. "You bought it today . . . for me."

Millie shrugged. "Well, what the hell. Wouldn't be the first time we swapped clothes."

"It's different now."

"You're right, it's different. I've got plenty, and I hate to see you looking so seedy when—well, not seedy, but . . . Darn it, you gotta look good! Everybody will be there in their glad rags and—"

"And I'll be in borrowed ones. I don't feel right taking things from you, Millie."

"I've never been squeamish about taking from you."

"Guess not. Nothing to take." Becky laughed.

Millie did not laugh with her. "Nothing? Do you know you're the only one besides me who ever visited Ma in that . . . that . . ." Her lips quivered, and she hesitated. "That place that turned my stomach every time I went."

"Oh, for goodness' sake, I only . . ." But Becky's voice trailed off as she remembered how Millie had loved her foolish, timid mother, how fiercely protective she had been of her.

"It didn't seem right," Millie said. "That when she was finally rid of Pa and could enjoy herself, she . . . just gave up. I don't understand it."

"Well, you have to understand that some things are out of even your capable hands. Besides, didn't we decide ages ago your mother is at peace wherever she is, happy that you are happy? Why are you bringing it up now?"

"Because I'll never forget her. And I won't forget that you kept going even after she didn't recognize either one of us. And now when I want to do you a simple favor—"

"All right! I'll wear the darn dress. Thank you."

"You're welcome." Millie smiled.

"But let's not make this a habit. I don't like misrepresenting myself!"

It was a good thing after all that Millie had gotten her the dress, since as things turned out, she wouldn't have had time to get to the cleaners. The next morning she had to leave early to drop Tommy at Kiddie Kamp and rush to Del Rio Junior High to substitute for Faye Hollis—again. She couldn't decide whether Faye was really ill, a chronic hypochondriac, or just a chronic goof-off.

Chronic stress, she decided later as she stood in Faye's classroom and watched her first-period English I students file in. Anybody who every day faced a pack of rapping, boisterous, loud-mouthed, gum-popping adolescents with all those know-it-all genes bursting out all over the place had to be stressed out.

Not I! I grew up in the projects.

She removed Faye's bullhorn from her desk, opened the roll book, discarded Faye's already-filled-out referral slips for troublesome students, and stood in front of the class. She spoke as softly as she possibly could and watched them strain to hear her. A couple of snickers were abruptly cut off by a shout from Sheeata, a student who had previous experience with her. "Shut up! We don't make no noise when Miss Smart here."

Roll call was its usual challenge, with the class roster reflecting not only current immigration patterns but also the current inventive trend in domestic names: Shereeka Jones, Ta Di Hunhy, and others. As she struggled to correctly pronounce Taminasheeka Smith's first name, a tardy student arrived, dancing backward into the classroom. He made a turn and stopped, gaping at her. "Who that lady?"

"She our teacher today," came a quick reply from one of the students. "She nice!"

"Thank you." Becky nodded to the boy who had spoken, and hastened to turn the compliment into a quick grammar lesson. "Always include a verb: 'She *is* our teacher today.' And I'm happy to be with you," she added before turning to smile at the newcomer. "Glad you could join us. Won't you have a seat?"

Her polite request evoked a roar of laughter from the class and a sheepish smile from the tardy student as he quietly took his seat.

Becky remained standing throughout the period. Experience had taught her that standing commanded respect. That, plus a soft voice, worked every time. She tried to follow Faye's lesson plan in her own way. She always encouraged student participation, which not only kept their attention but was an excellent teaching tool. As each student read aloud, she would quietly instruct and congratulate: "Watch the punctuation. . . . Excellent inflection . . . Pretend you are on radio or TV. Keep your audience interested."

Becky was fond of the Del Rio students, many of whom were from poor and/or dysfunctional families. They were the needy ones, and she took a special joy in teaching them. If she could impart just one bit of advice or instruction to help them survive, perhaps succeed . . .

"I've enjoyed being with you today," she said to her last class. And meant it.

She also anticipated the evening with a special joy. She was not often a guest at such a gala, and she was glad she would be there. Glad to be wearing borrowed finery, too, she admitted, feeling only a tiny bit guilty as she slipped into the fabulous dress.

Misrepresentation or not, she looked like a million bucks in the dress. That is, if Sam Hendricks's admiring eyes were any indication. And she felt good in it—right at home among the rich and famous in the glittering ballroom of Oakland's swankiest hotel.

Sam Hendricks was quite attentive and seemed to take pride in introducing her to everyone. He made her feel special. But then, he had a way of talking to other people, making an admiring remark or offering a compliment here and there, that made them feel pretty special, too, she guessed.

And Millie was right about the women, Becky thought, seeing the hungry adoring eyes of the bevy that hovered around him. An alluring, sweet-scented, beautifully bedecked bevy! That winning smile he bestowed on them wasn't exactly a brush-off. *Millie was right about something else, too—I'll have to be on my toes if I want him.*

Good heavens! Was she beginning to think like Millie? Deliberately scheming to catch a man?

Well, what was wrong with that? Any man as good-looking, charming, and prosperous as Sam Hendricks was worth catching, wasn't he? And she had to face it: This lifestyle wasn't hard to take. She enjoyed being at the mayor's birthday party, being entertained by Rob Peters, the famous movie star, even talking with him personally. She'd been cool, though. Hadn't even asked for his autograph, though for a few moments she wondered if maybe she should have asked. She could have pretended it was for Tommy or a cousin . . . somebody else.

She smiled at her crazy thoughts and sat back to enjoy the evening, a pleasant change of pace. *I could get used to this,* she thought.

Monday dawned very early for Becky, as she was again to be plunged into the hustle and bustle at Del Rio Junior High. Evidently this was to be another of Faye's long absences.

Not that I'm complaining. Faye needs the break, and I need the money. Maybe enough for another cocktail dress. Sam Hendricks was out of town on business but, before leaving, had engaged to take her to another event the following week. *Perhaps he does like me,* she thought, smothering a yawn, as she packed her lunch and coaxed a sleepy Tommy to eat his oatmeal. "Come on, eat up! I bet Joey and Skip are already at Kiddie Kamp. You don't want to be last, do you?"

Becky, as usual, gave her all to her students, and felt a bit drained by the end of the week. "Thank God it's Friday," she said to another teacher as she left school that afternoon. She made a quick stop at the grocery before picking up Tommy. At home she switched on *Sesame Street* for Tommy and placed the bag of groceries on the kitchen table, along with a pile of test papers and the day's mail. She was about to put away the groceries when she noticed the envelope with her bank's return address in the upper left corner.

It wasn't time for a statement. *What on earth . . . ?*
She ripped it open. A notice of insufficient

funds—a check in the amount of $59.85, made out to Saunders Plumbing, had been returned unpaid. Plus the bank was charging her a $22 fee for bouncing a check.

Her first thought was that the bank had made a mistake. She kept accurate records. Had to, on her shoestring income. She only wrote checks at the beginning of each month, taking out enough cash for daily expenses, and was careful to leave $150 in her checking account for a small emergency—more than enough to cover that plumbing bill. She decided she was going to complain to the bank, make them send an apology to that plumbing company, reimburse her and them for the bounced-check charges . . .

She pushed everything aside to make room for her last bank statement, checkbook, and calculator. She'd have the figures straight when she called the bank.

She tallied. Stared at the figures.

Tallied again. Blinked.

This is crazy, she thought. She couldn't have made a hundred-dollar mistake.

But you did, you dumb cluck! Had she pushed the wrong button, or—

"Can I have a cookie?" Tommy pulled at her skirt.

"May I please have a cookie," she automatically corrected before shaking her head. "What about an apple?" She reached into the bag for one, and rinsed it at the sink. She'd call the plumbing company . . . "Here you are." She gave him the apple and watched him scamper back to the TV. She'd have to make good on the check to the plumbing company, and to do that she'd have to take some money from her small savings account. She glanced at her watch. Four-thirty. The bank would be open till six that night.

She left Tommy in Cindy's care, along with hamburger and milk shake money for both. As she drove to the bank she wondered why the plumbing company hadn't called her. She hoped they wouldn't try resubmitting the check. If the bank returned the check once more, that'd mean another twenty-two-dollar charge, plus whatever the plumbing company's bank charged them.

She flushed with embarrassment and frustration. She couldn't afford mistakes like this one.

When the bank clerk informed her that the check had not been sent in again, she was relieved. She withdrew two hundred dollars from her savings, put one hundred in her checking account, and took the other in cash. She would go by Saunders Plumbing, reimburse them in cash, and get her check back. It was almost six. She hoped they would still be open.

As she drove down Dumont, looking for the address printed on the plumbing company's invoice, she thought about the worker they had sent out. Carl somebody? Such a pleasant man, and he had been so good with Tommy. She hoped he hadn't gotten into trouble because of her bum check.

Number 512 proved to be a narrow two-story building, hemmed in by a hardware store on one side and a beauty parlor on the other. A bell tingled when she opened the door to enter what appeared to be a combination office and reception area. No one was in the room, but as she moved toward the counter, a man came through the door in back of it. It was the same man they had sent out, Carl.

"I'm glad you're still open, and glad you're here," she said. "I want to apologize. I just found out I gave you a bad check. I hope you didn't get any flak about it."

"Flak?"

"From Mr. Saunders, or whoever owns this place."

"No." He smiled. "I'm Saunders."

"Oh. I thought . . . I didn't know," she floundered, feeling flustered, and somewhat irritated. If he was the proprietor . . . "Then why didn't you contact me immediately?"

"I was waiting."

"Waiting? For what?"

"The first of the month. Sometimes . . ." Now he was the one floundering, as if he were the culprit. "That is, some people—"

"Hope their paycheck will beat the check to the bank?" she asked. "I don't operate that way, Mr. Saunders."

He looked embarrassed. "It was just that I . . . I didn't want to pressure you."

She was touched. "That was kind of you, and I really appreciate it. I had made a stupid miscalculation. I'm sorry to have inconvenienced you, and I am here to clear things up. Let's see . . . fifty-nine dollars and eighty-five cents," she said, counting out the cash. "And here's ten dollars more to cover the bank fees—please tell me, was it more than that?"

"No. And I'm responsible for this charge, not you." He sorted out a ten-dollar bill and held it out to her.

She didn't take it. "I pay for my mistakes," she said.

"And I pay for mine."

"Don't be ridiculous. No reason why you should pay the charges for my insufficient funds."

"A business risk, which I should assume."

"Nonsense! I certainly will not let you—" She stopped, realizing they had been shoving the money back and forth. "Look, just take this money, give me my check, and—"

"Since we're going to argue about this, why don't we do it comfortably? Like over a cup of coffee?"

That made her look up. She had forgotten those beautiful, laughing eyes. Eyes that urged her to know more about him, to . . .

This is crazy, she told herself. For all she knew, he could be married with a dozen kids. "I don't think so."

"Come on. Take pity on a lonely bachelor."

Bachelor? Was he reading her mind?

"Eating alone gets lonely. I usually have dinner at Ma Sutton's place. It's just around the corner, and—"

"Thanks, but I really shouldn't."

"Shouldn't miss it!" He bent forward as if to confide a great secret. "Ma's from Georgia. Her barbecued ribs and succotash . . ." He smacked his lips. "Out of sight! Only real southern cooking I've tasted since I left Mississippi."

Mississippi. That accounted for that slight southern drawl, warm and rather enticing. She straightened. "It sounds delicious, but—"

"Wait a minute. We've got a problem here. What about this inconvenience you put me through? We haven't settled that yet, have we?"

She smiled. He'd been so nice about the bounced check.

"Well . . ." *This is ridiculous,* she thought. *I don't know one thing about this man!*

But again, it was as if he'd read her mind, for he added, "Ma Sutton knows me very well. She could tell you what a fine, upstanding citizen I am."

CHAPTER 4

What on earth am I thinking? Becky again wondered as she walked around the corner with him. She didn't know this Ma Sutton any better than she knew him.

The cafe they entered was small, only six booths and a counter with four stools. It had the standard commercial decor, but what gave it a cheerful, homey touch were things like the bright yellow of the booth cushions, the flowing tendrils of the fern next to the cash register, and the atmosphere itself, she decided, as each of the three other patrons smiled, nodded, or called a greeting to Carl, and Ma Sutton came from behind the counter to greet them.

"Hello, Carl. You're a little early tonight. And this young lady?" The older, rather plump woman smiled at Becky.

"Mrs. Rebecca Smart. I told her you'd give me a good reference."

"Sure thing." She beamed at Becky. "You can't go wrong with Carl. He's a good old southern boy," she added, as if that was the highest praise she could confer.

"Thank you," Becky said. "He also gave you an excellent recommendation."

"That's my boy! Now, you sit right here and see if I live up to it. Fish or ribs are tonight's choices. Both with succotash. Tea, coffee, or soda. I don't have a liquor license and don't want one," she said as she settled them in a booth and called a waitress to take their order.

"You were right," Becky said later. "These ribs are delicious, "And this . . . this . . . what did you call it?"

"Succotash."

"Very tasty. What is it? Corn and . . . ?"

"Lima beans, green peppers, tomatoes, and okra. A famous southern dish. Where've you been, lady?"

"Right here in California, I'm afraid."

"Never back east?"

"Only as far as Arizona," she said, thinking of the motor trip she and Tom had taken on their honeymoon. "I'm a lady of limited travel and limited knowledge."

"I don't buy that. Any woman who can teach school, take a lead in the church choir as well as the neighborhood block association, and take care of a kid all on her own can't be very limited."

She stared at him. How did he know?

He grinned. "You didn't think a bum check was your only recommendation, did you?"'

"Oh?"

"No, indeed. The check was a surprising and very welcome opportunity. I had already checked you out."

"Nosy, huh?"

"No! I just wanted to know—"

"And I don't know if I like the sound of that," she said, rolling her eyes at him. "Checked me out? Like a car you were thinking of buying?"

"More like a beautiful lady whom I'd like to . . . who strongly appeals to me."

She lowered her eyes.

"I wanted to know if she was married, single, involved. Things like that," he went on.

"I see. Your source?"

"Al Brown. Poker-playing buddy of mine . . . neighbor of yours."

"Oh." Al had given her the name of the plumber. "And did he satisfy your curiosity?"

"Not quite. All he could say was that you were beautiful, busy, and a widow. I'm still wondering about involved."

She smiled. "Well, you can't expect to know everything on such a short acquaintance, can you?"

"Guess not." He shrugged, took a sip of coffee. "All right. We'll begin with the small talk. What do you teach and where?"

"Everything and all over the district."

"Come again?"

She laughed. "I am one of those unfortunate fill-ins at the beck and call of a principal who has a teacher bail out on him or her, usually at the very last moment. I'm a substitute."

"That must be tough."

"Interesting."

"You like it?"

"I like teaching. But sometimes, on the spur of the moment, dealing with kids you get no chance to know . . . well, it can be difficult."

"Quite a challenge."

She chuckled. "The greatest challenge is the roll call."

"I can't believe that."

"Oh? Try to pronounce a six-syllable name from Thailand." She gave an example and watched him laugh. "Try to pronounce an eight-vowel name from Tonga." She liked seeing him laugh, liked the glint of humor in his eyes and the way the creases in his cheeks deepened when he smiled.

"I hadn't thought about that," he said. "You do have a great variety of foreign students now, don't you? Unfamiliar languages and unfamiliar names."

"Don't blame it all on the poor foreigners. Haven't you heard any of the creative domestic names that all seem to start with *La-* and end with *-eka, -isha,* and *-oka*? I do wonder whatever became of Mary, Martha, and Helen."

"Well, it's no wonder that you find your job interesting. Tell me more."

She enjoyed talking about her students to someone who obviously wanted to hear about them. Her recital ranged from funny to sad, from the bossy girl who resented a newcomer to the plight of a troubled or hungry kid.

"I like to keep a bowl of apples or a big bag of popcorn on my desk. A child can't learn when he or she's hungry. And some of those kids . . . well, you know."

"I know that any kid who lands in one of your classes is lucky."

"Thank you, sir. But . . ." She stopped, not knowing what to say. She'd been talking about the kids, not herself.

"You really care about them, don't you?"

"I suppose I do," she said. "At least I understand. I've . . . been there."

His eyes registered quick interest. "Tell me."

"Not another word! I've been talking and talking, as if you didn't already know too much about me. And all I know about you is that you're a good old southern boy!"

He grinned. "You want to know more?"

"I certainly do. If I'm going to—" She broke off. Was she going to see more of him? She blushed as the significant lift of his brow posed the same question. She evaded it. "It's your turn," she said.

"Fair enough. Let's see. Have you ever heard of Powtukit, Mississippi?"

She shook her head.

"Not surprising. Few people have heard of it. It's just a small coastal town where I was born, like my father before me, and his father before him."

"How did you land in California?"

"Pop. He brought me out soon after Mom died. I was still in high school."

"Oh." A difficult time to lose both mother and school chums. "That must have been hard for you."

"Not as hard as living where Mom had been. I was as eager to get away as Pop was."

"So you're not a good old southern boy after all," she teased.

"Sure I am. Roots are what count."

"So you and your dad just pulled up your roots? Why Oakland? It's a long way from Mississippi."

"Pop had done a short stint here when he was in the navy, and had taken a liking to it. And he said the pickings might be better here."

"Pickings?"

"Whatever work he could pick up." Carl chuckled. "Pop was what you'd call a handyman. I was his major assistant. We'd do anything, from hauling trash to plastering a wall."

"You must have been good at it," she said, feeling a spark of admiration. "Now you've got your own business."

"I inherited that."

"You did?" She stared at him, puzzled. He'd said his father was just a handyman.

"Not the business. The inclination."

"Inclination?"

"To be my own boss, determine my own income."

"I see," she said, thinking about it.

"Inherited it from my grandfather. No, from his father, I guess. It was an old family joke that my grandpa often told," he said, smiling. "Seems he started out one morning when he was a teenager, all bright-eyed and eager.

"'I'm going down to Mr. Landers's gas station,' he announced. 'I got a job.'

"'Get back in here!' his pa told him. 'You ain't going nowhere.'

"'But he's going to pay me three dollars a week!'

"'No, he ain't,' his pa said. 'No son of mine's gonna limit himself to three dollars a week . . . or any other paycheck. You choose your own work, set your own pay, my son. That way, the sky's the limit!'"

Now she was laughing at his exaggerated southern drawl. She could almost see the determined old man. "Good for him!"

"Yep," Carl said. "It was he who started the family trait. He was a great carpenter, but, well, he was unable to get a license, join the union, so he did odd jobs, too." He sighed. "Restrictions were also a handicap for Pop."

"But he managed in spite of them?"

"And very well. When he died five years ago, there was enough in the kitty for me to buy this building and set up my own company."

"Saunders Plumbing!" she chortled. "A tribute to your father, his father before him, and . . . You have a remarkable heritage, Carl Saunders."

"Do I qualify?"

"Qualify?"

"I'll put it another way: Are we going to see more of each other?"

"Oh. I hadn't thought . . . Perhaps." She looked down at her untouched dessert and coffee that had grown cold, and glanced at her watch. "My goodness, I didn't realize what time it was. Cindy will be wondering where I am."

"Cindy?"

"My baby-sitter. Thank you for a really delicious dinner, and I've enjoyed every minute," she said. "But I hadn't planned to be away so long. I'll have to get home pronto."

He stood up without protest. It was only after he had escorted her to her car and helped her in that he bent forward and asked, "What about Sunday? I often go fishing in a nearby river. Would you and Tommy like to join me?"

You and Tommy. It wasn't often that her son received such a treat. "I think he'd love it."

"What about you?" he asked.

"Oh, I'll come along," she said, laughing.

"And I'll love having you along," he said, touching her hand where it rested on the car door. "Pick you up at ten. Okay?"

She nodded and drove off, the touch of his finger still lingering on her hand, as intimate as a kiss.

◆

CHAPTER 5

Sunday was a beautiful day, perfect for sitting on a riverbank, a soft spring breeze wafting through the air, the rays of a bright sun warm on her back.

Tommy was beside himself, being on an excursion with another male, doing manly things women don't do. *At least this woman doesn't,* Becky thought. *How could he touch the slimy things?* she wondered as she watched him hand a squirming worm to Carl.

"Okay!" Carl baited the hook and expertly tossed the line into the lake. Then he closed Tommy's chubby little fingers around the fishing rod. "Hold on tight, now. Especially when you feel a tug. That'll be a bite. We'll whisk that fish out before he knows what's what!"

Tommy giggled, eyes wide and expectant.

Becky noticed that Carl also kept a tight hold on the line, as if knowing how far to trust Tommy's capabilities.

"How do you know so much about kids?" she asked. "You said you didn't have any brothers or sisters."

"Cousins. And, back home, more baby-sitting than I wanted to do," he said, chuckling. "Another reason I was glad to leave Mississippi."

"I don't believe that," she said, assessing his cheerful casual ease with Tommy, now leaning contentedly against his knee. "I bet you miss your family."

"At first, maybe. But, like old Booker T. said, you gotta let down your buckets where you are."

"And is your bucket pretty full?"

"Full of work, I'm glad to say. Yesterday I got a go-ahead to repair and maintain the sprinkler system at Lakeside. It's just a small retirement center, but it's my biggest contract so far."

"Congratulations! That's wonderful, Carl. Others will see your work, and I'm sure that will lead to bigger contracts."

"I hope you're right. And as it's coming from someone who's only seen me plug a leak," he added, smiling, "I do appreciate the confidence in my work, ma'am. Thank you."

"You're welcome," she answered automatically. But her confidence stemmed from the man himself . . . unmistakable integrity in the dark eyes, the firm set of the chin, the way his strong hand covered Tommy's. A handsome, thoroughly likable man.

"There must be more in your bucket than work," she teased, suddenly wanting to know what he did in his spare time, and with whom.

"A bite! A bite!" The squeal from Tommy broke into her reverie.

The jerk on the line had also alerted Carl, and,

his hand over Tommy's, together they reeled in the first catch of the day. It was the first of three fresh trout, all of which Carl cleaned and stored in the ice chest he had brought along. Again Becky noticed how neat and thorough he was about everything he did.

It was a perfect fun day, except for Tommy's tumble into the lake. A little bored with holding on to the rod, he wandered off to gather rocks, got too close to the bank, and slipped. He was only in for a minute, as Carl jumped in and scooped him out immediately. He choked, sputtered, and his little body convulsed with heartrending sobs.

"He's just scared," Carl said to Becky when she reached for Tommy, who kept a tenacious hold on Carl.

"No more than I was. If you hadn't acted so quickly . . ." She threw her arms around both of them, and her "Thank you" came out in a choked whisper.

A sloppy end, but it could not spoil such a perfect day.

Sam Hendricks phoned Wednesday evening. "I just got back into town. I hope you haven't forgotten about Saturday."

"Of course not." How could she? She'd been wondering all week what she should wear. A small dinner party at someone's home. Maybe the black dress could serve again. "I'm looking forward to it," she said.

"Good. And put next Thursday on your calendar, too. I'm to be the Man of the Year at a fund-raising function for the Children's Aid Society. They'll be roasting me, and I'll need a few cheerleaders in the audience," he said, chuckling. "What about it?"

"Sounds like fun." Black tie again. She wondered if she dared again wear the dress Millie had given her. "I wouldn't miss it," she said. Better not, she decided as she hung up. Appearing too soon or too often in the same attire was a no-no.

What to wear became quite a problem as invitations to attend some posh political or social affair with Hendricks grew more frequent.

"He really likes you," Millie said. "People are beginning to recognize that you're his steady. Now, if you play your cards right . . ."

Or manage to find something to wear, Becky thought, but didn't say it to Millie. She liked to solve her own problems. She solved this one in clever ways. She haunted the thrift and second-time-around shops for leftover finery, added a scarf, or wore a different top. She covered an old pair of pumps with the fabric she had cut off the blue dress, turning it into a stunning outfit.

"What do you think?" she asked as she modeled it for Millie.

"Exquisite!" Millie declared. "But, honest to goodness, Becky, you'd look good in a garbage bag. If I had your figure and your face . . ." She gave a sigh of pure envy.

"Will you stop that!" Becky shook her head in exasperation. For all the bravado and the queenly stance, Millie had never recognized her own attractiveness. "There's nothing wrong with your figure or your face."

"Cut the kidding."

"I'm not kidding. How many women can wear a size eight? Good features, too. And silky smooth skin!"

"Yeah, yeah, but still black as coal . . ."

"Don't yeah me!" Becky exploded. How could Millie still be sensitive about her skin color? "Black is not only beautiful, it's *in*!"

"Okay, okay, I'm beautiful," Millie said, laughing.

"Hal thinks so. He says you're the classiest dame in Oakland."

"He's right about the class," Millie said, examining her perfect manicure and running a smooth hand over her St. John knit. "And it doesn't come cheap. Remember that, Becky. Like I told you, if you play your cards right . . ."

There was no dress code on her excursions with Carl. She could go to dinner at Ma Sutton's in whatever she had worn to school that day; a pair of slacks was fine when they went to the movies, and so were jeans and sneakers when they went fishing.

She always wore an old pair of cutoff jeans when they worked in the garden. She wasn't sure how this had come about—something she had said about fresh vegetables and the small garden she and Tom had planted that first year.

"I'll give you a hand," he had volunteered. He turned up the soil and helped with the planting.

"You should have a sprinkler system," he said one day when they were working in the newly planted garden. "Stupid to have to drag out a hose every day."

"Oh, I don't mind. In fact, I rather enjoy it."

"Waste of time. In fact, you should overhaul your whole plumbing system."

"Oh, I will," she said as she yanked at the weeds rapidly appearing around her two tomato plants. "Someday."

"You ought to do it now, it would be cheaper in the long run."

"Maybe so. But my short-run budget is already overloaded."

"It could be managed." He sat back on his haunches and looked around. "I'll do an estimate. Might make an offer you can't refuse," he added, smiling at her.

She eyed him suspiciously. What was he saying?

"I'm sure we could make an arrangement that—"

"No, thank you," she said, her voice crisp. She wasn't sure what he was suggesting, but . . .

To her surprise, he roared with laughter. "Don't get so huffy. I wasn't offering to take it out in trade."

"I . . ." She swallowed. "I didn't think . . ."

"Yes, you did, darling."

She caught her breath. *Darling.* His soft southern

drawl gave the endearment a sweet potency that melted something inside her.

"Not that it isn't appealing," he said, "but I don't do business that way, sweetheart."

"Of course not. I don't mean to imply . . ." She floundered. "Darn it, Carl, you have been so kind and so helpful in so many ways." She gestured toward the expanse of garden. "I shouldn't like to impose."

"I don't do anything I don't want to do."

She stared, caught by his expression and voice. How could just the sound of his voice turn her inside out?

"Becky, the way I feel about you is in a category all by itself." He bent forward and pressed his mouth to hers in a light, almost casual kiss that blocked out everything but the rush of feeling that coursed through her. She clutched at his shirt, wanting to hold on to the rapture.

When their lips parted, he murmured, "Let's not talk of imposing or trade-offs. We're beyond that."

She jerked back to reality: her grubby fingers, dirt on his shirt, Tommy industriously digging nearby. "It's just that I wouldn't want to take advantage of a friend," she said with a slight emphasis on the last word.

"Gotcha!" he said, sounding amused. "No problem. When it comes to plumbing, I'm strictly business. And it's good business for you to upgrade your plumbing. Listen . . ."

"You ladies enjoy your luncheon," Hal said. "Tommy and I will be fine."

"Don't get lost on that golf course, Hal Banks!" Even in the very feminine, very fine coatdress she had donned for the luncheon, Millie's stance was that of a major pulling a private into line. "You know we have that dinner at The Mansion. If you make me late again—"

"I'll be here."

"And not at the last minute, for a change! It's embarrassing to be late like we were last night just because you—"

"Oh, Millie," Becky cut in, irked by the waspish drone. "Hal, it's sweet of you to take Tommy. Are you sure he won't be too much for you?"

"Of course not. He'll help me drive the golf cart. Come on, buddy."

"Coming. Gotta get my ball."

"Hey, that's a basketball. We're going golfing!"

"I know, but I'll just take it. Carl gave it to me," Tommy said, clutching the pint-sized ball. "He fixed a hook on the gate. Carl can fix most anything. He says . . ." His voice faded as he trailed after Hal.

Millie turned a suspicious eye on Becky. "Who is this Carl?"

"He's the plumber I told you about."

"Plumber?"

"Remember? I had miscalculated and gave him a bum check, and he was so nice about it."

"*Very* nice, I gather."

"It's quarter of. Hadn't we better be off?"

Millie picked up her bag, but she was not to be diverted. "You gave him a bum check, and he retaliates by bringing toys to Tommy and fixing things around the house?"

"Oh, for goodness' sake, Millie, he's doing some plumbing for me," Becky said as she climbed into Millie's car. "He's putting in a sprinkler system, and replacing some of those old pipes."

"I see. All that?"

"Well, he helped me get a home improvement loan. That gets everything in shape all at once. Plus that sprinkler system, too." Why was she explaining to Millie? It wasn't her business. But Becky found herself adding, rather defensively, "It does make sense. I'll have no more plumbing problems. Carl is doing an excellent job."

"Tommy certainly approves."

Becky did not miss the sarcasm. "Well, Carl's around a lot, and he does seem to relate to Tommy." She didn't mean to mention the fishing trips, but somehow Millie dragged it out of her. "I think it's good for Tommy to be with a male occasionally. Like today . . . golfing with Hal."

"It's not Tommy. It's how *you* relate that concerns me."

"Oh, my goodness. Carl is just a good plumber. And a good friend," she added honestly. She did not tell Millie how often he remained after the plumbing work to share snacks. Or the dinners at Ma Sutton's. Or that time they'd gone dancing. It was *not* Millie's business.

"Good. You have a tendency to be too chummy

with the wrong people and not chummy enough with the right ones." Millie smiled as she shut off the motor. "Which reminds me," she said, turning to Becky before leaving the car. "I want you to be especially nice to Kathy Morris today. She's president of the Circlets this year, and if you play your cards right . . ."

It wasn't that she intended to spend so much time with Carl. He was just around. A comfortable habit.

Comfortable? Well, she still melted at the sound of his mellow voice, and when he called her "darling." But hadn't she heard him speak in that same endearing way to Ma Sutton? He probably called all females "darling." Just an old southern custom.

At least there were no more casual kisses. She had seen to that on the night when things had gotten . . . well, not exactly casual.

They had shared a pizza after Carl stopped work that evening. After Tommy was in bed, they sat on the sofa and turned on the television. They did more talking than watching. Funny how she and Carl never ran out of things to talk about.

Just talking, and then . . . She couldn't even remember what she had said. Something about one of her students, she thought.

She remembered what Carl had said. "You don't even know what a loving, caring person you are, do you, darling?" She could hear the sincerity in his honey-sweet drawl, and it made her feel very special.

She remembered the way he had looked at her— the tantalizing promise in his magnetic dark eyes.

She remembered the feel of his arms around her, the pressure of his body against hers, the welcome warmth of his lips. The gentle touch of his hands teased, caressed, urged. Her body throbbed with exquisite sensations as long-buried erotic yearnings leaped to the surface. Passions that had been dormant all these years flooded through her. She was all weak, wanting, yielding womanhood.

"Mommy! Mommy!" Tommy's piercing cry had cut through her haze of pleasure.

She had broken away and rushed to the stairs, her heart in her mouth. Dear God, what had happened to him while she—

"I want a drink of water," he said, tugging at his pajama top as he descended the stairs.

The relief soothed, angered, and exasperated her. She drew a deep breath, but before she could say anything, Carl spoke beside her.

"I'll get it. Come on, buddy."

She was glad to let him take charge of Tommy. Alone in the living room, her hand over her mouth, she had tried to get control of her emotions, tried to think.

What had come over her?

Nature. She'd been a widow too long.

But she'd never been plagued—okay, aroused— by such powerful yearnings before. Not in the two years since Tom died.

Because you've been too busy, she thought. *Tommy, the house, work. You've hardly had time for any man. Now you're dating two men.*

Two men. Yes, she was also regularly dating Sam Hendricks, exchanging casual kisses with him. But his kisses hadn't shaken her to the roots like Carl's.

She was getting too close. Too intimate with Carl. She didn't want—

"Okay, he's back in bed. Almost asleep already." Carl moved toward her, holding out his arms.

"No!" She backed away.

He didn't say anything. He just looked at her.

"It's good that we were interrupted just now," she said.

"Oh?" His expression was blank, unreadable.

She forced herself to speak frankly. "I . . . I don't take physical intimacy lightly, Carl."

"Neither do I."

"I know." She looked earnestly up at him. "That's why . . . Look, I don't want to get involved with anyone just now. I wouldn't like to . . . to . . ."

"Give the wrong signal?" He touched a finger to her cheek, and she felt her pulse quicken.

She bit her lip. "I hope you understand."

"I'm trying, honey. I'm trying." He ran a hand through his hair. "But what you say and what you do . . ." It wasn't quite a grin, but an amused quirk tilted his lip. "Your signals do get a little mixed, darling."

He was laughing at her! "All right! All right! I have feelings!" she said, mad that she hadn't been able to conceal them. He knew as well as she that she had been ready to strip herself naked and go all the way. "But I'm not a silly teenybopper. Not even a carefree young woman with no ties or responsibilities. I'm a twenty-seven-year-old mother, for God's sake. I have to set standards for my kid as well as—"

"Becky, are you trying to tell me that you don't want to go to bed with me?"

"Well . . . yes, I guess I am." She felt winded, and rather foolish. She'd been out of the dating game so long. Did she sound like some prudish, old-fashioned nut?

"Now? Or never?"

"What?"

"These standards . . . restrictions. Might they be lifted at some later time? Say, when we know each other better, or perhaps have formed some mutual commitment?"

"I don't know." She thought of Sam Hendricks. Of Millie: *If you play your cards right* . . .

"Do you want to know?"

"What?" She was confused.

"Where do we go from here? Do we go the getting-to-know-each-other route? Or break off altogether?"

The thought of not seeing him at all was unbearable. "Couldn't we stick to being friends, Carl?"

"Isn't that what we are?"

"Yes. But what I mean . . ." She hesitated, deeply embarrassed. "Look, Carl, I—I'm pretty vulnerable right now. And when you touch me I . . . I don't want to start something I'm not ready to finish."

"I see. No touchy-touchy, huh?"

She nodded, feeling old. Out of date. Ridiculous. Now he did grin. "I'll try, darling. I'll try."

CHAPTER 6

"Becky, what about that plumber?" Millie asked.

"Oh, he's almost finished," she said. "Just a little more on the sprinkler system." She knew what Millie was asking, but she didn't elaborate, and she quickly changed the subject. "Sam asked me to go with him to the Governor's Ball in Sacramento Saturday."

"Wonderful! Wonderful! That means you're making headway, girl! Now, if you spend the night—"

"We're not. I've already told him we'll have to drive back immediately, no matter how late. There's Tommy. And the church choir . . . I'm scheduled to do a solo Sunday morning."

Millie looked thoughtful. "That's probably just as well. Best not to be too close till you're really close, if you get what I mean. And you're getting there, girl! The Governor's Ball! Aren't you excited?"

Yes, she was excited. There was no denying that she enjoyed the fabulous functions she attended with Sam Hendricks—posh affairs, so different from her usual routine, where she met different, often famous people, going different places.

Admittedly it did sometimes get to be a bit of a strain, like she was too busy keeping up with the Joneses instead of just kicking up her heels and having fun. But she wasn't trying to keep up with anybody. She wished Millie would just stop telling her to be sure to be especially charming to this or that important somebody. Sometimes she got sick of Millie's nagging and pushing. Just like she nagged her good-natured, easygoing husband. Hal must get pretty sick of it, too.

Oh, for goodness' sake. Millie means well, Becky thought. *She pushed Hal's business out of the doldrums, didn't she? And face it, Becky Smart, you never would have made it out of college without Millie's pushing.*

Anyway, what was wrong with being charming? She was nice to everybody, important or not, wasn't she? Even with her students, she always tried to say something that would make them feel good about themselves. People liked to be puffed up.

Sam Hendricks was good at that. He always seemed to know the right thing to say.

To the right people?

She thought about that. He wasn't quite as obvious as Millie, but he did seem to cater to people who could be of benefit to him.

So? Wasn't that part of being successful?

Anyway, he was nice to everybody. He was certainly nice to her—candy, and flowers, and taking her places—and there was no way he could consider her a contributor to his success.

She sighed and told herself to stop it, that she was being too critical. He was so modest and unassuming whenever he referred to himself.

But somehow it always leaks out, doesn't it? His impressive background, his impressive accomplishments.

So? she scolded herself. *He has no reason to hide his background . . . as Millie is prone to do,* she thought.

And so what if he reveled in his accomplishments and position, basked in the admiration and respect accorded him, enjoyed the adoration of all those women who flocked around him? She was in no position to criticize. She was as proud as a peacock that, out of all those adoring women, he had centered his attention on her.

Oh, yes, she liked all this attention from such a handsome, charming, prominent man. She liked being on his arm at those important functions among prominent people.

She did not stop seeing Carl. Why should she? She enjoyed him. They found so much to talk about, to laugh about. She always had fun when she was with him.

To tell the truth, after those posh affairs with Sam Hendricks, it was rather relaxing to be with Carl. Even comfortable, now that he was being a perfect gentleman about what he called the "touchy-touchy stuff."

It's as if he's carefully keeping his distance, she told herself one night as they drove home from a late movie. And what was oddest of all was that his restraint made her feel an overwhelming desire to touch him. She stared at his hands on the steering wheel. Strong hands, with a gentle, caressing touch that made her feel . . . She fought off the feeling, tore her eyes from his hands, and looked out at the almost deserted street.

Suddenly she saw something that made her sit up straight. Hal's car? Parked on this street at this time of night?

"Wait, Carl. Slow down. That car. I think it's a friend who might be having car trouble."

Carl's battered van was passing the car now, and she saw that it really was Hal. And Millie.

No, not Millie, she realized with a start as she got a clear view of the woman who lifted her face to kiss Hal.

"Don't stop!" she said to Carl, who had slowed and was about to pull in front of the car. "That's not someone I know."

"Are you sure?" he asked.

"I'm sure." *Sure we shouldn't stop, that is.* "Anyway, there's no car trouble." *Just a little hanky-panky,* she thought as Carl sped away. She looked back to see the woman get out of the car and hurry around the corner.

"You've been awfully quiet tonight," Carl said later as he walked with her to her door. "Something wrong?"

"Just a bit tired," she said as she stood with him to watch Cindy safely into the house next door.

"Then we'd better skip the coffee," he said. He

pushed back a lock of her hair, lightly touched her cheek. "See you."

She watched him walk toward his van. But what she saw was a woman lifting her face to Hal. A woman who was not Millie.

"Do you know what this means, Becky? Do you? When Sam Hendricks asks you to be hostess at a private dinner party in his condo—"

"Millie, it's no big deal."

"No big deal!" Millie's eyes rolled upward. "How can you say that?"

"There'll be only ten people, and he's having it catered."

"We're not talking about who's cooking the food, for God's sake! You're to be the hostess. Don't you understand he's making a declaration?"

"A declaration?"

"As good as a marriage proposal!" Millie said, as happily excited as she had been the day she had received her own marriage proposal from Hal.

"Oh, no. I doubt . . ." Becky floundered as she lost track of the conversation. Hal. Did Millie know? Did she even suspect?

"We'd better start planning."

"Planning?" Millie couldn't know. She was too happy, too complacent.

"For your wedding, stupid!"

"My what?" Becky was jerked back to the present. How did Millie get from one little dinner to a wedding?

"You can wear my wedding dress. You'd have to take it in quite a bit. But it's still gorgeous and will never be out of style. It cost way too much. Remember, I had already bought it long before Hal asked me."

Becky stared at her. Yes, Millie had bought her dress and planned the wedding long before the actual proposal. That was Millie, reaching for the stars.

No—grasping the star and running with it, long before it was there. Living in a future she envisioned.

"Oh, Becky, I just can't wait until you're Mrs. Samuel Hendricks. We'll . . ."

Becky listened to her friend fantasize about what they would do *when*. Was she so into the future that she lost sight of the present, was unaware that something was happening that would hurt her?

"You know you'll be on display, don't you, Becky? He'll be assessing you. Seeing if you'd be the perfect wife to handle these kinds of affairs."

Anyway, what do you know, Becky Smart? Becky rationalized to herself. *Maybe it was just a trivial one-night fling and it doesn't mean anything to Hal.*

"Didn't you hear me, Becky? I asked what you're going to wear."

"Oh. I . . . haven't decided. What do you think?" she asked, though she found it hard to concentrate on such trivia. Hal wasn't a trivial-one-night-stand kind of guy. She liked Hal, and of course Millie was her best friend. She didn't want either of them hurt.

She just hoped her ugly suspicions were unfounded, or at least greatly exaggerated.

"Yes," she told Millie. "I'll wear something spe-

cial that night. What did you say? Not exactly a hostess gown, but with an at-home look? And absolutely
smashing!" She nodded at Millie, wondering how
one achieved that combination.

This is nice, Becky thought as she moved about Sam
Hendricks's well-appointed living room, seeing that
each guest was happy, occupied, enjoying the delicious canapes and a before-dinner cocktail. So pleasant to be talking and laughing, participating in the
party, without having to run into the kitchen and
check on the meat or something. Nice to be just a
charming, unflustered hostess.

She guessed she was doing it right. She couldn't
help but notice Sam's eyes following her every move.
Watching. Approving?

What was it Millie had said? . . . Assessing.

At least Millie approved. She had taken one look
and given her the thumbs-up sign. And Hal had
winked as he whispered, "Right on!"

That made her feel good, too—seeing Millie and
Hal together in the usual way. No sign of troubled
waters.

"Everything is lovely." The governor's wife beamed
at Becky. "And such a congenial group. I'm enjoying
myself immensely, my dear."

"So am I," Becky said. "I am so glad you could
come," she added, thinking of the governor's heavy
schedule.

"Oh, we wouldn't have missed it. We adore Sam.
He is such a talented man, and so involved. I don't see

how he does all he does. He told us you helped arrange this little gathering. That was sweet of you."

"Thank you. I loved doing it." All she had done was discuss the menu and select the flowers, she thought as the state's First Lady gave her a pat on the arm and moved away. But he had told the governor that she helped arrange the dinner? She caught her breath. Was this, as Millie had said, a kind of declaration?

For a moment, her head in a swirl, she imagined herself as Sam Hendricks's wife, moving in pomp and ceremony, arranging little parties. A piece of cake!

At least, she thought, smiling to herself, it wouldn't be quite the same thing as when she and Tom, or she alone, entertained: all the cleaning, scrubbing, and ironing beforehand, then looking and feeling frazzled as she tried to cook, serve, and make conversation all at the same time.

Yes, a piece of cake, just looking pretty and being charming. Her head still in a swirl, she moved toward a woman who was standing alone and looking almost out of place. "Mrs. Alston, how beautiful you look. I love the color of that dress. . . ."

As the evening progressed, she had the feeling that Sam did approve. At the end of the evening, she knew it. He stood with his arm lightly but possessively around her as they bid the guests good night.

And when they were alone, he said so. "You were wonderful, my dear. All that I could wish."

"Thank you. But I really did so little."

"Don't you believe it. This was—purposely, I

admit—a rather diversified group. You pulled them together, made them all feel comfortable. There's quite a trick to that, and you're good at it."

"Well, thank you," she said again, not quite sure what he meant, but feeling pleased—and, as his arms drew her closer, just a bit giddy.

"Yes, you're a very special lady, Becky," he murmured as his mouth descended to hers. His kiss was possessive, demanding, and arousing. "This has been a special night. We're not ready for it to end, are we?"

She hardly heard him, so busy was she trying to analyze her feelings. She had been a widow too long. That a kiss from any man could tempt her to . . .

"No need to return home at this hour, my dear. Stay with me, and in the morning—"

"No, I couldn't." She had pulled herself together and was thinking rationally. She gave the usual excuses: Tommy, the morning choir. "And I don't relish sneaking out of your place in the morning."

Maybe it was this last comment that convinced him—after all, appearances counted. Anyway, he did not demur. He took her home and bid her a polite but possessive good night. "There will be other evenings," he said. "Perhaps you might join me on a trip to the Vineyard. I'd like you to meet my folks."

Another declaration? she wondered as she closed the door behind him. *Meet his folks? Perhaps another assessment,* she concluded.

"You were perfect!" Millie said the next day. "Did you see the way Sam watched you? He was about to bust his buttons, he was so proud of the way you handled things."

"He did say he was pleased."

"Pleased? He was crowing like a rooster, making sure everyone knew you were his lady. That lobbyist, Patty Roster—she's been hot after him, you know—was green with envy. Now tell me what happened afterward. Did he pop the big question?"

"Not exactly."

"What do you mean, not exactly? And wipe that silly smile off your face. We're talking serious here."

"Well, all I got was an invitation to spend the night."

"Shucks, that's routine, honey. But I hope you . . ." Millie paused, a stricken look on her face. "I mean . . ."

"I didn't."

"Good." Millie's relief was evident. "I know we're nearly in the twenty-first century, but don't discount that old saying, 'Why buy a cow when you're getting the milk for free?' It's as true today as it was a hundred years ago. Maybe even more true today, now that morals and shotgun marriages are plumb out of style. You listen to me," she said to Becky, who was practically rolling with laughter. "Cut that out, will you? Like I said, we're talking serious."

"It's the way you put things, Millie."

"I'm telling it like it is, girl, and it ain't no laughing matter." She gave Becky a level look. "Are you still seeing that plumber?"

"Carl? He . . . he's about finished now."

"I asked if you were still seeing him. And you know darn well what I mean!"

"I . . . yes, we do go out occasionally. I like him. We always have fun."

"We're not talking about fun. We're talking about your future, and your future depends upon the choice you make right now."

"Choice?"

"Between Sam Hendricks and a plumber. You do know what it would mean to be married to Sam Hendricks, don't you?"

She did. She listened as Millie listed all the advantages of being married to a man like Hendricks, but it was hardly necessary. She had heard it all before.

"You do like him, don't you?" Millie asked.

"Of course." How could she not? He was handsome, courteous, and kind, and yes, she was physically attracted to him.

"And really, Becky, you must think about Tommy, and what a man like Hendricks could do for him."

Indeed, Sam had commented on how bright Tommy was, a candidate for a really good university. Maybe business or law, he had said, reminding her that he had connections at Yale. It was hard to think of her baby at a university, much less as a man with a career. But she did realize the exposure he would have through Hendricks.

"If you play your cards right, you're in with Sam. And you ought to stop playing around with that plumber."

"Oh, for goodness' sake, we're just friends."

"These platonic friendships can get out of hand sometimes, honey."

She stared at Millie, remembering. Things *could* get out of hand.

"You don't want to be unfair to the poor guy, do you?"

When Becky thought about it, she realized that she really was being unfair to Carl. She didn't want to hurt him. She would have to break things off with him, tell him that she was seriously involved with someone else.

And she should do it that night. Hal had taken Tommy to a movie, and he and Millie were keeping him all night as they often did.

She and Carl had planned to go to a movie. But maybe she would just fix dinner and . . . well, just talk.

Maybe it was time to say goodbye to a beautiful friendship.

CHAPTER 7

She would miss Carl, she thought as she drove home. He had become almost . . . well, almost like family.

But Millie was right. She shouldn't be unfair to him. He had been fair to her, hadn't he? Nothing beyond a touch on her cheek, and maybe a tug of a lock of hair, since that night. But the way he looked at her and the way he said *darling* . . .

Dear Lord, she had to be fair to herself, too! Little insignificant things like that seemed to touch her inside, twist her thinking, more than a physical touch. And if she was going to marry Sam . . .

Now she was thinking like Millie! Way ahead of where she was.

Well, all things pointed that way, didn't they? Sam had asked her to set a time when she and Tommy could go with him to Martha's Vineyard to meet his folks. That was as good as a proposal, wasn't it?

Stop! Stop thinking like Millie!

But she couldn't. She kept hearing Millie's words: "You'll never get another prospect like this one, honey! I can see you now, on his arm, going into the

White House to meet the president. Sam Hendricks is going places, girl, and I can tell he wants to take you with him!"

It was a thrilling prospect for a woman who'd hardly been out of California. For Tommy, too. Yes, she would like to be his wife. And, from all indications, he was on the verge of asking her.

She had to clear the decks.

Carl was a friend. In the short time since they had met, he had become her best friend next to Millie. But, as Millie had said, platonic friendships could get out of hand.

Nobody knew that better than she. She had to break off this friendship. And she had to do it in a way that would not hurt Carl.

She planned carefully what she would say. Cooked a special dinner. On impulse, she removed the books and papers that were usually scattered on the little round table that stood in the dining area of the living room. She draped it with a long skirted tablecloth, then set it with flowers, candles, and her best china.

This would be a special night. Their goodbye would be a festive occasion, like all their happy times together.

Her hair was still damp from the shower when the doorbell pealed. She slipped into the long red checkered dress she had picked up at the second-time-around shop, and hurried downstairs.

She opened the door to find Carl on the stoop, removing his boots.

"Stopped at Lakeside to check on those guys

doing the sprinkler system. Muddy as hell out there—didn't want to track it in," he explained as he stepped inside, leaving the boots on the stoop. He gazed at her and gave a low whistle. "You look luscious, darling!"

"Thank you."

"Not exactly dressed for this weather, though."

"I thought we might stay in tonight," she said, reaching for his jacket.

"It's wet. I'll put it in the laundry room." He walked back and laid the jacket on the dryer. Then he followed his nose into the kitchen. "Smells mighty good," he said.

"I hope it is," she answered, her attention on what she was stirring. "I followed Ma Sutton's recipe very carefully."

He peered over her shoulder. "Succotash! I knew I recognized that smell."

"Will you get out of here!" She slapped his hand and replaced the lid. "You're spoiling my surprise."

"But I am surprised! And mighty pleased. This beats hamburgers and a movie all to pieces."

"I thought you'd like a good old southern dinner. The kind you introduced to me that first night at Ma Sutton's when I came to settle my bum check. Remember?"

"Yeah." He forced himself to say it casually, but how could he forget that night and the bum check that had brought Becky into his life? He hoped she would be a part of his existence forever. But she didn't know that yet, and he had promised to tread carefully, to give her time.

That was hard. She was so damned responsive to any intimate touch. So warm and soft and yielding. She would respond to his caress, but then suddenly she'd catch herself and slam on the brakes. This on-off business drove him crazy, and so he'd decided it was best not to touch her. He'd wait until she was ready.

And he hoped she would be ready someday. But he knew she was seeing someone else. He'd figured it out from something Tommy had said the day he dropped by when she was out. Then he had seen her picture in the paper with some big shot at the Governor's Ball.

That didn't surprise him. He wouldn't be surprised if there were a dozen guys after her. She was one in a million.

But . . . she was still seeing him, wasn't she?

Yeah, and he meant to hang in there till she told him to buzz off.

Suddenly aware of the quiet, he asked, "Where's Tommy?"

"Hal took him to some kids' movie, and he's spending the night with them."

"Oh." They were alone. He'd have to keep a tight zipper on his emotions. *And on my pants,* he thought.

"What's so funny?" she asked.

"Nothing."

"Well, wipe that silly grin off your face, and get out of here. You're getting in my way," she said. "Go into the living room and wait."

He glanced at the kitchen table, where they usually had their snacks. What was going on?

"Out!" she said, giving him a little push. "Dinner's almost ready."

The first thing that struck him was that the living room was more orderly than usual. Then he saw the table . . . the candles, the roses.

He felt the jolt in the pit of his stomach as it hit him: She *was* trying to tell him something.

She was ready!

Well, damn! Why didn't she just say so? Why all the to-do?

She was surprising the hell out of him tonight. All this build-up was getting to him. He was all fired up, and as nervous as a schoolboy on his first date.

If she wanted a romantic atmosphere . . . his Becky could have whatever she wished. He bent to the logs in the fireplace and had a fire blazing by the time she came in. "Open this, will you?" she asked, thrusting a bottle of wine into his hands. "Oh, you've started a fire. How nice!"

He was still nervously fumbling with the opener when she called over her shoulder, "Everything's ready. I'll get the salads."

By the time she returned, he had himself in hand and was pouring the wine.

"Good," she said. "Now, sit down and enjoy this scrumptious meal I prepared especially for you."

He sat and lifted his wineglass. "To us."

She touched her glass to his and gave him such a dazzling smile that his heart turned over. He was trying to play it cool, but the atmosphere was getting to him: the glow of the candles on her face, so beautiful and rosy, framed against the stand-up collar of that red thing she wore . . . The hell with the meal. He wanted to take her in his arms and—

"That's what I want to talk about," she said. "Us."

Talk? For a moment he was confused. Then it hit him. *Of course, stupid! You didn't think all this ceremony was for a one-night romp in the hay, did you? We're thinking commitment, buddy!*

God, didn't she know he was gone, totally committed almost from that first day?

"You haven't touched your salad."

He took a mouthful. Crisp, tasty. "You . . . said you wanted to talk," he prompted. Then he realized that he should start, tell her how much he loved her. "Becky, you know how I feel about you."

"Yes. You've been the very best friend I've ever had, Carl. These weeks we've known each other . . . Oh, for goodness' sake, you're not going to eat that salad. Give it to me. I'll bring what you like!" She jumped up from the table, took their plates, and disappeared into the kitchen.

She was nervous, too, he thought. Naturally. Total commitment was serious business after being on her own for two years. and with a child to consider. Didn't she know that Tommy meant as much to him as to her?

"Here you are, sir." She set a steaming plate before him. Fried chicken, whole-grain rice in good old creamy gravy, and succotash. "And don't you dare tell me it's not as good as Ma Sutton's."

"Better," he assured her after a sample. "Best I've ever had." To tell the truth, he hardly tasted the food. He was too elated by the thought of sitting with her, like this, each night for the rest of his life, of taking her in his arms and kissing that rosy mouth that curled so invitingly against her perfect white teeth. He watched the pulse beating in her throat and could hardly contain himself. "About that talk," he said, wanting to have things settled between them.

"No! Not now," she said, fumbling with her fork, then putting it down to take a sip of wine. "I've worked hard on this dinner. We need to concentrate and enjoy." She smiled at him, picked up her fork, and made a great pretense of eating heartily.

Damn, she was nervous. More awkward than he had ever seen her.

Down, boy, he told himself. *Give her time.* He changed the subject. "You know," he said, "I don't know if that last guy I hired is quite up to par. I have to check on every little job he does." It was hard, but during the rest of the meal he stuck to small talk. He told her about his work, and she talked of her students.

By the time they finished, she seemed to have regained her composure. She stood and reached for his plate. "Now for the dessert."

But his composure had gone. He quickly moved around the table and put his arms around her. "No. It's time to talk," he whispered against her ear. He trailed kisses along her temple and cheeks as he drew her to the couch before the fire. "I've so much to tell you, darling."

"Wait. There's something I must tell you," she cried, her hand over his lips.

The slight touch drove him wild. He kissed each fingertip, and then the palm of her hand.

"Oh, wait!"

But her cry was muffled against the pressure of his mouth. He was done with waiting. And when he felt the instant response, the eager yielding of her body against his, the passionate hunger in the pleading moans that escaped her lips, he knew that she too was done with waiting.

With gentle, tender caring, he moved to pleasure them both.

She could no more have stopped what was happening than she could have stopped breathing. She was lost in a rhapsody of feeling . . . the sweet intimacy of his caressing hands, the ripples of erotic delight mounting and burning within her, the rushing flood of wanting.

Her arms tightened about him, and she cried out in exultation as her body ignited in the powerful, blissful surges of fulfillment.

Afterward she rested her head against his shoulder, feeling strangely contented.

"Happy, darling?" The honey-sweet drawl roused her, as if from a deep sleep. To wakefulness. To reality.

To the shock of what had just happened.

"Now, sweetheart, we can talk."

Talk?

She sat up, made a valiant effort to get herself under control. Dear God, what had she done?

"Carl, I . . . I'm sorry." She reached for her clothes.

He also stood and began to dress. "Sorry?"

She couldn't look at him. "I . . ." How could she explain what she couldn't understand herself? She had been alone too long. Too close to him. "I didn't mean for this to happen."

He didn't say anything, and she forced herself to look at him. His expression was unreadable. Blank.

"I . . . I didn't want this to happen," she said again, through dry lips. "That's why I planned tonight . . . to . . ." She had to tell him. She had already bungled. "I . . . We were getting too close. I thought we should break off."

"Break off?"

"Oh, Carl, I'm very fond of you. I really am. That's why I wanted to make tonight special."

"A special goodbye?"

"Yes. I didn't mean to . . . to . . ."

"My fault. I misread the message." A wry smile twisted his lips. "Your signals tend to . . . to get a bit crossed."

"I'm sorry."

"So am I, darling. So am I."

When she looked up, he was gone.

CHAPTER 8

Millie glanced around the luxurious tearoom at the Royal Hotel, but there was no sign of Kathy Morris. Late as usual.

"Madame?" the hostess inquired.

"Morris . . . I think there's a reservation."

"Yes, indeed. Right this way."

Big waste of time, Millie thought when she was seated at a small table near the window. *I'm chairing the Circlet's fashion show this year. Kathy's got as much sense of style as a brass monkey. But Madame President has to poke her finger in every pie, the big show-off! Oh, there she is.* She smiled at the approaching woman, noting the suit. Saint Laurent, but a shade too tight. Not the style for her, anyway.

"Sorry I'm late, Millie, but the scholarship committee meeting went on and on." The plump woman sighed as she sank into a chair opposite Millie. "Lord, I'll be glad when this year is over. It's running me ragged, and with so much going on. Liz, poor thing, has taken a leave, you know. Girl, did you hear about her . . . ?" By the time their salads were set before them, Millie had heard all the lowdown on "poor Liz." Kathy had a way of highlighting her pity with colorful, juicy tidbits.

"That's too bad," Millie said, thinking she would take Liz some flowers, take her out to lunch. She knew what it was like to deal with an alcoholic in one's family. "Now, you said you had some suggestions about the fashion show?"

"Oh, yes. Let's see . . . You say Fanny's dealing with the Boutique?"

"Yes, and Sue's been talking with someone at Miller's. They're not up to Boutique standards, but maybe for shorts and swimwear . . ."

The discussion went on for some time before Kathy asked, "Who're you getting to handle the publicity?"

"Why, Jan La Rue, of course," Millie said.

"I don't think that's a very good idea."

"Oh?" Millie was surprised. "I know she's not Circlet. But she did a good job last year. We're lucky to get a professional at such a small fee."

"Professional? That so-called public relations outfit of hers?" Kathy sniffed. "Lily La Rue's into relations all right, but they're not always either public or professional."

Millie hesitated. Kathy obviously had a thing against La Rue. "Well, that's not our concern, is it? She did an excellent job for us last year. Besides, she agreed to act as emcee."

"Agreed? She volunteered, my dear. Lots of big shots in our audience, and she knows it. Oh yes, she was anxious to emcee . . . make contact! For Miss La Rue."

Millie smiled, took a sip of wine. "That's business, isn't it?"

"Is that what you think? Business? In that take-a-good-look-at-me-dress? The way she throws her skinny hips around with that slutty come-and-get-me walk? The eye contact with the men? Didn't you notice?"

Millie fiddled with her salad. Was Kathy trying to tell her something?

"Look, Millie, I . . . I've thought about this a long time. I'm not sure I should say anything. But I thought . . . well, if I were in your place, I'd want to know. Oh, Millie, this is embarrassing. I don't want to hurt you."

But you're itching to hit me with the juicy details. I know the look. "Fire away, Kathy. You can tell me anything."

"Well . . . it's about Hal."

"Oh?" There was no mistaking the poor-Millie inflection. She braced herself.

"And Lily La Rue."

It hit like a bolt of lightning. She remembered all the late meetings, the lame excuses. She took a swallow of wine, fought to still her pounding heart. "Sounds as if you've been listening to some stupid rumors, Kathy."

"Not rumors, Millie. Fact. Your Hal has been seeing a great deal of Jan La Rue."

"Of course he has." Millie dug into her salad with every appearance of relish. No way was this bitchy gossip getting to her! "He's been handling her affairs, and—oh, Lord, forget I said that!" she exclaimed, a hand over her mouth. "Our law business is strictly confidential, you know."

"Business? At her apartment in the middle of the night?"

"You mean he's been seen? And we've tried to be so careful." *I'll kill the wretch!* It was hard to maintain her cool with that one thought raging in her mind, but she managed. "Kathy, don't repeat it, please. The fewer people who know about this business, the better."

"What do you mean?" Kathy asked, obviously puzzled.

"I mean his having been seen sneaking into her apartment may rock the boat. We've tried to do everything under cover."

"Under cover? What?"

"Oh, I shouldn't be talking to you like this. Listen, Kathy, this is strictly confidential, and you'd better not breathe a word." Millie bent forward to speak as if in the greatest confidence. "Lily La Rue's affairs are so messy, so dirty, and so complicated that the greatest secrecy is required." The bigger the lie, the more believable, Millie thought as she broke off.

"Yes? Go on." Kathy leaned forward, expectant.

Millie shook her head. "I mustn't tell you. It wouldn't be right."

"But I don't understand."

"Of course you don't. But I can't disclose such lurid indiscretions. You wouldn't believe what we lawyers go through to protect our clients. I can't tell you the questionable places I've been, at the strangest times," she added with a significant lift of her brow.

"Well, I hope you're . . . that is, I'm glad it's what you say, and not . . ." Kathy's face revealed her indecision. To believe or not to believe? Millie also saw shock and greedy curiosity in the other woman's face. One hand brushed the table, as if to smooth things out. "I didn't want to tell you, but . . . well, I was concerned."

"Of course you were, and it was sweet of you to speak about it. I'm glad we had this talk, so you know there's nothing to worry about."

"Yes, I'm so relieved. You never know about people, do you? Lily must be in a tizzy about this . . . this . . . ?"

"Poor Lily." Millie sighed. "But let's not talk about it anymore, Kathy. I mustn't air her dirty linen. Hal would kill me. Now, let's see. Have we finished with this fashion show business?" She pasted on her happiest, most complacent smile. She hadn't been labeled "Madame Queen" back in high school for nothing!

The rage consumed her. It robbed her of all reason. All sense of time.

No, that wasn't true. She was keenly aware of time. Each toll exploded in her breast as the clock in the downstairs hall struck the midnight hour. He wasn't home yet.

An image of Hal wrapped in the arms of that

hussy was as clear to her as her own empty king-size bed. The image hurt, and she blocked it out. She kicked aside her discarded pumps and resumed her pacing.

At two o'clock that afternoon she had stopped back at the office and been told, "Mr. Banks is at the golf club."

Just as well. She couldn't kill him in front of the whole eagle-eyed staff. Couldn't even tell the sneaky, low-down bastard what she thought of him.

At two-fifteen she dialed the club. "He's on the course, Mrs. Banks."

She spent the next hours listening woodenly to a client; thank God she had only one appointment scheduled for that afternoon. She tried to read the legal documents on her desk, but the letters swam before her, dissolving in her tears.

Five-thirty. She dialed the club again. "Yes, Hal Banks was here, but he left—about five minutes ago I think."

She sped home. She would kill him . . . beg him . . . Like a child, she mopped at her eyes.

He wasn't home. Like many a night during the past month.

Didn't you notice? Kathy had asked. Dear God, she hadn't! She'd been too involved in the important business, the social amenities. All that was nothing compared to the ache in her heart . . . the terror . . . the fury.

She paced her bedroom floor, intermittently calling his beeper number. No answer.

She dialed his car phone a dozen times, always getting the same recording: "The customer you have called is not available at this time."

She had also called a certain other number—one that by this time had been burned into her memory. One where a sultry voice intoned over and over again on the answering machine, "Lily La Rue Public Relations. We are unavailable at this time. Please leave your name and number and we will return your call as soon as possible."

Finally she could stand it no more and her whole being burst into flames. With one swift movement, she hurled the phone against the wall, smashing it to bits.

The nightmare jerked her awake.

Becky sat up in bed. Her gown was damp. She wiped sweat from her face, but she was cold, still shivering with terror. Just as on the night it had really happened. When it hadn't been a dream.

It had been so many years ago, one of many nights when something like that had happened. Why would she dream about it now?

The dream had been so vivid: Millie and her mother banging at their door, Mrs. Parks's face swollen and dripping with blood, four scared women piling furniture against the door, bolting the windows.

Then, later, Millie with an iron pipe in her hands: "He's passed out now. I'm going to kill him."

It had taken all the strength and willpower Becky

possessed to talk sense into her fiery-tempered fifteen-year-old friend, to coax her back to bed.

Why now? Why had Becky had a dream so vivid that she couldn't shake it off?

Millie was in trouble. She knew it.

She dialed Millie's house over and over but always got a busy signal. A busy signal . . . like a warning bell.

She didn't hesitate. First she called Cindy's house. "Mrs. Baxter, I have an emergency. Could I bring Tommy over? I don't think he'll awaken."

Ten minutes later she was speeding toward Millie's house.

She was just about to turn into the driveway when she had to brake abruptly to keep from colliding with the oncoming car. The other car lurched to a stop, and Millie flung open the door and ran toward her.

"Millie! What's wrong?" Becky cried.

Millie looked strange and disheveled, standing there in that smart suit, sneakers on her feet.

"Damn! It's you," Millie said. "I thought you were Hal." She turned and strode back to her car before Becky could say another word.

Becky switched off her motor and rushed to Millie. "Wait a minute! What's wrong?" There was no answer, but Becky managed to get into the passenger seat of Millie's Porsche just before Millie stepped on the gas.

"Slow down, Millie! What's the matter? Has something happened to Hal?"

"Something's going to! Just as soon as I get my hands on him! I'll kill him!"

"Not if you kill us first! Stop it, Millie. Slow down! Do you want a cop to stop you?"

Her words must have penetrated, for Millie released her pressure on the gas pedal a little. Becky tried to keep her voice calm and reasonable. "What's the matter, Millie? Talk to me. Come on, tell me. What's wrong?"

"Everything!" The cry was like the whimper of a hurt child. "She's trying to take my husband, the bitch!"

Becky's heart lurched. *She's found out about that woman. Somebody must have told her, and now she's all riled up, liable to do anything!*

This is all my fault. I should have told her. Nobody knows Millie as well as I. I could have softened the blow, prepared her so that she wouldn't go off the deep end.

"Listen, Millie . . ."

But Millie wasn't listening. She was talking, her voice muffled, her speech rich with obscenities as she went on and on about that slander-slinging Kathy bitch, and that slut who was trying to get her hands on Hal. "And she's not! I'll kill her first. I'll kill them both!"

Becky tried to reason with her. She interjected calming words, cautioning her to slow down and watch the road, as Millie drove on.

Then she saw it. Hal's car. Right where it had been on that other night, with that woman.

Dear Lord, was Millie going to smash into it?

But Millie hadn't seen it. She was turning the corner that the woman had scurried around. She brought the car to a stop in front of a modest one-story house. The street was quiet and dark. A few cars were parked by the curb, but there was nobody in sight. Becky reached toward Millie to restrain her from whatever she intended to do.

But Millie was out of the car and running toward the house, picking up something as she ran.

Becky cringed as a stone hit the front door of the house with a resounding *thump*.

CHAPTER 9

Becky was out of the car in a flash.

"Are you crazy?" She grabbed Millie, propelled her back to the car, and pushed her into the passenger seat. Millie was now too distraught to move, and Becky managed to drive rapidly away before anyone came out to see what was causing all the ruckus.

When she had gone a few blocks, Becky looked over at her friend. Millie was bent over, sobbing uncontrollably, all the fight gone out of her.

What to do? Becky didn't want to take Millie home in this state. She knew how her moods could suddenly and dangerously shift. When Hal walked in, she might fly into such a rage that she'd hit him with any object near at hand. That certainly wasn't an approach likely to repair a failing marriage.

Or had it already failed? How far had Hal's relationship with this other woman gone? Could Becky have headed it off if she had warned Millie?

Forget that, Becky told herself. *Deal with now. If Hal gets home first, he'll see my car there but not Millie's. He'll wonder and call my house.*

If he shows up, we'll think of something, she decided as she drove to her own house. She needed time to talk some sense into Millie and calm her down before she took her home.

Once inside the house, she led Millie to the sofa. "Sit here. I'll get you some . . . brandy, I think." That's what they always gave distraught persons in old novels. She fumbled in the kitchen cabinet for that bottle Carl had brought one night, hoping it was still there. Yes, there it was.

Millie almost knocked the glass out of her hand. "Leave me alone!"

Becky carefully set the glass on the table. "Look, Millie, you need—"

"Don't tell me what I need, you dummy!" Millie was on her feet now, back in her fighting mood. "All I need is to get my hands on that thieving whore! And I would have if you hadn't . . ." She glared at Becky. "You! You stopped me. Dragged me away from that whore's house."

"I certainly did."

"Why don't you mind your own business and stop poking into mine, you meddler! That sleazy bitch is after my husband! But she won't get him. I'll see to that. I'll whip her ass till it ropes like okra!"

"That's 'hood talk, Millie."

"Damn right. That's where I'm from. The damn whore doesn't know who she's messing with! I'm going out there and—"

"All you'll do is make a fool of yourself. I won't let you do that."

"You think you can stop me?" She pushed Becky aside and looked wildly around. "Where are my keys? I'm going back out there and—"

"Sit down and listen to me!" Becky gave Millie a push that sent her reeling back onto the couch.

"Don't push me!" Millie started to rise, but was stopped by a stinging slap across her face. "Becky, you . . . you slapped me." She stared at Becky, her eyes filling. "You're my friend, and you . . . you . . ."

"I'll do whatever I have to do to keep you from losing everything you've worked for."

"That's why I've got to get out there. Don't you understand? She's taking him away from me." The tears were falling now. "I've got to stop her."

"Do you want to make a laughingstock of yourself?"

"She's already doing it. I tried to tell Kathy it wasn't that. I told her . . ." Millie began to laugh now, with the tears still raining down her cheeks. "You should have seen Kathy's face, Becky, trying to decide what to believe. Only I need to get to that Jan La Rue and—"

"Confirm all the gossip? Here, Millie, take a sip of this." Somehow she coaxed Millie to drink the brandy and simmer down a bit. She talked in soothing tones, trying to make her realize what was at stake.

"You're not in the projects now," she finished. "You're Mrs. Harold Banks, who resides on Vista Lane in beautiful Oakland Hills. You're an attorney at law, a partner in Banks, Burroughs, and Banks, and part owner of the new Banks Building."

"Stop it!" Millie cried. "Stop it! Why are you talking about all that? That's nothing!"

"Nothing?"

"Didn't you hear me? She's trying to take my Hal!"

Becky couldn't close her mouth.

"My own darling, sweet, funny Hal! You know him, Becky . . . how he's always laughing and making jokes. Never mean, never even fussing about anything." She bent toward Becky. "I didn't know that kind of man existed. You remember Pa, Becky? Always scowling and ready to bust you in the mouth all the time. Hal's not like that. Not at all. He's so kind and gentle, and never mad about anything. You know how he is, Becky."

"Yes. I know." But she hadn't known that Millie knew and appreciated it. Millie . . . reaching for the stars. Money, position. But . . . "You really love him, don't you?"

"Love him! Oh, Becky, I can't live without Hal. I won't let her take him. I won't!"

"Listen to me, Millie. Your fight is not with that woman. You need to concentrate on Hal."

"You're right! He's cheating on me. I'll kick his—"

"And not with a baseball bat!"

"What do you mean?"

"I mean a man like Hal doesn't seek another woman unless he's missing something at home."

"Becky, how can you say that? You of all people know what I've done for Hal. The contacts . . . They'd never have had that building if it hadn't been for me. I've worked hard."

"For what you wanted."

"For what *I* wanted?"

Becky nodded. "And what did you call it a minute ago . . . all that nothing?"

"Okay, but it's not nothing. If I left it to Hal, he wouldn't do anything but play golf and make love!"

"Uh-oh."

"Don't look at me like that! We do make love." Millie paused and blinked. "Okay, okay, maybe we've slacked off a bit. When you work like hell all day and have to keep up a tight social pace, it takes a lot out of you."

"Bingo!"

Millie might have been distraught and irrational, but she wasn't stupid. A few more minutes of straight talk, and she had her priorities in line.

By the time Becky drove her home, Millie had regained her composure and was back to her usual in-control self. "I know exactly what to do. Hal will never know I even heard about that hussy. I'll keep him so occupied, he'll . . . Do you know what I'm going to do, Becky? I'll book a cruise. No, I'll make a two-week reservation at Sea City—you know, that fabulous golf club. He can play golf all day, and I'll take care of the nights." She was smiling when they reached her house.

As Becky was ready to drive home in her own car, Millie called out to her. "Hey, I just thought of something else. Wait a minute," she said, digging into her purse. "You take these. I won't need them."

Becky looked at the packet. Birth control pills!

• • •

Becky returned to her bed, exhausted. But she couldn't sleep. Her mind was in a whirl, still on Millie.

That dream. She had known Millie was in trouble, and she was glad that she had gone to her. Glad she had been able to calm her, restore her confidence.

But was it too late? Hal was not a one-night-stand type of man. Even with all Millie's verve and determination, would she be able to lure him back?

Maybe not.

Immediately Becky told herself that she wasn't going to think like that. Had Millie ever before failed to get whatever she went after? She was as hot after Hal now as she had been when she first saw him. And Hal had always wanted a child.

Becky smiled, thinking of Millie dumping her birth control pills.

No, not dumping them! Giving them to me. Since when have I used birth control? I haven't had the need. . . .

And then it hit her. That night with Carl! Dear Lord, she hadn't even thought about it. She had been so carried away, she hardly knew what she was doing. She could easily have gotten pregnant.

Well, she hadn't. That had been confirmed last week. She was lucky.

Lucky? Not to be carrying Carl's child?

What was she thinking? She hadn't seen Carl since that night a whole month ago. Why couldn't she get him out of her mind?

She had made her choice. And, from all indications, so had Sam. And she liked him. She had been seeing him more frequently since Carl's departure, and everything was going so well.

Only . . . was something missing? A bit of carefree fun?

Oh, for Pete's sake, you make the fun! That's what Sam needs—Tommy and me.

But a small voice inside her asked, *And what about the passion?* For a full minute she was gripped by the memory of the all-consuming passion she'd felt with Carl. The feel of him. His tender, gentle touch.

She shut it off.

Think about Sam, she told herself. The next night was an especially big one—the economic summit. Business tycoons from all over the country would be in attendance, and Sam was to be the keynote speaker. He had arranged for her to be seated on the podium beside him. That really said something, and she had bought a special dress for the occasion.

Next month they were to visit his folks at Martha's Vineyard. That was really going to be fun. Tommy would love it, and so would she. She pictured long lazy days on a sandy beach, and tried to sleep.

Day came too soon, just as she had dozed off. But she couldn't sleep in. She had to go next door for Tommy.

She thanked Cindy's mother and explained her emergency. "A friend got sick during the night. But she's fine now," she said, crossing her fingers, hoping it was true.

The day didn't go well. To begin with, Tommy

upchucked his breakfast all over the floor and her. A heck of a way to begin preparing for that night's posh affair, she thought, yawning as she mopped the kitchen floor on her knees.

However, after that, Tommy seemed fine. He did cling to her more than usual, but she managed to do her nails, wash her hair, and was ready, as promised, by five-thirty.

Cindy arrived, prompt as usual.

But Tommy did not, as usual, race to greet his favorite baby-sitter. He stayed by his mother's side, his thumb in his mouth.

When Sam Hendricks arrived and they tried to leave, all hell broke loose. Tommy, screaming to high heaven, wrapped his chubby arms around her legs and clung.

Becky bent to him, anxiously thinking of the morning's vomiting. Was he sick? She was also concerned about his tears staining the sequined silk of the costly dress, and conscious of Sam's impatience.

"He was a little sick this morning," she explained. "I thought it was just an upset stomach, but this is not like him. Maybe it's an indication that something is seriously wrong."

"An indication that he's quite spoiled, I think."

"Perhaps. But I think you'd better go on without me," she said, still trying to pry Tommy loose. "Cindy, get the thermometer from the bathroom, please. Sam, I'm sorry, but you'd better go by yourself."

"That's impossible! Really, I hate to say this, but

you must be more firm, Becky. Tommy, come here."
He moved forward and took a firm grip on the child.
"Your mother is going out for just a little while, and
you are to stay with Cindy. Do you understand?"

Carl was reluctant as he drove toward Becky's house,
but he couldn't leave those tools there forever. He
needed them.

Might as well get it over with.

Over and out.

In front of her house he saw the Mercedes. The
big shot was there.

He started to turn back, but then decided that
this was better. Easier. Just the plumber coming to
pick up his tools.

He denied to himself that he wanted to get a
good look at the man. Who was he to judge if he was
right for Becky?

He heard Tommy's belligerent yells before he
reached the house.

"Go away! Leave me alone!"

What was going on? The door was ajar, and he
didn't hesitate.

First he saw Becky, dazzling in a long dress that
shimmered and sparkled. But her face was anxious as
she bent toward Tommy, who was kicking at a man
holding him well away from his impeccable tuxedo.

"What's going on?" he asked, hardly realizing he
had spoken aloud.

That voice! Becky's heart lurched. She looked up,
and for one crazy moment all she could see was Carl.

She wanted to run to him, bury her head against his chest, feel his arms around her.

Tommy had the same thought. He ran to Carl, arms outstretched.

The strong, muscular arms did not enfold him. "Why are you acting like a brat?" Carl demanded.

Ten minutes later Becky was sitting beside Sam in the Mercedes as he headed for the banquet hall.

"We'll make it in time," he said. "Good thing that guy dropped by."

"Yes." *Oh, yes!* She had missed him, but she hadn't known how much until she'd heard the sound of his voice, seen his face.

"Who is he?"

"Carl. Carl Saunders," she said, the sound of his name like music to her ears.

"Well, he sure took charge of your boy."

Your boy. That was how Sam always spoke of Tommy: as a kind of appendage to Becky.

Carl always treated Tommy as a person apart, even from her. Yet he recognized that he was still a young child and needed both cuddling and direction.

She smiled, thinking of how Carl had calmly reasoned with Tommy. "Mommy's going to leave you and you're sick? How sick?" And, after a mutual inspection of the thermometer, "Not sick at all. You love Mommy and want her to have a good time, don't you? Why don't you say goodbye very nicely, then you and I can work this puzzle. How about that?"

Her thoughts were interrupted when Sam spoke. "I hate to say this, Becky, but I do think you have a tendency to indulge your Tommy."

"Oh . . . perhaps you're right," she said quietly. Then she added, "But I guess I have been leaving him alone quite a bit lately. Maybe he feels neglected, and—"

"Not now, Becky. I have to concentrate on my speech."

His speech, she thought, turning to look at him. *Not Tommy. Not even me. Except as an extension . . . in the right dress, with the right demeanor to enhance his position and social prestige.*

And what about you, Becky Smart?

Choices.

It came to her with a shock. She had made a choice. She was trying to marry a man just because of money, position, and social prestige.

All that nothing, as Millie had said.

And, indeed, that was about all she knew about him. Oh, he was kind, and . . .

But she didn't want to think about Sam Hendricks. She wanted to think about love. About Carl calling her "darling" again, in that soft southern drawl. About Carl taking her in his arms and . . .

They were at the hall. She forced herself to respond to the biggies, to be charming. She joined in the resounding applause after Sam's speech, though she hardly heard a word.

Speech over, she watched the admiring women surround him. Watched him eat it up, and respond in kind. He would never miss her, or any one woman.

She flashed back to Carl. Had she lost him?

Apprehension battled with anticipation. Would he ever call her "darling" again?

STEPPIN OUT WITH ATTITUDE

Sister, Sell Your Dream

Anita Bunkley

Bestselling novelist and motivational speaker Anita Bunkley shows women, especially African-American women, how to get their talent, service, dream, or product in the spotlight. Filled with short exercises and useful tips, this handy guide demonstrates how to zero in on the three Ds—desire, discipline, and drive—and provides a step-by-step program that offers both practical and emotional support. With *Steppin' Out with Attitude* every woman can gain the confidence she needs to go for it!

ISBN 0-06-095288-1
$12.50 ($18.50 Can.) trade paperback

HarperPerennial
A Division of HarperCollinsPublishers
www.harpercollins.com

THE NEW NOVEL
FROM *NEW YORK TIMES*
BESTSELLING AUTHOR

Connie Briscoe

A LONG WAY FROM HOME

From the *New York Times* bestselling author of *Sisters & Lovers* and *Big Girls Don't Cry* comes a lyrical and moving novel—a multigenerational story of slavery, freedom, and the indestructible bonds of love and family, witnessed through the lives of three unforgettable women.

"A wonderful read! . . . Connie Briscoe provides a fascinating peek inside the world of a proud family that refuses to let the turbulent times in which they live destroy their dreams for happiness and freedom. The strong women who leap from the pages of her book are unforgettable . . . readers will cheer for them."

—Anita Richmond Bunkley, author of *Girlfriends*

ISBN 0-06-017278-9
$25.00 ($36.50 Can.) hardcover

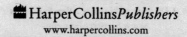 HarperCollins*Publishers*
www.harpercollins.com

$\mathcal{E}$VERYTHING SHE WANTS
Angela Patrick Wynn

"**Angela Patrick Wynn is an author to watch.**"
—Anita Richmond Bunkley,
author of *Balancing Acts* and *Girlfriends*

D riven, with a stubborn streak a mile long,
Renea Peaks is sure she can take care of her
14-year-old brother Brian, finish college, and
launch her career. But her well-ordered plan
doesn't include family trouble or a budding
romance. Determined to be a self-sufficient
woman of color who can handle it all on her
own, Renea discovers that she doesn't have to
sacrifice everything she needs in order to hold
on to everything she wants.

"**I am pleased to recommend this debut novel.**"
—Rosalyn McMillan, author of *Blue Collar Blues*

"**A sweet and utterly engaging read.**"
—Sharon Mitchell, author of *Nothing But the Rent*

ISBN: 0-06-101363-3
$6.50 ($8.50 Can.) paperback

HarperPaperbacks
A Division of HarperCollinsPublishers
www.harpercollins.com

TREAT YOUR BODY & SOUL WITH THESE INSPIRATIONAL BOOKS FROM NOTED AFRICAN-AMERICAN WOMEN

BODY & SOUL
The Black Women's Guide to Physical Health and Emotional Well Being
Linda Villarosa, editor

A NATIONAL BLACK WOMEN'S HEALTH PROJECT, *Body & Soul* is the first and only self-help book specifically written to address Black women's health concerns. Seeking to end the damaging conspiracy of silence about the realities of Black women's lives, this essential resource gives voice to the physical, emotional, and spiritual health experiences of Black women today.

ISBN 0-06-095085-4
$20.00 ($28.00 Can.) trade paperback

IN THE SPIRIT
The Inspirational Writings of Susan L. Taylor
Susan L. Taylor, *Essence*™ Magazine, editor in chief

Sisterly, informed, and inspirational, Susan Taylor shares insight and advice on personal growth and fulfillment. In this collection of twenty-two essays she challenges readers to transcend fear, to face inevitable challenges with courage and spirit, and to use change as an opportunity for growth.

ISBN 0-06-097645-4
$9.00 ($12.75 Can.) trade paperback

HarperPerennial
A Division of HarperCollinsPublishers
www.harpercollins.com